PROPERTY OF

Alice Hoffman is the author of thirteen novels, including *At Risk, White Horses, Turtle Moon, Practical Magic, Here on Earth, The River King* and, most recently, *Blue Diary*, many of which have been bestsellers in the USA and Germany, and she has also written screenplays. Alice Hoffman is married with two sons, and lives in Massachusetts.

ALSO BY ALICE HOFFMAN

Alice Hoffman

PROPERTY OF

V

VINTAGE

Published by Vintage 2002

2 4 6 8 10 9 7 5 3

Copyright © Alice Hoffman 1974, 1975, 1976, 1977

Portions of this book appeared, in somewhat different form, in *American
Review 23*, *Best of Playgirl*, *Fiction*, and *Ms.*

First published in Great Britain in 2002 by Vintage

First published in the United States in 1977 by
Farrar, Straus and Giroux, Inc

Vintage
Random House, 20 Vauxhall Bridge Road, London SW1V 2SA

Random House Australia (Pty) Limited
20 Alfred Street, Milsons Point, Sydney,
New South Wales 2061, Australia

Random House New Zealand Limited
18 Poland Road, Glenfield,
Auckland 10, New Zealand

Random House (Pty) Limited
Endulini, 5A Jubilee Road, Parktown 2193, South Africa

The Random House Group Limited Reg. No. 954009
www.randomhouse.co.uk

A CIP catalogue record for this book
is available from the British Library

ISBN 0 09 942919 5

Papers used by Random House are natural, recyclable products
made from wood grown in sustainable forests. The
manufacturing processes conform to the environmental
regulations of the country of origin

Set in 10½/12 Sabon by SX Composing DTP, Rayleigh, Essex
Printed and bound in Great Britain by
Bookmarque Ltd, Croydon, Surrey

With thanks to Maclin Bocock and Albert J. Guerard, and to Patricia Crowe, for many kindnesses during the writing of this book

January

I

Night of the Wolf

I

"Look," I said, "I'm going with you."

Snow was falling and the moon was howling light onto the Avenue. It was a night for skidding tires and Orphans on the street. I waited for his answer.

"Get lost," said Danny the Sweet.

"Danny," I said, "what kind of an answer is that? That's an answer I won't accept."

"Eh," said Danny, "you got no choice but to accept it."

I considered words of persuasion. "Hey," I said, as we stood in the doorway of Monty's candy store with the darkness of a January night surrounding us. "I can take care of myself."

"What do you know?" said Danny the Sweet. "Girl, you know from nothing."

But did I care? This was no time for loose talk from this eater of Milky Ways, from this driver of a fifty-seven Pontiac. No.

"I know enough." I smiled.

The Sweet leaned against the stone of Monty's doorway and sipped ginger ale. Inside Monty was closing up for the night, chasing away the neighborhood corner kids, muttering over a gin and tonic, and wiping the linoleum counter clean with an ancient dishcloth.

"That sounds like a threat," said Danny the Sweet.

I was silent, and I smiled at my old friend the Sweet.

"If you are threatening me, I got only this to say, said the Sweet, "don't try it."

But I knew Danny the Sweet, and I had no fear. I lit a cigarette and exhaled the smoke into the winter air.

"Girl, what you think you got on me?" Danny gulped ginger ale. "You can't prove nothing."

"What I got on you," I said, "would make your mama cry." I exhaled slowly.

"You talk too much for me to take you anywhere," said Danny.

A weak argument. Hadn't I watched him change the oil of his Pontiac enough times? Hadn't I coughed my way through drugstores, hacking madly and buying up shelves of Romilar and dozens of candy bars for the Sweet?

I was silent.

"You know you do," said the Sweet.

"Hey, I'm no fool," I told him.

Danny the Sweet turned his back on me. "You see this?" he said. I could see clearly in the reflection of neon the words written in red and gold on the back of his jacket.

THE ORPHANS

Danny turned around to face me once more. "They don't take no trash," he confided.

"I'll behave." I smiled; any lie to meet the Orphans.

"Especially not tonight," continued Danny.

Tonight was a night remembered in the doorways of candy stores all along the Avenue. The Night of the Wolf. The hour when the Orphans went hunting their enemy from the south end of the Avenue – the Pack; a night to celebrate when the snow is covering alleyways and the moon shines white.

"I swear it, Danny," I said. "I won't cause trouble for you."

"Maybe if you showed some respect for me," said Danny the Sweet.

Ah, he wanted me to pay for an introduction to the Orphans. What the hell, I'd fake it.

"I respect you," I said.

"Eh, you never have." Danny unwrapped an Almond Joy. 'Since we were kids, you never have."

Well, that was true. But I liked him anyway; even if the mixture of codeine and chocolate had rotted his brain.

"You all think you're smarter than me," said Danny.

"Ah, Danny, I never said you weren't smart. I never said I didn't respect you."

Ice was forming on my boot, Monty had already dimmed the neon of the store, and the Night of the Wolf would soon be over if Danny didn't stop eating chocolate and feeling so stupid and sad. What more could I say? I wanted *this* Night of the Wolf, not any other – this night, when I was seventeen and the air rose like smoke from the gutter and the ice shone like glass upon the street.

"Hell, you're one of the Orphans, aren't you? You think they would have you if you were dumb?"

They would indeed; Danny was always good for a ride or an alibi, I knew that. But Danny the Sweet didn't have to know. What the hell.

"Yeah." Danny nodded. "Yeah." He smiled.

Good. I had talked him into temporary smartness.

"Let me go with you," I said.

"This one time," warned Danny the Sweet. "O.K. But only this one night."

That was all I needed; for I knew that this was my night; full of smoke and winter and wolves. This was my night.

"Anything you say, Danny," I told him.

The hour was growing late; and Monty sat somewhere in the darkness of the candy store, drinking one gin after the other, and the corner kids stood at a safe distance from us, warily reading the emblem upon Danny's back. "Anything you say," I repeated.

Danny nodded and began to walk down the Avenue; I followed. "You're not taking your car, Sweet?" I asked.

"Are you crazy?" he said. "Are you crazy? This is a secret meeting of the Orphans. The Pack could easily follow my car, see? We walk."

I followed him through the mazes of alleyways that led to wherever the Orphans were.

"Remember not to look at anyone," said Danny. "And whatever happens, don't say a word to the Dolphin."

So the Dolphin would be there tonight. I hadn't thought of that. How could this idiot Danny the Sweet take me where the Dolphin would be?

"What if the Dolphin talks to me?" I asked.

Danny the Sweet stopped in his tracks. Snow fell, and as Danny fumbled for a cigarette, our boots were covered in white. We stood now somewhere close to the City Line, in the territory known as the Orphans', north of an invisible line that stretched across the Avenue.

"Honey," said Danny the Sweet, "don't worry about that. The Dolphin ain't going to talk to you, see? No one's going to talk to you. If you and me both is lucky, no one will even notice your presence. The Orphans is particular about who they address themselves to. So just shut up."

"Drop dead," I said to the Sweet.

"Now, now," said Danny. "You are just a girl, and not even the Property of the Orphans gets to speak at meetings, see?"

"Hah," I said. What had the Property to do with me? Those girls in mascara and leather and silence who belonged to the Orphans.

"Look," said Danny. "After McKay, the Dolphin is the main man. And the Dolphin talks to few."

O.K., I thought. Why should I be offended by the words of the Sweet? It was not everyone who got to sit in the same room as McKay and the Dolphin on the Night of the Wolf. Especially McKay. Why should I lie? This was the night I had waited for; to finally meet McKay. What did I care about the Pack? What did I know of revenge or of blood on the streets? It was McKay, President of the Orphans since the death of Alf Cantinni four years before, whom I cared about. So I said to Danny as we walked in the snow, "You tight with McKay?"

"Sure," said Danny. "Doesn't he call me brother?"

"Doesn't he call everyone that?" I asked.

"Hah," said Danny the Sweet.

"How well do you know McKay? I mean, he really talks to you?" I said.

"Cease with the questions," Danny said.

The Sweet didn't have to respond to my questions; and he

6

probably didn't know any answers. I knew that secrets surrounded the Orphans. All that I knew of them I had heard from Danny, or from the liquor-coated stories Monty told each morning as we had coffee at the counter of his store and he repeated rumors that had blown in through his door off the wind of the Avenue.

Like the corner kids, I could only read the Orphans' colors on the backs of their leather or denim jackets. Jackets I had seen loitering on the corners, loafing outside the Tin Angel Bar, hovering at the doorway of Monty's.

McKay – I knew something of him. I had memorized the lettering on the back of his leather jacket.

PRESIDENT OF
THE ORPHANS

I could conjure the name, the sound of his boot heels on cement; I could recite the number of the license plate of his '59 Chevy in my sleep. McKay – President of the Orphans at seventeen, sworn into office on the night of Alf Cantinni's death. An hour after Cantinni had totaled his Corvette, the Avenue knew that McKay was now President; for four years the Avenue had known the name of the leader of the Orphans.

First in line was now the Dolphin; and secrets surrounded him like ice-coated cement in the streets of January. About him, I'd rather not know. Some said, and perhaps it was Monty who began the story, that it was the Dolphin himself who had begun the Night of the Wolf some years ago. Some said that was how the paintings on his skin had begun. But some said a lot of things.

All I knew was filtered through Danny the Sweet and Monty; so I took it all through a haze of cough syrup and gin. I wanted to see for myself, now – enough of leaning over the Sweet's aging Pontiac to catch the details of the Orphans' activities while I was splattered with oil. Enough of deciphering the brogue and the lies of Monty's stories as he mixed up milk shakes for the corner kids, and rumors for me. I wanted to find out for myself.

Now we reached the edge of City Line; the last border of the Orphans' official territory. The Sweet hesitated. "From now on," he said, "you blind."

"Sure," I said. But I was tracing road maps, alley maps, the drawings of frantic directions on the lining of my jacket pocket. "Sure," I said.

We walked past St. Anne's. Lights flashed colors and the sound of a Temptations record poured onto the street from the chapel.

"Knights of Columbus," said the Sweet. "To keep us off the street on the Night of the Wolf."

We were now conspirators, so Danny the Sweet winked at me. Groups loitered on the steps of the church; bottles of Thunderbird wine cloaked with brown paper bags were passed from one dancer to another. As Danny and I walked on, the crowd let us pass by with mumbled words about the Orphans and stares at the colors of Danny's jacket. Danny the Sweet turned up his collar against the wind, and he winked at me once more.

Those dancers should have known what kind of Orphan was Danny the Sweet. Maybe that was why I felt no fear as we turned into an alleyway off the Avenue a block away from St. Anne's. Did I imagine that the Orphans were all like Danny? Smarter, maybe, but with kind, chocolate-covered hearts.

Danny stopped.

"The clubhouse?" I whispered.

He nodded. "Forget you ever saw it," he said.

It was the basement of Munda's City Line Liquor Store. The home of the Orphans. But as Danny climbed down the cement steps to the basement landing I lingered behind.

"Hey, hey," whispered Danny the Sweet.

I followed; and then I rested my hand on the cold metal of the banister and hesitated.

"Hey." The Sweet's voice rasped.

So I followed. What could I do? Sometimes it's too late; sometimes you walk down the steps, frozen with ice, your hand resting upon the metal banister. You walk into darkness where no neon reaches. "Danny?" I whispered.

"O.K., O.K.," answered the Sweet.

I found Danny's arm and held on to him, and we waited outside the door of the Orphans' clubhouse, both of us knowing that the door would open without us knocking our fists upon it. Sometimes you know when doors will open; you have only to walk up to them and wait.

The light spilled out onto the cement where we stood. I was holding tightly on to the arm of the Sweet, who was sipping ginger ale and blinking his eyes.

"What are you, Sweet, waiting for July?" someone said.

Danny the Sweet giggled. Always an inappropriate response, a giggle, when caught in an act of fear. Even I knew that much.

"Admiring the ambiance of your surroundings," I said. What the hell, as Monty often said, a word was often the best defense.

"Oh, yeah?" The voice at the door sounded nasty.

"Who is that?" I whispered to Danny the Sweet.

"Only Tosh," whispered Danny, and I could see now the shaven head of one of McKay's most feared soldiers. "He's not so tough." The Sweet gulped more ginger ale.

"Evening, Sweet," said a voice behind us on the stair.

Danny turned. I stared at the cement, as advised.

"Evening, McKay," I heard the Sweet say.

So. McKay. I forgot cement, and Tosh at the doorway, and melted ice seeping into my boot. I forgot fear of alleys and the lyrics to all the songs I ever knew. And I remembered only how many girls in Brooklyn and Queens had carved McKay's name into their thighs with slick razor blades. His name in hearts on subway trains and in toilets. President Of. McKay. I could not help but turn.

"Cold Night of the Wolf, brother," McKay said to Danny the Sweet.

"Sure is," mumbled the Sweet.

I forgot myself, forgot that I too stood in that cold stairwell with Danny and McKay. McKay – well, he didn't look evil, but he sure looked bad. His long dark hair fell upon the collar of his leather jacket, his face, unlike so many of the Orphans', was unscarred; I could now understand why so many legs had been marked with the initials of his name.

And then I remembered I was there in that alleyway, for McKay's eye had seen me, and he nodded. I owed it to the Sweet to keep quiet, so I only nodded back. McKay walked past us in that beam of light which fell from the clubhouse door. The letters, red and gold, glowed on his back, the pink motorcycle goggles he wore gleamed electric. McKay opened the door of the clubhouse wider, greeted Tosh, and then, his back to us, the letters "President Of" spotlighted, McKay spoke.

"If you are hip to the ambiance," he said – McKay actually formed those words in his throat, "wait till you see the décor."

So McKay had heard me, had addressed himself to me. Perhaps I should have been surprised, but I was seventeen and the moon was circled with frost and I could not have imagined McKay not speaking to me. I could not have imagined the Night of the Wolf did not belong to me. Danny the Sweet, however, was taken aback; his jaw was slack and his eyes blinked.

"You are causing a draft," said Tosh, who had come out onto the landing to grab the Sweet by the jacket collar and lead him into the basement. I followed – Tosh or the Sweet, who knows? One Orphan jacket looks like any other after you've seen "President Of."

Sometimes you know whether or not it's your night. Sometimes you don't. I wasn't sure. And as I stepped into the clubhouse that first time, I did take McKay's advice. I checked out the décor, mainly because I didn't want to look anyone in the eye. Orange crates and mattresses, wooden chairs and posters with ripped corners advertising car races and demolition derbies, some with McKay's name in small print along with a description of his Chevy. Pillows and cushions and smoke. Your basic basement clubhouse, I assume.

Except for the fact that the basement was populated with Orphans and the Property of the Orphans. I had never seen them all together in one room. One small room with a ceiling of water pipes steaming, one room full of leather and dark

10

eyes and smoke. And now, as I sat on a cushion near Danny the Sweet – I didn't even want to look the Sweet in the eye – I thought of only one thing. Leaving.

And then McKay spoke. He sat on a crate near the cement wall, boots propped up on a footstool, his long hair constantly pushed back as he ran his hand along his forehead. He smiled into the darkness of the room, and I thought no more of leaving.

"Brothers," he said. The noise in the basement began to subside; the air itself seemed to clear of smoke.

Around the room I could see the figures of the silent Orphans. Tosh, with his shaven head, just released from the Joint after eighteen months to five (the charge – arson; the target – his brother-in-law's Mustang), lounged on the floor. Not far from Tosh was T.J., another of the Orphans' soldiers. Small and pale with wispy blond hair, T.J. crouched upon a mattress. The rumor was that T.J. kept losing parts of himself. First a hand, as he leaped toward a freight train and an attempt to travel free to Elizabeth, New Jersey. And then some toes as a Harley, driven by one of the Pack, gave him a dancing lesson. And now I saw he wore a black patch over his left eye. With anyone else I would say the patch was for effect, but T.J.'s eyeball was probably rolling down some alleyway.

Most of the other Orphans – Jose, Little Doug, Menza, and the rest – I had seen racing their cars on the Avenue or loitering in one doorway or another. But now in the dark, in the cold, in the night, with the jackets of their colors, with their sunglasses, their cigarettes, and their closeness to me, I knew why their names were only whispered on the wind of the Avenue. And now they were the fifteen or so shadows that lined the walls of this one room, the room I was in. And then up against the farthest wall: the Property of the Orphans. They sat in a line, in high black boots and darkness, all of them silent with their eyes on McKay. I had often seen the Property in Woolworth's, where scarves flowed into their purses and eyeliner jumped from the counters into their jacket pockets. I had often seen them on one street corner or another, silently waiting for the Orphans, with the insignia upon their backs:

11

PROPERTY OF
THE ORPHANS

The Sweet was right: the Orphans ignored me, but I could feel the eyes of the Property as they turned occasionally from McKay to steal a glance at me. All right, I was looking also. I recognized Starry. Her reputation as a loner, as a fighter, as the Number One Property, was known all along the Avenue. Tonight her pale hair was pushed away from her face and she wore no make-up. She looked no more than fourteen, though she was probably closer to twenty. The way she drank from a bottle of tequila, the way her pale eyes surveyed the room, made it obvious that she was no child.

Near Starry sat Irene La Hoy, who smoked a cigarette while she chewed gum, and who weighed at least twice as much as Starry. Irene also had a reputation on the Avenue, for more than her weight. She was known for her kindness to runaways, drifters, dogs, losers; she was known as a good cook and an easy lay. The rest of the Property were no more than shadows to me in the darkness of the room; six or seven of them sat behind Starry and Irene.

"Brothers," McKay began once more. "Evening on this Night of the Wolf." Murmured greetings echoed his words. "Tonight," said McKay, "we take care of the Pack. Tonight the Pack sees the strength of our colors."

Not bad, I thought.

"Tonight," McKay said with a smile, "they can run, but they cannot hide."

"That's no lie," agreed Tosh.

"Hear what I say," McKay continued. "This night is owned by, belongs to, the Orphans, and the Orphans alone."

General agreement was ensuing, and Danny the Sweet whispered, "Ain't he something?"

And then, somewhere close by, glass broke on the street. McKay held up his arm to silence us. Could it be the Pack's attack? I wasn't unfaithful to McKay, but I could live without an introduction to the Pack, particularly in this, the territory of the Orphans.

The door opened and Martin (the Marine) Storm walked quickly into the clubhouse. He stood at attention and saluted McKay with a nod. "Sisters." He then nodded to the Property.

"What's cooking out there on the street?" T.J. asked, pulling on a jacket sleeve, at a hand that was not there.

"It's Munda's," said Martin. "Some kids from over the church dance broke the windows."

"No alarms?" asked McKay.

"None," said Martin.

"The Man ain't there?" asked Tosh.

McKay laughed. "What are we waiting for? We gotta protect our landlords."

On that signal the Orphans flowed from the clubhouse and up the stairs.

"Stay here," said Danny the Sweet as he followed them out.

"Hah," I said. "Not a chance."

"You heard me," said the Sweet.

But Irene La Hoy was already grabbing my arm, and who could refuse the power of her grasp?

"Stick with the Property," Irene said, and she winked.

Out on the street Josh, Jose, and some others had chased away the dancers who had broken into Munda's. Now Orphans flew through plate glass, grabbing fifths and howling laughter in the dark of the liquor store. Irene La Hoy loosened her grasp on my arm, and she bolted her weight through the broken window.

Starry had walked up behind me. "Hope she don't get stuck," she said, laughing.

Starry and I followed the path of Irene and the sound of smashing bottles. The smell of alcohol was alive in the air and Starry and I watched Irene La Hoy charge the rack of potato chips. Grabbing bags of Wise and Chee-tos, she tore one bag open with her teeth and began to munch wildly. And then Starry silently disappeared to fill her jacket pockets with tequila and Harveys Bristol Cream.

Irene's mouth grew slack as she stood in the store

13

surrounded by mad laughter and the noise of the Orphans tossing bottles onto the tile floor. Her head turned quickly and she knocked her fist on her skull. "What," she cried out, "no dip?"

As Irene began to rummage through a freezer case in search of clam and onion, I felt lost, surrounded by howls, and completely alone. So I walked to the back of the store to search for cartons of cigarettes and to escape the noise of the Orphans.

"A drink?" I heard him say.

It was McKay, seated on the top of the farthest counter, watching the riot that surrounded us, and calmly sipping Dewar's from a crystal wine glass. Leave it to McKay to find crystal in this mess of broken bottles and Orphans. He was something, all right.

"I don't know," I said. "There's not even any dip in this place."

McKay smiled as he poured some whiskey into another glass. He nodded, and yes he was something. So I smiled and accepted the drink.

"How come you're here with the Sweet?" asked McKay. "The Sweet's all right," he continued, 'just a matter of him having no brains."

"So they say." I sipped from the wine glass.

"You belong to him?" McKay said.

"I don't belong to anyone," I said. McKay smiled down at me. Amused? We'd see if McKay stayed amused. "I belong to myself," I said. I belong to myself; not bad. Not bad at all.

"I see," said McKay. He sipped and drummed a rhythm on the counter top with his palm. Under and above McKay's eyes the color was rose.

"Tonight," I said. "What happens tonight between the Orphans and the Pack?"

"That's my business," he said.

"I see," I said.

This was getting nowhere.

"Why don't you be here when I get back?" said McKay. He was staring ahead into the air, into the mass of rioting Orphans. I assumed he was addressing me.

14

"Did you say something?" I said.

"Be here," said McKay.

I would have considered waiting for McKay if he were rowing a small boat to the Galápagos Islands had he merely coughed in my direction. I thought I might find something to fill a few hours while I waited for McKay to drive to the south end of the Avenue and back once more.

"I'll consider it," I said.

McKay smiled, but his smile disappeared when I said, "You sure you're coming back? Kid Harris ain't no child, I hear."

Kid Harris was the President of the Pack, and a name not to be mentioned in McKay's presence.

"I said I'm coming back," McKay said quietly. "And I said be here. But you always got a choice."

I needed no persuasion, but had I, his words would've been enough. McKay sipped his drink amid the rubble of Munda's Liquor Store.

"I'll think about it," I said.

"Think no more," said McKay.

"I'm used to thinking," I told McKay. He turned to stare at me. "But only occasionally," I said.

"Have another drink," said McKay.

I could see Danny the Sweet carrying family-size packages of M & M's and searching the store frantically for me. I was wondering what to do with his worry when Danny's eye found us.

"Don't do that to me," said the Sweet, nervously popping M & M's.

"What?"

"Disappear like that. Jesus."

"She can take care of herself," said McKay.

Really? I winked at the Sweet, but he still looked worried.

"Relax," McKay told him.

"I don't know," said Danny and he stared at us. "I just can't decide between plain and peanut."

"Decide later," said McKay. "Because, brother, it is now time to get these here boys together. And you is the man for the job."

Danny nodded wildly. "Sure," he said. "Sure, McKay."

I followed McKay from the store, tripping once or twice over trash, and bottles, and Orphans, as we walked out into the night air. It was still winter out there; and as we stood together in the alleyway, ice surrounded us and calls and cries were alive in the night.

Later I told Starry that I had not been afraid. That was, of course, a lie. Because on that night, in that alleyway, with McKay's arms holding me, in the half-light of the liquor-store neon, I saw the Dolphin's face for the first time.

"Evening, McKay." The Dolphin's voice was soft and I could not locate him at first.

And then I saw him before us as he stood against the stone of the alley wall, his eyes covered by black sunglasses, the leather of his jacket glowing in neon. Slowly he smoked a cigarette. I could see the famous tattoos upon the skin of his wrists and throat.

"Evening, Dolphin," said McKay.

"I see the liquor's free," said the Dolphin, and McKay laughed. "But you might think that the time for games would be over. This is a serious night – if these boys can understand the word."

The Dolphin came toward us and I moved closer to McKay. On the Avenue it was whispered that the Dolphin originated the Night of the Wolf on a January night when one of the Pack threw a vial of acid into his face. On a night of frost, and moon, and bitter cold, and the slick cement of the streets. And the story ends with the Pack boy never seeing another sunrise over the Avenue again. So they said. And over the counter of the candy store Monty had whispered that the blue butterfly which covers the scar that was the Dolphin's cheek was born on that same night. That butterfly which glowed tonight like ice.

"You playing games, too, McKay?" the Dolphin said.

"There's a time for that," McKay answered.

"And there's a time to get rid of her," said the Dolphin. He hadn't looked at me yet, and he didn't when I spoke.

"That might be easier said than done," I said, and I leaned close to McKay so that I could feel the outline of his hip against me.

16

Danny the Sweet would have cried at the words I spoke, would have vowed, once again, never to take me anywhere. McKay only smiled.

"I doubt that," said the Dolphin, and he continued to stare at McKay. "I could get rid of that girl so fast no one would remember seeing her." The Dolphin stroked his face. His lip curled and the blue butterfly seemed to flutter. Like moving ice.

I merely nodded at the Dolphin and placed my hand on McKay's shoulder. Enough of words – the Dolphin's message to me was clear. Let mine be the same. I lit a cigarette and threw the match into the gutter. McKay took the cigarette from me and inhaled.

The Dolphin said to McKay. "Whenever you say it's time, it's time."

"I say now," said McKay.

McKay knew that the Sweet could never get the Orphans together after all that free liquor. Hell, Danny the Sweet couldn't even get himself together. But when the Dolphin walked toward Munda's, McKay and I both knew it would be minutes before each Orphan had climbed into a Chevy or a Ford; only minutes before keys would be turned, motors started, and the race down the Avenue begun.

"You know you don't have to wait for me," said McKay.

Why did he keep insisting I had a choice? How many hours of watching McKay from second-story windows, how many pages of dialogue planned, how many ways to scrawl his name had I known? There was no question of choice. There had been none when I stood with my hand on the banister of the clubhouse steps. There had been none from the first time I saw him.

"I want you to know that I don't take any Property," McKay said. He combed his hair. "I find it too constricting."

"Really?" I said. "You gonna make me cry," I told him.

"I will," said McKay.

Did he think so? And I kissed him; for the first time I kissed him.

"Wait," I said. "Wait, and then we'll see who cries."

"I'll be back before morning," said McKay; and already the

17

Orphans had left Munda's to start their engines. The search for the Pack on this Night of the Wolf had begun. The Dolphin was driving the black '59 Chevy that McKay owned and raced. He skidded the car to a stop at the curb and the engine strained.

"McKay," said the Dolphin.

The door of the Chevy sprang open and McKay slid into the back seat. He leaned deep into the custom-velvet upholstery and rested his head against it. It was difficult to know where the eyes of the Dolphin stared, but they must have focused on McKay's image in the rearview mirror, for the minute McKay nodded his head slightly the Chevy took off, fast as light, down the Avenue. The other cars belonging to the Orphans followed in procession and the street ice flew through the night air like bullets. And I stood, and waited in the night.

Look, I was in love.

What more can I say? Oh, I was a fool. Is that it? If that's what you want me to say I can't say it. Listen. It wasn't only McKay. It was all of them, each one. Even the Dolphin, in a way. From that night on I thought of nothing but the Orphans, nothing but McKay. That's how love is, isn't it? Song lyrics and printing the name hundreds of times on hundreds of pieces of paper.

Ah, I see. You can't forget that all of the words are draped in black leather. Then don't forget. If you want to know about dope, I'll tell you about dope. You want words about sex, I can tell you those. Anything you want to know. I can spill my guts, I can tap-dance on signal. And I can lie, like I can dance. Words about orgies and betrayals and knife fights in the street. The location of the Avenue, the address of the clubhouse. If you want me to lie. Because the truth is McKay was in love with his vision of the Orphans, with his vision of himself. And I was in love with them both. That's all.

I fell in love with them on that night, though I suppose I had been even before I knew any names. I could not help it, because the spell was cast, the mood was set, and with the wind of the Avenue moving around me and the ice shining like mirror, there was no choice at all.

18

Do you see? Do you see McKay on that Night of the Wolf? Sitting in that Chevy, leaning against the maroon upholstery, smoking a cigarette, chasing his enemy through the darkness of the night? You see the scarred Dolphin driving the Chevy along the Avenue? His black-gloved hand upon the wheel? The Sweet, a codeine smile on his face. Possibly he sat in the front seat with the Dolphin that night. I don't know. I didn't see everything, I can't tell you every detail; from where I stood I saw only the red glow of taillights moving down the Avenue.

From where I stood I could only hear sighs, words that were a story of love. Nothing more than that. And nothing less. And so I waited in the alleyway. I waited for some time, smoking a cigarette, watching for the morning, for McKay. But morning was still hours away, and I remembered that it was winter, and that I was cold. So I made my way back to the clubhouse, and for a second time opened the door.

Soft radio music played and the voices of the Property of the Orphans rose above the song lyrics. Starry stood in the middle of the room, her pale hair floating in a circle as she swung her head and drank from the bottle of tequila which was now almost empty. When I entered the room, when the cold air and the slamming of a door followed me and announced my presence, the Property of the Orphans became quiet. Starry gulped from the bottle until it was drained, then she turned and saw me. She smiled.

"Welcome, sister," she said.

II

"We have a responsibility to the Orphans," Starry said.

I nodded, lit a cigarette, and looked at the clock on the wall. They had surely reached the south end, the Pack's side, of the Avenue by now.

"We got a reputation to uphold," Starry continued.

"I know I do my best to keep my reputation," said Irene La Hoy. There was laughter. We all got her double entendre, there was no need for Irene to poke me and giggle.

"It's nothing personal," said Starry. "If McKay wants to

see you some, that's not my business. But you talk trash about the Property and we'll punch your heart out."

Was that all? So this was Starry's game – getting the new girl. I'd rather not play. I only wanted to wait for McKay and be left alone. So I smiled.

"Personally," said Starry, "I like you."

"Oh, yeah?" I said. Did she think her opinion meant something to me? "Why?"

"Why not?" Starry said. "I like you until you prove me wrong. I've made mistakes, but I trust my judgment."

She was like they said, pretty tough for a girl only four feet eleven and ninety-something pounds and with strands of uncombed pale hair, and no particular Orphan to protect her. It was rumored that Starry didn't need anyone to protect her; she defended herself.

"I won't cause no trouble if you don't cause me none," I said.

"Don't get so hostile," Starry said. "Like I say, nothing personal, long as you know you're nothing to the Property and that the minute McKay wants you gone, girl, you gone."

"Fine with me, sister," I said. The minute McKay wanted me gone I would permanently erase the basement and all its occupants from my memory forever.

Irene La Hoy was fixing salami on rye and whiskey sours from packaged mix – all taken from Munda's. I accepted a drink and a sandwich. Irene smiled at me. Well, there was one on my side. Wait, did I have a side? What did I care? The Property was nothing to me, I was waiting for McKay.

Starry called an informal meeting of the Property to order. I could see what had made Starry the Number One Property – she belonged to no one but herself, with her first allegiance to the Orphans. Before the death of Alf Cantinni, the Number One Property was always the Property of the President. But McKay had changed all that; Cantinni was dead, his Property, Wanda, had run off to Florida with some college football hero, and McKay was not one to take Property. That left Starry. She was the toughest, the smallest, the smartest of the Property. I'd say the Orphans had gotten a fair deal. Particularly when comparing Starry with the rest of the

Property. I looked around and could now give names to those who were only shadows before.

Leona I had seen wandering about on the Avenue; she was Tosh's Property. Like Tosh, Leona had a special droopy-eyed look about her; on him the look was mean, but Leona just looked tired. Her long dark hair fell across her face, and she mechanically rubbed at her nose and then twitched the muscles of her cheek.

To Leona's right was Gina, who worked behind the counter at Monty's mixing egg creams and stealing from the cash register. Gina and I had a speaking acquaintance. Often I said to her, as she attempted a short-change, "You owe me a dime."

Often she had said to me, "What you listen to Monty's bullshit stories for, anyways?" Gina was the Property of T.J.; constantly wondering and worrying over which part T.J. would lose next had created the permanent affectation of batting eyelids.

"Hey, Gina," I said – after all she had seen me at the counter of Monty's often enough, so I thought I might attempt a conversation – "I don't particularly want to be at a personal meeting of the Property. It ain't got nothing to do with me."

Gina gazed at me as though for the first time. "So, don't listen," she said. That I could have told myself.

Did I want to know the details of Irene's abortion? Did I care about the Property of the Pack? The others, whose names I was learning – Black Susan, Marie, and Kind, the quietest of the Property who had a particular smile when she looked at McKay – did I want to overhear their personal conversations and give them just cause to later punch my heart out? So, I blocked it all out with pages and photographs from *Rona Barrett's Hollywood*.

After some time, I noticed that only a few of the Property remained in the basement. Even Leona was now gone, and Starry, Gina, Irene, and I were quiet, and waiting. Starry sat down on a cushion and listened to me rustle the columns of gossip.

"I have to do that,' said Starry.

"Do what?" I asked. I wasn't about to make anything that sounded like an apology easy for her.

"I'm really too short to be in charge of the Property," Starry said. She opened a new bottle of tequila. "Hell, anyone in this room could take me, easy. So I put some meanness in my style. You understand, it's nothing personal."

"Sure," I said.

"It all has to do with height." She nodded.

What good would it do me not to understand Starry's words? "Sure," I said. "Nothing personal."

"If you want to be with McKay, that's cool with me. Even if you are a nobody."

"Thanks," I said.

"Now, some will have you understand, seeing how I'm the Number One Property, that there's something between McKay and me. Bullshit. It's only that we're both the best. When Cantinni was wasted, McKay was voted in. When Wanda split, I got voted. in. Now, if you want to keep your eyes open," Starry said, "you look out for Leona and Kind. They're the bitches. And Kind's got her eye on the Number One slot, no matter what she got to do to get it."

Starry needn't have wasted her campaign speech on me: I wasn't about to become involved in the politics of the Property. I had noticed Kind's green eyes on McKay, but she had been a shadow to me then, and as long as McKay didn't look back, she would remain a shadow.

"Thanks for the advice."

"It ain't really advice," Starry said. "It's more like a warning. See, McKay is gonna make you cry. But since somebody will, it might as well be McKay. At least he looks good." Starry winked.

"I'll remember that," I said. "And you remember that I'm not Leona, and I'm not Kind, and I'm not aiming to be the Number One Property. The truth is, I don't give a shit about the Property."

"You're only interested in McKay."

I believed I could see the beginnings of an understanding. "Only McKay," I said, and Starry nodded.

So we waited in the clubhouse and the hour grew later. The

moon was falling, and the Night of the Wolf was outside the door. We knew this and we pretended not to know. I turned page after page of the magazine, Irene and Gina traded jokes, and Starry sat with her knees drawn up tightly, sipping tequila and staring into the air. Gina and I waited for particular Orphans, Irene for any Orphan. But Starry should have been out there in the Avenue. I could see from the white of her clenched fist that she waited to hear details of a battle she should have been a part of. She would fight to stay Number One Property, but she would have fought still harder out there on the street where she belonged.

Outside we could hear the screeching of tires. Perhaps because of the whiskey I had drunk, perhaps because of the lateness of the hour, I had fallen into a restless sleep. I dreamed for a while, and somewhere in that dream I heard the door of the clubhouse open and clatter against the stone wall of the basement.

"Get the door!" Starry screamed. But it was too late, as it always is by the time a forgotten lock is remembered. I awoke to see the Pack walking down the stairs of the Orphans' clubhouse. I awoke cursing that fool, Danny the Sweet, for having brought me into the Night of the Wolf.

"Get them out!" shouted Starry. But who was there to do that? Irene had sipped too many whiskey sours, eaten too many sandwiches to do anything but wail. Me? This was none of my business. Sure I was on the Orphans' side, but I also had nothing against the Pack.

There were only five of them. Although I had never before seen him, I could tell Kid Harris was among them. I hadn't expected this. I lit a cigarette – what else was there to do? Starry rushed the Pack and was thrown against the wall easily by one of Kid Harris's gloved hands. I decided to smoke my Marlboro and wait and see what happened. There's a time to make a move, and there's a time not to. Starry stood against the wall, hand on her hip, and she too lit a cigarette.

One of the Pack shut the door of the clubhouse and we could hear the click as the lock was bolted.

"Howdy," said Kid Harris. The enemy of the Orphans stood before us in black leather and boots with his red hair long on the shoulders of a pink shirt. I agreed with Starry's sentiment as she spat on the floor of the basement, inches away from the Kid's boot. His black-and-pink wardrobe, his use of the friendly Western vernacular, and the sneer on his face were all repulsive.

"Do that again and I'll break your head," Kid Harris told Starry. Now that I was completely awake, and as Starry sat down heavily on an orange crate, I could see blood on Kid Harris's face and marks of battle on the others. Yes, surely the Pack and the Orphans had already met. The knife wound on Kid Harris's face was fresh and he held a handkerchief to the gash. "See this?" he said to me.

"How can I help but see it?" I said.

Kid Harris raised his arm in the air. When he brought his hand down before my face, a knife had been clicked open.

"See this?" Kid Harris grinned.

I nodded.

"The Dolphin's gone and cut one too many tonight," he said.

I nodded. And I agreed.

"Someone's gonna have to pay for this." Kid Harris touched his face. "I won't take the blame for the death of Cantinni that happened years ago. I won't be the target of the Dolphin's vendetta. Someone will pay."

"Ah," said Starry, "you was so pretty before, and now you is ruined." She laughed loudly.

Irene and Gina looked with widening eyes at Starry as she continued to laugh at Kid Harris. The girl was tough, but why bother? There was no defense against the Pack, and anyway, Harris was after the Dolphin. No need to protect the Dolphin; that was how I saw it. But I knew Starry saw it differently. She had a responsibility to the Orphans.

"So that's the way you want it," Kid Harris said.

"Man, I wouldn't want it any way, not from you," said Starry.

Kid Harris walked to Starry, looked down at her, and hit her in the face with his fist. None of the Pack moved. I could hear something like a cry escape from Gina. Starry had known what would happen. She was ready, and had been

24

quietly waiting for the force of Harris's fist.

I was not. I began to think – if she lost any teeth, who would pay? The Dolphin? McKay? X rays would be expensive, caps even more so. Starry only looked up at Kid Harris, the blood trickling from her mouth. She didn't move. Maybe she swayed just a little, but she held herself straight and stared into the face of Kid Harris.

I picked up the bottle of tequila and stood.

"Bastard!" I cried and smashed the bottle on the wood of a chair. I was beside myself now. Look, I had never before seen anyone hit a girl as small as Starry. "How many more scars can fit on your face?" I said. Where was I finding these words?

"None that you'll put there." Kid Harris had turned to face me, and he laughed.

"I'll cut you," I said as Kid Harris walked toward me.

"You won't," said Kid Harris.

Whether or not I would did not matter. I knew this when I looked down. The bottle was not the jagged and murderous weapon I had intended, for the glass had merely splintered, leaving me holding nothing but glass fragments and streaming blood on the palm of my hand.

Now I began to laugh. My palm with blood running across the lifeline. Me, here in the clubhouse of the Orphans, avenging Starry because of her height, defending myself with splinters of glass. Me: the antagonist of Kid Harris. I couldn't help it, I laughed in the Kid's face.

It was then that he hit me. I fell onto the floor, the cement was cold against my back. Looking up I could see only the smile on Kid Harris's face as he raised his arm. And I wondered if the knife was in his hand, if he had tired of waiting for the Dolphin and had decided to substitute my face for the Dolphin's.

I was not afraid. If anything, I was curious. Would he cut me? Wouldn't he? Would I cry out? What had the death of Alf Cantinni, a name whose face I had never known, to do with me? What had any of this to do with me?

"Starry!" A voice called from outside the clubhouse door. Harris stopped his hand in mid-air; the Pack stood at attention.

25

"Starry, honey, you in there?" said the voice.

Kid Harris nodded at Starry. "Who is it?" he whispered.

"Jose," said Starry. "Only Jose. I was supposed to wait for him." But the voice outside the door did not sound like the voice of Jose.

One of the Pack walked to the door on a signal from Harris. "Don't," said Starry. "Don't open the door."

Harris only smiled and walked away from me to pick up an unopened bottle of liquor from the floor. "We'll see one Orphan dance now," he whispered.

One of the Pack opened the door and cold air rushed into the clubhouse. I arched my back, leaned on my elbows, and realized, perhaps at the same time as Kid Harris, that Starry was never supposed to meet up with Jose. Starry was grinning and Kid Harris turned on his heel.

"Keep the door locked," he shouted. But it was too late. Jose would not be at that door alone. And it was too late.

Not Jose, but McKay stood in the doorway.

"So, we find the Wolf twice on one night," said McKay.

I tell you this was it. If I wasn't sold on McKay before, I was now.

The Dolphin now stood beside McKay, and never could I have imagined greeting the Dolphin's presence with a smile, with a sigh. The Orphans, in full colors and in silence, waited behind the Dolphin and McKay. The Pack edged away and looked nervously toward Kid Harris for an order, any order. No, this was not their night.

"It's only fair," said Kid Harris. "You know what's honorable, McKay."

"Honor?" said McKay. "Is it honor I find when I walk into the Orphans' clubhouse and find the Pack? When I find the Pack in my territory? Is it honor I find when I see that?"

I turned to see where McKay pointed. But he pointed at me, and I remembered the cold of the floor and I rose to sit near Irene and Gina.

"Why," said McKay, "was she on the floor?"

"You talk!" said Kid Harris. "The Orphans fight like rats in the sewer, come to *our* territory to do destruction, take down Ralph when he ain't prepared – what do you expect? A

26

thank-you card?" Kid Harris rubbed at his face. "And this,' he said, stroking his wounded face, and looking at the Dolphin, "this I won't forget soon."

The Dolphin smiled. 'You weren't supposed to forget," he said. "No, indeed. You were not supposed to forget."

I could see Danny the Sweet now, and Jose. Two or three of the Orphans were missing, it had been a hard Night of the Wolf. Outside, morning noises were beginning on the Avenue. The cover of darkness was lifting and the Night of the Wolf was almost yesterday. Almost.

"Enough for one night," said McKay. "For a man without honor we got pity." McKay smiled.

"Fuck your pity." Kid Harris tried to smile as calmly as McKay did.

"Pity for defeat," whispered McKay. The Orphans laughed. "Pity for the Pack who are only good for fighting with the Property."

"I got mine tonight," said the Dolphin. He lit a cigarette and blew the smoke into Harris's face. "I can get the rest of him some other night. When he don't expect it."

"I have no pity," said Starry. And she walked toward the Dolphin and McKay. McKay nodded when he saw the blood on Starry's face; one of her bottom teeth had been knocked out and her nose dripped blood. McKay removed his motorcycle goggles; he touched his hand to Starry's cheek.

"Yes," he said. For an instant his eyes found mine. "Yes," said McKay again.

Tosh and another Orphan guided Harris to the wall of the clubhouse. Harris stood with legs apart and hands up against the stone of the wall.

"The Night of the Wolf is over," called out one of the Pack.

"Not for me," said Starry. She stood close to Harris and then she picked up a wooden footstool and handed it to McKay. McKay nodded, and waited for Starry to leave the basement. When she had shut the door behind her, McKay walked toward Harris.

"Brother Wolf," McKay said. "You'll touch no one with those hands when I'm through."

McKay raised the stool and brought it down on Harris's

hand. Again. And again. Tosh held the hand against the cement and Harris cried out in anger and then in pain as the bones broke under McKay's hammering. Now Tosh held Harris's other hand against the wall. I had to look away.

Danny the Sweet found me. He placed his arm around my shoulder and produced a Milky Way and a Kleenex.

"Hey, Sweet," I whispered; and I leaned my head on his shoulder.

"I'm sorry," said Danny.

"I'm not," I said, and I touched his face where it had been bruised under the eye. "I'm really not," I told him. It was true, whatever I was, sorry wasn't part of it.

You see, I was waiting for McKay.

2

UNDER THE SPELL

I

I KNEW NO chants, no charms, no words of love. So what could I do? There was the chance that McKay might not even remember my face. What then? I wasn't one to take chances, to take risks. I knew only what words could often cast the most effective spell, but which words to work on McKay? I wasn't sure.

McKay drank coffee, and the window of the clubhouse had been unshuttered so that the morning light fell across him like bars. Few Orphans had left the clubhouse. Figures moved upon the mattress, and shadows talked quietly in the corners of the room. Danny the Sweet snored for a while, his head resting on my knee, and then he slept deeply and soundlessly. I had waited for that, and I slipped a cushion under the Sweet's head before I stood and walked toward McKay.

It was still early morning, not more than seven, yet it seemed hours ago that Kid Harris and his Pack had been escorted from the basement to be dropped off on some dawn-dark corner of the Avenue. After Irene had painted the cuts on my palms with iodine, I had slept, while the private council of McKay and his soldiers – the Dolphin, Tosh, and Jose – whispered in the darkness of the threat of retaliation. I found I cared less and less about sounds out there on the Avenue. Kid Harris's slap had made me a quick convert to the Orphans' regiment, and I cared for nothing that existed outside the walls of the clubhouse.

But now I needed some words, some potion, some magic

29

that would affect McKay. I walked to where McKay sat. He was alone and quiet and watching the dance of last night's street in the air before him.

"I know better now," I said.

My words brought McKay back from the streets of last night, and he smiled.

"Meaning what?" he asked. His voice was softer than it had been last night, but the smile was the same.

"Meaning, I know not to ask if you're sure you'll be back."

I had wanted those words to flatter McKay. But the grin on his face made it clear he thought I was stating the obvious, that I had merely wised up and seen the light of his truth.

"I don't exaggerate, if it can be helped," he said.

"I see." I watched McKay as he watched me, grinning with enjoyment at seeing me wordless. Maybe it was the lack of sleep, maybe it was McKay not telling me how wonderful I was to stand up to Kid Harris, more likely I was angry at not knowing the words I needed. Whatever it was, I had had it with the Orphans, with the smoke that filled the room, with McKay. I had had it with waiting for McKay.

"To hell with you," I told him.

McKay sipped coffee. The lines of laughter were at the corners of his eyes.

"Did you hear me?" I said.

"I heard you all right," McKay said, and he offered me a cigarette.

"Did you know," I said as I accepted a light for the cigarette, "that I was on the floor last night when you walked in because I was fucking Kid Harris?"

The lines around McKay's eyes deepened. I could tell he was hiding his grin within the coffee cup.

"And that I liked it?" I said. "And that I told him he was much better than any Orphan could be?"

"You told him that?" McKay smiled.

I was silent. We stared at each other. "There is no way to get you angry, is there?" I said.

"There is, darling," said McKay.

I doubted that. How could he, the President of the Orphans, let me talk such trash to him? Furthermore, what the hell did he care, anyway?

"Really?" I said. "What? You tell me what would get you angry."

"Try leaving," said McKay.

I didn't believe that one for a minute. "Leaving?" I said.

"That's right," McKay said.

All right, then. I walked to the door, and I didn't hear McKay's angry shouts. I opened the door, and there was no maddened rage. I walked out of the clubhouse and into the street.

The air was cold and clear; snow reflected white light into my eyes. So I lost out with McKay. So? If nothing else, I could call a bluff. If nothing else, I could let him know I was no fool. Leaving, hah. Although, I admitted, there in the light of the Avenue, it wasn't a bad line.

At least I had had a chance. If nothing more I had taken the opportunity to tell McKay to go to hell. How many could say that? So? So, all I wanted now was coffee and a seat at Monty's counter, that was all. But standing outside the Orphans' clubhouse, I began to cry. No sound, only tears. The door of the clubhouse slammed. I could hear the echo of boot heels on cement, and McKay was beside me.

"You don't listen, do you?" he said.

"I can hear," I said.

"What's this?" McKay was referring to the tears. I had told him we would see who cried, well, now we saw. So I began to walk down the Avenue. I knew McKay wasn't one to follow. But he didn't have to follow, he simply held my arm, and although my feet kept on moving, I realized that the rest of me wasn't going anywhere. I didn't have a chance. I wasn't going anywhere.

"I said, what is this?" said McKay.

McKay was angry now; his voice grew quiet. I was certain McKay's anger had surfaced not with my leaving the clubhouse, but because I had involved him with something that had to do with tears.

"I feel it's really none of your business," I said.

"Perhaps you haven't heard," said McKay, "that I never involve myself in what ain't my business."

31

He was wrong. I had, indeed, heard that. He never got involved unless it was a matter of defending his honor.

"The hell it is," I said.

"Accept it," said McKay. "This is my business. You are my business, and that's all there is to it, whether or not you want it that way."

McKay lit another cigarette and handed it to me, and maybe he smiled, I don't know. And he couldn't have known that acts of kindness made me cry. That cigarettes being lit and offered to me when I cried could make me sob. So I did. McKay studied the effect of winter lighting, and the nuances it could lend to the shadows upon a Chevron station. He waited until I could take the cigarette from him.

"What you need is coffee," said McKay.

"That's not what I want," I said.

"Yeah, coffee." He nodded. "I know you ain't used to the ways of the Orphans. All right, last night was hard for you. You think Starry enjoyed it?"

McKay led me toward the Chevy and opened the door. I sat in the car and he began to shut the door after me, still muttering about the soothing effects of coffee. I held the door open.

"What I want," I said as McKay stood in the street, one arm leaning upon the glass of the car window, "is for you to fall in love with me."

"No," said McKay.

"No?" I said.

"No. I don't go in for that," said McKay. "That falling in love, I don't go for that."

"All right," I said, as he closed the door of the car. Through the black-tinted windshield I watched him walk to the other side of the Chevy. "All right," I said, as McKay opened the door of the driver's seat and was there beside me. "Then I'll take what I can get."

I had faith in McKay, so I closed my eyes, and in the warmth of the Chevy, with my head leaning against the velvet upholstery, I heard only the lullaby of the Chevy engine. McKay could decide what direction to go; I needed more sleep.

I awoke on the George Washington Bridge.

"McKay," I said. "Why are we on this bridge?"

"We're going to safe territory," said McKay. I was beginning to doubt him.

"Where's that?" I asked.

"Clifton, New Jersey," he said.

"I see," I said. "Clifton, New Jersey, is safe territory."

I did trust McKay; it was his sense of direction I thought a bit strange.

"Hey, girl, you see T.J. after the Night of the Wolf?"

"No." I had assumed that T.J. was somewhere gathering pieces of himself off the street.

"No," said McKay. "And you might not see him soon again. You want to see him, check out the critical ward, and you just might see him there. What do you think, this is a game?"

"Hey, where was I last night?" I said. "Where was I, drinking champagne? I got hit, you know. I almost got cut."

"Almost," said McKay. "What do you know? Do you know that Cantinni was murdered by the Pack? Wasted by their treachery? Do you see the scar the Dolphin carries? That was just innocent fun they had with you last night? You say you think occasionally? Then think what would've happened last night if Starry hadn't of thought fast and said she was meeting Jose. Just think."

I was thinking. Yes, Starry had acted fast. But it was McKay whose hand had knocked upon the door. I looked at him. He was concentrating on the lanes of the bridge, for a wind had come up and the Chevy edged first toward the divider and then into the lane to our right. McKay was driving as he must when he raced the Chevy. We were flying over the near-empty lanes of the bridge.

"Could you pull over?" I said.

"Honey, I don't trust the Pack for shit, for all I know they could've followed us. Clifton is safe territory."

For that matter, so was the George Washington Bridge.

"Could you pull over?" I said.

"Are you going to be sick?" said McKay.

"No."

"Because if you're going to be sick, I'd rather you not do it in the car, see? It messes up the car, see?"

McKay kept his foot on the accelerator. Wind and the steel columns of the bridge passed us by.

"I race this Chevy, and you can't race a car someone's been sick in," said McKay. "Particularly not when the upholstery's velvet. Don't let my talk of the Pack scare you sick, girl. And not in the car, that's all."

"Yes," I said. "I'm going to be sick. Pull over."

I had no intention of being sick. The thought hadn't entered my mind. Had it, I would not have thought twice about McKay's upholstery. And I felt no fear of the Pack. So they were not playing games – well, neither was McKay. No, I was not afraid of the Pack. I only knew I'd rather be with McKay there above the Hudson River than in a room across the street from the Greyhound Station in Clifton, New Jersey.

McKay turned the Chevy into an emergency parking area – one telephone and cement.

"I'd rather not go to New Jersey," I said.

"Sure," said McKay. "Sure, I understand. You ain't being forced to go anywhere with me."

"That's true," I said and moved closer to him.

"Do I understand?" said McKay.

"I have no idea, do you?" I said, as I unbuttoned my jacket.

What do you expect? I had no previous history of seduction on the George Washington Bridge. Or on any bridge, for that matter. I had no previous history of seduction at all.

"McKay," I said, and I sat with one leg raised, so that I could unzip my boot. "I want to fuck you, but not in New Jersey."

I used those words because I knew McKay would smile when he heard them. And he did. I would not use words that would make him turn away and say, "No. Not me. I don't go for that." I pulled my T-shirt over my head. I was afraid to tell McKay that if it wasn't him it would be no one, and so I was silent. I held my arms around McKay and felt the touch of his hands on my shoulders, and then across my back.

And as I lay with McKay on the front seat of the Chevy, I forgot we were parked on the George Washington Bridge. I forgot the Hudson River below us. McKay unzipped my jeans and I thought I would tell him once, only once, and say the words so softly that perhaps he might not hear.

"McKay," I whispered, as I pulled my jeans off and felt him move as he unbuckled his belt. "There has never been anyone but you."

Whether or not he heard me, I didn't know. But for some words the saying can be far more important than the hearing.

I unbuttoned McKay's shirt. He still wore the Orphans jacket and the black leather pressed against my breasts.

"McKay," I said. "McKay, honey, take off your jacket."

"No," he said, and he kissed me. For the second time, he kissed me.

"Why not?" I whispered.

I felt McKay hard against me. Because I knew the answer to my question without McKay speaking, I felt fear. "Can't you forget?" I whispered. And I knew the answer: that there was no time, not even now, when McKay could forget the Orphans.

"Darling," said McKay, and I could barely hear him. "Darlin'," he said, and McKay was inside me now, "I am always prepared."

And no, we did not get caught fucking on the George Washington Bridge. No maintenance crews peered through the black-tinted windows, and no tow trucks dragged the Chevy away. I did not shiver, with McKay's jacket thrown about my bare shoulders, as the Highway Patrol forced McKay to stand with his hands upon the roof of the Chevy and his back unprotected by the colors of his jacket.

No. Sometimes love is made on the George Washington Bridge and the traffic still flows by and the radio music plays on without interruption. No sirens flash, no gale winds rise off the Hudson. I did not love McKay any more than I had when I watched him from second-story windows without knowing the color of his eyes.

Sorry if I disappoint you, if you wanted to hear sirens or see flashes. And are these sights and sounds expected because of youth, of leather? It is so easy to forget being young when young; easier still when cloaked in black leather. Was McKay young? Twenty-two, and his body, you've seen some of it, still young. But the skin and the muscles and the blood know the streets at midnight and at dawn, they know Chevy engines and honor. Do you call that young? We did not. For it is easy to forget that we were once young when we didn't even know it at the time.

A matter of perspective? Perhaps. That morning on the bridge would the driver of the tow truck have known I was in love? Could he have known how young McKay was? But why ask you? You passed us by that morning without seeing McKay's eyes or feeling the touch of his hand on your skin. If a warning had been tossed from the window of a Jersey-bound Ford, I would have smiled and wrapped my legs around McKay, and smiled again. If the note had had scrawled across it: "This is a matter of perspective. And you're not seeing," I would have turned to McKay with a wink and a nod. If the telephone that waited in the frozen cement of the emergency parking area had rung, I would never have answered. Of course, it is easiest to forget what is never known. And that telephone could have rung for hours.

See us, surrounded by cement and wind. Against the bed of maroon velvet. The winter and the Chevy and youth hidden by language and leather. See how little I knew; not even the letters of my own name. Only McKay, and the sound of the wind upon the roof of the Chevy.

Because he held me closer, and because he whispered love in my ear without saying a word, I loved McKay as the colors of the Orphans jacket covered me.

II

McKay drove the Chevy back toward the city. What did I know of Manhattan? Manhattan may have been the city, but New York was Queens, Brooklyn, and Long Island. And I didn't need knowledge of highways and exits; I had faith in McKay.

Because McKay had stopped all verbal communication, and was concentrating on avoiding scratches on the finish of the Chevy while driving at sixty through Manhattan streets, I lit a cigarette and sang along with the radio lyrics.

"McKay," I said finally, when I had seen enough tailgating of taxis, enough running of yellow lights, enough sprinting of pedestrians from out of the path of the Chevy, "why are you going downtown?"

McKay shrugged and pointed to the Winstons on the dashboard. I handed him a cigarette and struck a match and tried to ignore the screeching of tires that seemed to follow us. McKay inhaled and kept his eyes on the street. Let him think this was Daytona, what did I care? And I didn't take his silence personally. Last night had been long, and this, I assumed, had not been a typical morning for him. Anyway, I knew McKay to be a man of few words. Did I look angry? For McKay had thrown his cigarette out the window and rested his hand on my leg. Did I look as though his silence offended me or had McKay heard the words of love I had spoken?

"Occasionally I like to think, also," said McKay.

"All right," I said. "About this morning or last night?" I said.

"Last night." McKay smiled.

And although he smiled, I knew that was no joke. "Thanks," I said. "Don't spoil me with your charm."

"The Orphans did what they were expected to do," McKay continued.

"You won." I shrugged.

"There's no winning," said McKay. "There's only defending your honor. You do a good job of it, or you don't."

"Honor," I said.

"Yeah, that's right," said McKay. "What do you think it's all about?"

I didn't know.

"Shit," said McKay. "It's honor. Like when I race this Chevy." As opposed to what he was doing now? "You think I race for money?" said McKay. "Shit, I could make more money pulling a job on one liquor store than I can in a month of racing. It's knowing you're the best, see?"

Well, I knew he was the best; everyone on the Avenue knew it. Seemed as if McKay was the only one who didn't know it.

37

"You don't have to prove nothing to me," I said.

"What do you know?" said McKay.

"What about Cantinni?" I asked.

"What about him?"

"There's talk on the Avenue that somebody tampered with his car, fixed it good, the night he had the accident. The Pack?" I asked. "Was it the Pack?"

"There's a lot of talk on the Avenue," said McKay, and he lifted his hand and drew away from me.

Another subject to be avoided. What was not?

"Why are we stopping?" I said as McKay double-parked the Chevy. I had a right to know at least that much.

"Picking up the Dolphin," said McKay.

I moved away from McKay and rested my cheek against the cold glass of the window. Why did being with McKay have to include the Dolphin? I stared out the window. "Where are we?" I said.

"Harlem," said McKay.

The Dolphin certainly moved around. With whom and for what, I didn't want to know. If I had known the subway lines I would've asked McKay to let me off at any street corner.

And so I was silent as McKay double-parked the Chevy on 123rd Street alongside a Corvair.

"Honey, you afraid to wait in the car?" he asked.

I wasn't, but where McKay went, I wanted to go. "Yes," I said.

I walked with McKay. The street was quiet, except for some shadowy figures who rested up against the icy shelter of storefronts or doorways. It was too cold for almost anyone else; it was certainly too cold for me. I slipped my hand into McKay's jacket pocket. "Is that really what you want? To be the best?" I asked him.

"What else is there?" said McKay.

I hadn't thought of it that way. "Second best?" I laughed. McKay rolled his eyes and didn't bother to answer.

We walked to the cement stoop of a dark apartment building. Rust from the fire escape fell like red confetti as McKay pulled open the glass door of the building. I followed McKay through the darkness of the hallway and stopped

38

when he did. McKay knocked twice with his fist.

"Who there?" a voice said through the peeling green paint of the door.

"McKay," was the answer. I held his arm tighter. It was colder in that hallway than it was out in the street and I began to shiver.

"Nothing to be afraid of," said McKay.

"It's just the cold," I told him. McKay smiled and touched my face with his fingertips and must have known that I wished I were still in the Chevy, smoking cigarettes and waiting for him.

"It's no stranger in there," said McKay. "It's only a cousin of Jose's. A friend of the Orphans."

Some cousin of Jose's. What did I know about Jose? How could I be comforted by his familial relationships?

"Hey, boy," said the figure in the open doorway. "The dude has been waiting on you." Jose's cousin, a thin black man in a denim jacket, motioned us to enter the apartment.

"Been busy," said McKay as we walked inside.

"I see." Jose's cousin nodded to me.

"Far as I can tell, Flash, you haven't seen nothing for years now," said McKay.

"That's a fact," said Flash.

The light was dim in the apartment, but I could see the Dolphin, in sunglasses and T-shirt, seated on a couch in the middle of the room. And even in this dim lighting, I could see clearly for the first time the colors on his skin. His arms were painted with red and green, covered by panthers and crosses and flowers with no name. On his chest a peacock, whose colors reached up in feathers to his neck. Not an inch of visible skin was bare of illustrations, not an inch without color.

"McKay," said the Dolphin.

"Brother." McKay nodded. "Jose." McKay nodded to a figure that sat in an armchair, in darkness.

"McKay, you taking goddamn Property?" said Jose. "What you bring her here for?"

McKay walked toward Jose and switched on an electric light so that his face could now be seen. "You say something

39

to me?" McKay said quietly. Jose blinked his eyes against the light. "I don't think I heard you. You say something to me?"

I could feel Jose's fear and the anger of McKay. Was McKay defending me and my presence in this uptown apartment? Could this be something like love? Or only honor once again?

"He didn't say nothing," said the Dolphin.

"Hey, my cousin's crazy," agreed Flash. "He didn't say nothing."

Jose nodded.

"I didn't think I heard anything," said McKay.

I was impressed. And more. Could this be the same McKay I had laid not more than an hour ago in the front seat of a Chevrolet? McKay who with a few words could bring about intense hearing loss in these three in this Harlem apartment?

McKay smiled. "Brothers, it's time we be going."

"That is true," said the Dolphin. He slipped his jacket on over the tattoos that covered him like a rainbow-colored shirt and nodded to Flash.

"You be cool now," said Flash. "And see me next week."

The Dolphin nodded again and McKay and I followed Jose and the Dolphin out into the street.

"If you get tired of him," Flash called out to me, "you know where to find me."

"Don't expect me to look," I said.

Flash laughed. "You just don't know what good is when you see it, girl."

I looked up at McKay; I disagreed with Flash.

The Dolphin and Jose were already sitting in the front of the Chevy, the Dolphin at the wheel.

"McKay," I said as we neared the car, "is Flash something special?"

"He thinks he is," said McKay.

"He's no Orphan," I said.

"But he knows a little magic," said McKay.

"Him and the Dolphin," I began, but we had reached the Chevy now.

"Don't ask no questions," said McKay.

McKay opened the door, and we got into the back seat

40

together. The Dolphin started the engine and began to drive down the street. Jose turned to face us. "Got some good reefer," he told McKay.

"Fine," said McKay.

"Got some good hash. Man, that shit tastes like perfume."

The Dolphin was driving through a tunnel now, and the light was of night or of no time in that tunnel. Jose lit a thin paper cigarette and passed it to McKay.

"What is that?" I said and Jose laughed.

O.K., so I didn't know about quality drugs. I only knew the dope of childhood – airplane glue in brown paper bags, breathing in and out in schoolyards and parking lots littered with the useless bodies of model airplanes that would never be constructed and would never fly. Bottles of cleaning fluid, of medicine, and of wine. I was no connoisseur.

McKay dragged on the joint.

"Try it," Jose said to me.

McKay handed me the joint and I inhaled. Exhaled. Nothing. I passed it to Jose. The Dolphin ignored us, he paid no attention, his eyes remained on the traffic signals, the tollbooth, the expressway. Maybe the Dolphin didn't like the communal touch of a joint.

"This reefer's not bad," said McKay. "It'll do."

"Not bad?" said Jose as he rolled another joint. "Man, Flash sells a nickel bag like you've never seen."

I passed the joint to McKay, but he waved it away, and I smoked the rest myself. Nothing was happening. What was the big deal? I could get a better buzz from swallowing a bottle of Midol.

"I'm not high," I said to McKay. He smiled.

The Dolphin still said nothing. I could see the silence around him as he drove, black-gloved hands on the steering wheel.

"McKay," I said. "You know, you have a very interesting face." He did. More so than ever before.

"Yeah," said McKay.

"Very interesting." I nodded.

"But she's not high," said Jose.

"You know," I told Jose, "a face defines a personality."

"I'm hip," said Jose. "If you knew all the personalities of all the dead people in the world, especially the great ones, you could change the world."

That was brilliant. "Yes," I said. "Yes, you're right." Brilliant. I stared out the window at the movement of the highway. "What did you say?" I asked Jose.

"Dolphin," McKay said, ignoring Jose and me, "how are we on money?"

"We could stand to have some more," said the Dolphin.

"I'm going to be racing the Chevy, but that won't pay shit."

"I've been making money, if you want to get in," said the Dolphin.

"No," said McKay, "that's your money. That has nothing to do with the Orphans. No, I was thinking of pulling some sort of job."

"Why bother?" said the Dolphin.

"You know," said Jose, "Flash sells some damn good reefer."

"Flash?" I said. "What did you say?" My hearing was not what it might have been. The words spoken in the Chevy seemed to float by me like air.

"I got a job in mind," said McKay.

"If that's the way you want it," said the Dolphin.

"It's an easy job," said McKay.

"A bank?" I asked.

"Don't be smart," said McKay.

"With a motorcycle," I said. "You could ride up to the teller on a Harley, and that would mean a real quick getaway."

"You still not high?" McKay asked me.

"McKay, I'll say it once," said the Dolphin, "you're asking for trouble with her." I could feel the Dolphin's eye on me in the rearview mirror. "I'll tell you once. You start bringing her around with you, she starts knowing too much, and you got trouble."

"O.K.," said McKay, "you said it once."

I might have said a word to the Dolphin, but I knew he wouldn't answer and Jose began to talk about getting all the great dead people together at a conference.

"There could be regional conferences, first," said Jose.

"Like all the great dead people from Texas, say. You hip? And then from Paris, say. Then the greatest of the great dead people could meet at a general conference."

"Shut up, boy," said the Dolphin. "You talking bullshit trash."

"Hey, man, this is important stuff. It could change the world. Sort of like a U.N. for dead people."

The Dolphin raced the Chevy past the skeleton of the World's Fair.

"And New York City," said Jose. "Man, forget it. We got the cities covered as far as dead people go. Lefty Gomez and those mayors, what's their names? The Irish one, Walker, he was great. La Guardia. And then my cousin, who was pushed off a roof. *He* was great, man. Now, he had good reefer. You think Flash's pot is something?"

"He sure can babble," I whispered to McKay, who nodded.

"You get them all together, see. Kenny, that's my cousin, and the two mayors, and Lefty. *Oye*. Terrific. We got the best. See, we could even take control. Yeah, New York City could control the main conference. And then we get someone like Nancy Sinatra to be the guest speaker."

"She wouldn't come to the conference," I told Jose.

"You think she wouldn't speak there? Shit, she'd be only too happy to."

"Jose, she's not dead," I told him.

"That doesn't matter," said Jose. "She'd hear about the free liquor we was serving."

"Jose, enough," said McKay.

"Not wine," said Jose. "The Orphans got too much class to serve wine."

"Jose, enough with your conference. Keep your conference plans a secret. Have a surprise guest speaker, and don't tell us about it now."

"Man, it would be great," said Jose.

"You see what happens when you involve assholes in business matters?" said the Dolphin.

"It would be," I said.

"You gotta be loose," said the Dolphin. "Or you find out you lose. You gotta travel alone."

"I thought you were going to say it once," said McKay.

"McKay," Jose said.

"I know. I know," said McKay. "We got the best dead people in the world in New York City."

"The greatest," said Jose.

"Yeah, and if you don't want to be one of them you'll know this is enough with your goddamn conference plans."

"McKay," I whispered with my eye on the Dolphin. "I don't like him referring to me that way."

"Don't listen," said McKay.

I turned away from him as the Dolphin drove the car off our exit; the Avenue was before us. What more could I say to McKay if he wouldn't even defend me? And who needed him to defend me, anyway?

McKay moved his hand up along my thigh and between my legs. "You gotta look at me sometime, girl," he whispered.

We traveled along the Avenue. I knew McKay was right. The Dolphin slowed the Chevy as we neared Monty's, and I could see the Pontiac of Danny the Sweet, and the gathering of Orphans at the doorway of the candy store.

"Sometime, you gotta look at me," said McKay.

As the Dolphin pulled the Chevy up to the curb I turned to face McKay, and I stared into his dark eyes. The Dolphin and Jose opened the front doors of the car and cold air rushed into the Chevy. It seemed that now that I had begun to look at McKay, I could not look away.

"What you staring at?" said McKay.

I was staring at myself; myself reflected in the dark of his eyes.

"You," I said, and it seemed I could not turn away.

3
IN THE MOOD

I

"WHY YOU WANT to make me worry?" said Danny the Sweet as I sat on a stool at Monty's.

"Danny," I said, "I've told you before. Don't worry about me. I'm not your responsibility. So just don't you worry."

I had left McKay at the doorway, standing in the cold with the Orphans to discuss the Night of the Wolf and, I assumed from the hushed voices and gesturing, the threat of Pack retaliation. Danny sat alone in Monty's, swinging his long legs and turning the stool right and then left. The corner kids had not yet been released from school and Monty cleaned the counter top with an old dishrag and winked at me as I entered the store and sat next to Danny. For Monty winking was an easy task; his eyes, morning, noon, and especially in the evening, were red and heavy with drink. Monty had a light hand when pouring syrup over a sundae, and a heavy one when pouring gin into a glass of tonic. His long white hair floated to his shoulders, and his eyebrows were long enough to intertwine with his lashes. The drink and the lashes gave Monty no choice; even when he wasn't winking, he was winking.

"The Sweet's been sitting here and worrying and worrying, the poor dear boy," said Monty.

"Go on," muttered Danny.

"Ah, Danny," I said and I winked back at Monty, "please don't be like that."

"Like what?" said Danny the Sweet.

45

"Like the Sweet that you are," I said.

"I ain't sweet," said Danny. "All I is is practical."

"You're out of your head," I told him. "There's nothing to be uptight about. I can take care of myself."

"Oh, yeah," said Danny. "What do you know about the Orphans? You don't know what's what."

"The way of the world," said Monty, and he poured coffee into the chipped porcelain mug he had set before me. "The way of the world upsets the poor dear boy."

Danny rested his elbow on the linoleum of the counter and knotted his hand in a fist, leaving his third finger free. "You know what this means, old man?" he said.

"I believe I do," said Monty. "It only serves to reiterate my preceding statement." Monty winked at me. Cruel, to use language like that on poor Danny. All the Sweet could do was nod.

"All the old man is saying, Danny," I began.

"Hey, I *know* what he's saying," said Danny.

"Is that you're too sweet, and too worried, and you should quit yelling at me for what ain't your business."

"I see you ride up with McKay," said Monty.

"That goes for you too," I said to Monty. "You too might find it much easier to mind your own business."

"But far less interesting," said Monty. "If you knew my business you wouldn't mind it either. Only so much concentration can be utilized in divvying out pieces of Bazooka bubble gum and wiping the counter clean."

I sipped coffee and looked through the frost of the door pane at the gathering of Orphans.

"It's no secret you're fooling around with McKay," said Monty. "The word travels fast down the Avenue. Particularly when it travels in a '59 Chevy."

"I drink your coffee every morning, but I'm telling you this," I said to Monty. "Don't push me."

"Already association with McKay has produced a marvelous effect," said Monty.

"Do you want to sell me a pack of Marlboros or do you want to give a personality evaluation?" I said.

Monty smiled and slid a pack of cigarettes along the

counter. I lit one for myself and one for Danny, who sat with his head resting upon his long thin hands.

"I understand, no intimate knowledge of course, I try to mind me own business" – Monty smiled – "that it was a particularly hard Night of the Wolf last night. Night o' the Wolf, I'm remembering hearing last night titled."

Danny sat up straight, the Orphan in him aroused.

"What do you know about the Night of the Wolf?" he demanded.

"Boy, I know nothing but that which is carried down the Avenue by the wind. Only rumor and innuendo."

"Keep it that way," said Danny.

"That means he don't know shit and is pumping you for information," I said to Sweet.

Danny turned to me. "Hey, I *know* it."

Then the three of us were silent; and as the familiar odor of syrup and Lysol surrounded us, I swung around on the stool so that I could see out the door into the street where stood McKay, the Dolphin, Jose, Martin the Marine, and Tosh. The Dolphin was moving his lips and McKay was nodding to words I could not hear.

"No, no, no, no, no," said Danny, and he pounded a fist against his head.

I swung around to face him as Monty dropped a glass into the suds-filled metal sink.

"Danny," I said.

"Why did I bring you with me?" cried the Sweet. "If anything happens to you, it's my fault. There just ain't no reason for me being so dumb. But that's the way it is. I shouldn't have brought you to the Orphans, but that's the way it is. I'm dumb, and I didn't think anyone would notice you, and you'd quit bothering me about McKay, and now I gotta be honest and admit how dumb I am."

"Shut up," I said. "Danny, shut up. You're just acting nuts, so shut up."

Danny stopped pounding his fist to his head and was quiet. But he continued to mutter softly to himself and his eye had the faraway look of codeine.

"Now, stop it," I said. "What the hell. You ain't dumb and

47

neither am I. I stood up to Kid Harris and I'm O.K. Just look at me."

Danny stared mutely at my face.

"See?" I said, and he nodded.

Monty's eyes winked furiously as he dipped his hand into the sink fishing for pieces of broken glass.

"If he acts like a maniac, the poor boy, I want him out," said Monty. "I'll miss his business, but no maniacs in here. Not in my place."

"Look," I said to Sweet, "you know McKay. Doesn't he call you brother?" The Sweet nodded. "You ain't responsible for introducing me to your brother." Danny listened to me and his pale eyes were wide and blank with his old sweet stare. "You know McKay's a man of honor," I said and Danny nodded. "So just you quit it. I can take care of myself."

"My boy, Danny," said Monty, as he poured more coffee into my cup. "I know McKay since he's but a child. I knew his uncle Red Stuart in the six counties. We came to New York together, if you must know the truth. Shared many a sea-tossed night. He was a man to swear by. And you yourself know the Orphans as well as any man. So why pound upon your head like a mad dog or an Englishman? You'll hurt yourself, boy. Go out, take a walk, smoke a cigarette. Above all, keep your mind clear, free from manias, and aired in the cold of the street."

Monty was telling him to get the hell out, and Danny nodded.

"I'm going out in the street for a while," Danny told me.

"Sure," I said, and Monty and I watched the Sweet edge his way out of the store, passing by the corner kids who had entered the store and were now rushing the candy counter. Danny paused to pick up a few bars of chocolate and lay some nickels on the counter. "If you need me," he said, "I'll be out on the street."

The door closed after Danny and we could see the Orphans wave him away from their conference. Monty poured himself a drink and said, "And you never did meet a bigger liar, a craftier thief, than Red Stuart."

"Come on," I said.

48

"It's true," he said. "Oh, lord, did that boy, he was a boy at the time I knew him, lie. What stories he told. What deals he did make. What stolen articles he did fence."

"Go on, you like the sound of your own words," I said.

"That's not the point in question," said Monty, as he drank the clear liquid he would have the corner kids believe was Seven Up or water.

"Now, I'm not saying the boy McKay is a bit like his uncle," Monty continued. I wrinkled my nose, but I didn't mind listening to Monty's words. I had listened to most of his stories at least once before. And now a new character or two to intertwine with Monty's continuing plot: Ireland, civilization, and Monty's various roles in its founding and continuance. There was little truth in his words, but sometimes his words were punctuated with a little magic. So I listened to him now.

"What are you saying then?" I asked.

"The Orphans are not for you," said Monty. "Oh, I've heard McKay is a man of his word. Yes, yes, a man of honor. As Red, his uncle, was well known as a liar and, you'll excuse me, a thief, so is McKay well known for his honor. That is the problem. As you should never trust a liar so should you never trust a man of honor. Those two are the worst of mankind."

"So you warn me against McKay?" I said. "And what of the Orphans? So I'm with McKay, that doesn't mean I'm with the Orphans."

"The Orphans are known for their black-hearted thievery. What stories travel down the Avenue on the wind I keep to myself. But McKay and the Orphans are not to be separated. Be with one, and you be with the other."

"You is a fool, old man." I smiled.

"Trust the fool. Always trust the fool." Monty took a chain from around his neck. Upon it dangled a silver locket. He opened the locket and within was a tooth edged in silver. "Look," he said.

Nothing but a locket and a tooth, rotted with age or decay.

"Disgusting." I laughed.

Monty flipped the locket shut and held the chain out to me.

"A charm?" I asked and Monty nodded.

"This," said Monty, "is the tooth I went and had punched out of me mouth by the aforementioned bastard, Red Stuart. You see, armies can spring from the tooth of a beaten man.

"Why for me?" I asked. "Why give the charm to me?"

"I might say it was an inducement for you to work behind the counter so I could get rid of that damn Gina, who is robbing me not quite blind," said Monty.

So he knew about Gina.

"I aspire to better things," I said.

"No doubt," said Monty. He sipped at his gin and mixed up egg creams for the corner kids who had sat down at the front end of the counter. "Let's just say I offer you the charm because I'm wondering if you'll be smart enough to take it. If you're not, you're not. And if you are, well then, you deserve its magic."

I was not quite sure how to pass this test of perception. "I'll see you on this," I said, and I slipped the chain around my neck.

Monty nodded and slid the egg creams down the counter top barroom style. "Tony, ya little bastard," he called out to one of the corner kids, a dark-haired boy of thirteen or fourteen, "get them airplane models out of your pockets before you're banned from this here store forever more."

"I said I'll take a chance on this magic of yours," I told Monty.

Monty raised his glass to me. "All right, then," he said. "I've done my part. Now, do what you will; it's no business of mine." He drained the glass of gin and returned to the sink full of dirty dishes and ran hot water so that steam rose into the air of the candy store.

"You're crazy," I said, but Monty ignored me, and the sound of his humming and the sound of glass and water and porcelain, drowned out my words.

Monty was as bad as Danny the Sweet, maybe worse. Danny knew how dumb he was. Monty admitted he was a fool. A chocolate addict and an old gin drinker. What did they know? Why should I listen to them when they spoke McKay's name? A fool and a dummy, both thinklng they knew something about McKay, about the Orphans, about me. Why did I rate the worry and the charm? Could it be that Danny the Sweet was ready for worry? That he needed an object, a me, to center his codeine hysteria upon? Could it be that Monty had planned to give up that old tooth, and had planned to endow it upon the three thousandth patron of the candy store? Perhaps I just happened to open the door of the Chevy and to walk into the candy store at the moment of fear and of magical benevolence.

I sat quietly, smoking cigarettes and listening to the wildness of the corner kids who had been trapped in classrooms all day and were now making up for it. And then Jose walked through the door and swaggered past the corner kids. He knocked the hat of one of them to the floor and the kids quieted down, though some mumbled curses when they knew Jose was too far away to hear them.

"Meeting adjourned," Jose said as he leaned on the stool next to me. "And a good thing too, man. I was freezing my ass off there. McKay says high-priority meetings are more secret when they ain't secret, Next time, I hope we meet in a sauna, man." Jose rubbed his hands together. "Old man," he called out to Monty, "give me a vanilla Coke and a pack of Camels."

"Did you see Danny the Sweet?" I asked Jose.

"Yeah, sure, he's out there," said Jose. "They wouldn't let him listen to any business matters, but they need him for a ride to the hospital and to stand guard outside T.J.'s room."

Monty slammed a glass of Coke on the counter top. "Drink up, fast," he said.

"T.J.?" I said.

"Yeah," said Jose. "He got it bad. Them Pack are something. Attacking a one-arm. Shit. A knife in the kidney. See, that's one part T.J. can't afford to lose. Now, Tosh, he got a tough wound. Knife mark down the side of his head. Since he bald, he now cool."

"Maybe you shouldn't tell me. What would the Dolphin say if he thought I knew too much?"

"Girl, I could care less," said Jose. "This is one Orphan who is his own man."

The door of Monty's opened and it was Tosh. Jose was

right, Tosh's shaven skull was now scarred with a long knife mark.

"Jose," Tosh called, "who told you the meeting was over? Get your ass out here."

Jose smiled at Monty and me, gulped his Coke, and walked toward the door.

"Your own man," said Monty.

"Shut up, old man," said Jose. "Duty is calling on me, hear?"

"Don't say a word," I told Monty. "Hear me? Not a word."

Monty only smiled.

I could see now that the meeting was breaking up. The locket at my neck swayed slightly as I walked from the store. I watched McKay. I waited, smoking cigarettes and watching circles of air move above the Avenue. I touched the locket, the charm, and looked into the Avenue where, between the alleyways and the empty lots, there was said to be magic. Who said there was magic? Who knows? I said it, everyone did. Herbs that can be boiled down into tea serve as potions. They can keep away the bark of the dog at morning, the howl of the cat at night. Magic grows like weeds in the cracks of the Avenue sidewalk. It flowers there, and it goes to seed. But this is small magic, difficult to see, for it rarely grows strong enough to climb like ivy, like vines over the glass of storefront windows.

The big magic is there as well. It is cheap, it is not difficult to find. It is patented in liquor stores, in drugstores, in uptown apartments where it is cut with strychnine or sugar. This magic is terribly easy to see, unless one is blind. And control of the spell, and control of the mood, is due to this big magic. It too keeps away the bark of the dog in the morning, the howl of the cat at night. Only much more effectively, much quicker, and surer.

The Avenue is littered with wizards. Sometimes, often, they are in disguise. A Cuban woman of eighty once sat blinded by some island disease in the doorways of abandoned buildings on the north side of the Avenue. But she was not Cuban, nor was she an eighty-year-old woman. She was the magic that sent Sandor Inez to the slammer for life on the charge of robbery, assault, and causing heart attacks by earthly forms of big magic.

Hard to tell – with magic, with charms. Some big, some little. Difficult to categorize, until, of course, the consequences are seen. The little magic only causes a smile, but the big magic always seems to end up in the slammer or at a wake.

I've seen through some disguises, I've known some magic. Look, who hasn't? You see Monty and he's a fifty-two-year-old drunk behind the counter of a candy store on the Avenue. So his name is above the door, and he calls himself by the name. Did you ever see his passport, birth certificate, proof of his brogue? But I had seen Monty add up the letters of my name and cast toothpicks upon the linoleum counter top to figure out my date of birth. So I laughed at the charm, but I didn't deny its worth. I had no talent for magic, but I could spot it in others. To survive on the Avenue, there can be no tripping over the forms of sleeping wizards; there can be no stumbling on the cracks of the sidewalks.

About McKay? I didn't know. He must have had some talent or else he would have tripped long ago over leather and bottles and witch doctors and dust. When I looked into his eyes I felt there might be some spell there. As I watched the Orphans gather around him, gutter smoke and steam hissing as it rose in the cold air, I thought there might be the whispering of chants. Although I had no talent in magic myself, I could spot it in others as a cobra spots a sparrow, as a sparrow spots a cobra. I could always see it in the eyes.

But about McKay, I didn't know. I would have to judge the magic by the consequences. Those consequences which are the after-magic: the mood induced, the spell, the jail sentence, the act of falling in love, the words remembered. The way to finally tell the big magic from the little. The too late, the of course, the last step of the spell.

They were walking away. The engines of Orphan cars were started. The Dolphin moved away from McKay, and as he did shadows were cast that might have caused white magic to appear dark, and black magic to glow blinding light. McKay was alone now. I threw a cigarette to the street, stepped on fire with my boot, and slipped the locket and chain from around my neck. I held the charm and waited. When McKay nodded I placed the tooth in the lining of my jacket pocket and walked toward him.

"I got some runs to do," said McKay.

"All right," I said.

"Alone," he said.

"I'm no trouble at all," I said.

"Honey, this ain't no game. This is a condolence call to the Pack."

"You're crazy," I said. "What was that talk about Clifton, New Jersey? What was that talk about safe territory?"

"No one messes with a condolence caller, that's all there is to it. So it's safe."

"Anyone specific in store for your condolences?" I asked.

"Only Ralphie of the Pack," said McKay. "Only the Christian Brothers Funeral Home across the street from St. Francis'."

"What for?" I asked.

"Darling, it's a wake I'm talking about," said McKay.

"McKay."

"I told you this weren't no game," said McKay.

"I want to go with you," I said.

"You don't want to go," said McKay. "Because you don't know what it's like. You don't want to go with me."

"It's not fair that you have to go alone."

"It wasn't fair that the boy got wasted, either."

"But alone," I said.

"Hey, that's the way it is," said McKay. "Someone gets wasted and I'm the one to go. And go alone."

"Am I supposed to just wait for you?" I said.

"Remember. I never forced you to wait."

No, he never did. But whether McKay knew it or not, he did not even have to ask me.

"Then don't ask me to wait now. Take me with you."

McKay lit a cigarette and was silent for a few moments.

"Get in the car," he said.

I did and McKay started the Chevy and pulled into the Avenue.

"You got a black dress?" he asked.

"No. And no pearls either," I told him.

"Gina will have one to fit you," McKay said and he smiled. "You'll do fine without pearls, but you be with the Orphans and you gotta get yourself a black dress."

"I don't like that talk," I said.

"You want me to lie to you?" said McKay. I shrugged. Why not? I didn't mind lies.

"Anyway," I said, "I'm not with the Orphans. It's only you and me in this car."

McKay smiled at that.

I took the charm from my pocket. I opened the locket to show McKay the silver-edged tooth. "A gift from Monty," I said.

"I seen that," said McKay. "The tooth of a dragon fought by some knight on the west coast of Ireland, ain't that what the old boy says?"

"No," I said. "The story I was told was that it's a tooth punched out of Monty's very own mouth by your uncle, Red Stuart, aboard a ship in mid-Atlantic."

McKay laughed. "I never did have no uncle by that name. And that sure wasn t the story I got when Monty offered it to me."

"And you turned it down?" I said.

"And you accepted it?" McKay smiled.

"Monty seemed to think I could use some magic."

"Even if you could, that there tooth won't be strong enough magic."

"Maybe I won't need no black dress after today."

"Then that there dragon's tooth is stronger than Monty thinks, darlin'. Else he wouldn't dare be giving it away."

"All this locket means" – I moved closer to McKay and touched my lips to his face – "is that if I'm protected by this charm, you are too, as long as you're with me."

McKay pulled the car off the Avenue and into an alley. We were going to T.J.'s apartment. "Is that a threat?" he said, and then McKay kissed me.

"No," I said. "It's only magic."

II

Gina wasn't at T.J.'s apartment, and we knew from the tear-covered Kleenexes in the corners of the room that Gina was most likely standing her own guard outside T.J.'s hospital door. McKay looked through the closet and found, finally, a black linen dress that was too large, and too short, and too lightweight for winter. I slipped the dress over my head in the darkness of the apartment and stared into a mirror. I could barely recognize myself in the darkness, but when McKay's face appeared in the mirror near mine I saw mine smile at his.

"Won't Gina mind if I borrow the dress?" I said.

"Nah," said McKay and he placed his hands on my shoulders. We spoke to each other's mirror images. "She's grief-struck, and she shoplifts all her wardrobe from Robert Hall, so she don't even know what the fuck she's got in the closet."

McKay had changed into a black suit and a white-and-black print shirt. He wore the Orphans jacket about his shoulders like a cloak.

"Tell me why," said McKay, and he held his arms tight around me, and pressed his body close to mine, and spoke with his mouth against my neck, "I'm letting you go with me."

I watched myself and McKay in the mirror. "It's only love," I said. McKay moved away from me and raised his head, though his arms were still around me.

"Don't use that word again."

"I didn't know it would frighten you so."

"I mean it. If we're together for a while, then we're together. It ain't nothing more than that, and I want you to know that right now. I will tell you no lies. If you're in trouble I'll just turn away."

An honest man, McKay. But I had taken no vow of honor, and so I said, "I'm not asking you for anything. I am not one of the Property, and I'll be with you only until I want to be with you, no more. I can't help it if you're in love with me. That's your problem."

McKay laughed. "Think you're smart," he said, and he

turned me around so that I no longer looked in the mirror. "You think you're real smart."

I threw my jacket over my shoulders to cover Gina's dress, tied a scarf around my head, and let McKay know I was ready to go by walking from him and opening the door of the apartment. We walked into the street toward the Chevy that waited with engine running and exhaust streaming into the cold air.

"We hit the wake first," said McKay.

We drove down the Avenue into the territory of the Pack. Far down the Avenue we stopped before a building of stone, surrounded by crosses and angels and several black Fords. A line of limousines waited in silence. I could hear organ music from some other funeral or wedding filter through the glass and cement of St. Francis' as McKay double-parked the Chevy before the Christian Brothers Funeral Home. I walked away from the Chevy with McKay.

"Let me kiss you before you do this," I said.

"Do what?" McKay stopped and let me kiss him, and he lit a cigarette to share with me before we entered the funeral chapel.

"Go to the wake of one of the Pack."

"That's what's to be done," said McKay. "I accept your kiss, but, girl, you don't know shit. Anyone gets wasted and they are honored, they should be honored, even if they is one of the Pack. If I skipped out on the wake it would be defeat for the Orphans. I couldn't walk the Avenue."

"I see," I said. "But you'd turn away from me any time there was trouble."

"You fight like this Pack boy and I'll sit in at your wake."

"I'll look forward to it."

"Then again" – McKay smiled – "I never fucked this dead Pack boy in the front seat of the Chevy."

We walked on. I figured those were McKay's brand of words of love. I was learning to leave love and honor out of the words I spoke to McKay. He didn't want to hear love and I couldn't understand his words of honor. So I kept quiet, and held McKay's arm. We reached the steps of the chapel.

"I don't expect anything from you," I said to McKay.

"Good," said McKay as we reached the steps of the chapel.

"Except that you don't turn away," I said.

And McKay couldn't argue that, for as we walked up the cold cement steps, Kid Harris sat upon the railing, guarding the door of the chapel with three of his Pack. In a shiny black sharkskin jacket and ruffled pink shirt, the Kid waited.

McKay only continued to walk up the steps. I could see now that the Kid's hands were wrapped in white, covered with bandages like a mummy, encased in casts of plaster and gauze.

"Harris," said McKay, and he nodded.

"McKay," said Harris, and the Kid tipped his head of long orange hair.

I looked not at McKay, nor at Harris and the other Pack, but through the doors of the chapel at the rows of metal folding chairs.

"This is no longer a game," said Harris.

"It never was," said McKay. "You knew that."

"But death is something else again," said Harris.

"Cantinni was a death. T.J. may soon be a death."

"Nothing was ever proven. Prove that the Pack was at the scene of Cantinni being wasted. Where's the evidence? Some lousy brake fluid drained from his 'Vette? Anyone could have done that."

"The evidence is in the air and it is common knowledge," said McKay. "You knew this was no game, and you know it better now."

"McKay, this is the beginning of the end for you, my friend."

"Brother Wolf," McKay said to Harris. "I can't stand here all day and listen to your loose talk and your jive."

McKay walked past Harris on those stairs and I followed. The Pack was ready to spring on a signal. McKay alone, there'd not be another chance like this for them soon. One wink, one movement of a finger from Harris, and McKay would not make it through the door of the chapel. I was, and had been, and would continue to be, ready to turn heel on a signal from McKay and find a bottle of Dewar's, and forget condolences and honor.

But McKay walked on. Harris nodded and said, "Now we talk. Now you go through the doors of the chapel to kneel before a soldier of the Pack. You walk free through the door, and free out of it. I admit you got some guts coming here alone like this without your soldiers. But McKay, you're going to lose anyway. You're going to lose it all. Everything, including those guts of yours."

McKay only smiled. We walked through the wooden doors of the chapel, and as the doors swung out behind us, and then clattered, we entered the overheated warmth of the room where the weeping of family and friends of the Pack blanketed the air.

The room was alive with the odor of wreaths, the smell of salt water, with the whispered chants of remembering. In the front row, before the casket, sat the family of the Pack. A young woman in a heavy black veil, who must have been Ralphie's sister, wailed and rocked back and forth in her chair. Behind her a row of the Property of the Pack – a row of girls in tears, mascara in thin wet lines upon their faces. The men of Ralphie's family and the boys of the Pack sat in brown metal chairs around the altar where the coffin lay.

McKay and I walked toward the coffin. As we moved down the aisle toward the altar I could hear McKay's and the Orphans' names whispered, and the word "murderer."

"Darling, you are my charm," whispered McKay. "You make me seem even more respectable than I already am." He smiled and increased the pressure of his hand upon mine. But I barely heard McKay's words, words that I would have memorized at another time. I could hear only the whispers, see only the coffin before us.

I had no previous acquaintance with dead bodies, with coffins, with curses and prayers. What did I know of the look of someone without life? I was afraid to walk farther, but McKay held my arm tighter, and I followed.

We knelt beside the coffin, and I crossed myself as McKay did, but I kept my eyes closed.

McKay whispered, "Honey, just don't look, is all." But my eyelids wouldn't listen to his words and I looked. It was just a boy, young and seeming more alive than anyone else in that chapel of death. He smiled. His eyes were closed and he smiled. I thought I saw his chest move.

"Maybe he's alive," I said to McKay.

"Not a chance," whispered McKay. "He ain't gonna get up and dance no more."

I wanted to touch the boy in the casket. I wouldn't have wanted to when he was alive, but now I wanted to reach out and touch him. His face. To touch him and see if he would move, could turn his smile into a laugh.

I was busy concentrating on the face, and McKay was staring straight ahead into the air. Neither of us heard someone come up behind us as we knelt.

"Murderer," she cried, and lifted the veil from her face. "Do you know what he is?" the sister cried out to the room. "A gangster. A murderer." The sister pounded a fist against her heart.

From the corner of my eye I could make out the row where the Property of the Pack were sitting. Not one of them moved. Only stares and the slow movement of their tears.

"You come and desecrate what's holy," said the sister. "You, you murderer, dare to kneel at my brother's coffin. You dare to come here and bring some tramp with you to kneel before what's holy. I know what you are," she cried.

Now I found I could not unkneel, and as McKay stood I could not look up at him. I could only stare at the boy's frozen smile. The curses of the sister fell like hailstones; I could no longer distinguish one word from another.

McKay stood. "I am here to honor him, not to curse him," he said quietly to the sister of the dead boy I could not stop staring at, because he was so young. I could not believe he had ever been one of the Pack. I could not believe that he had ever worn the Pack's emblem of the head of a wolf in colors of turquoise and gold upon his back. Or that he had laughed, had howled on that Night of the Wolf.

"Oh, God, you're making me sick," cried the sister. "You being here in the same room is making me sick."

"Death" – McKay spoke the word so low that I could barely hear – "is only a mystery."

"There's no fucking mystery to a knife in the ribs," cried

60

the sister. "And you can't make it be, even if you want to."

"I am here only to honor that which was your brother," said McKay.

"Murderer," said the sister, and threw herself at McKay. I moved closer to the coffin, edging toward the safety of the wood.

Kid Harris and his soldiers walked down the aisle. The room was alive with curses and wailing and the sound of heavy shoes on the wooden floor. Now the priest, whom I had not seen before, held the figure of an old woman in black so that she would not fall. McKay stared into the air as the sister of the dead Pack boy beat her fists against his chest and wailed the word "murderer" again and again so that I could not get her voice out of my ears. McKay did not move, did not protect himself from her fury, and I could do nothing to get him away to the safety of the Avenue, to the safety of some familiar place. I could not move.

"Leave it be. Leave it be, now," Kid Harris said to the sister, holding her off from McKay. Untouched on the Night of the Wolf, McKay now bore a line of crimson on his right cheek, beneath his eye, a gash left by the fingernails of this woman, the sister.

Now I stood up. No one noticed me and I did not feel afraid. I walked to McKay and stood beside him, and waited for him to turn. But he did not; he continued to stare into the air. Then he said, "She can't understand." And Kid Harris laughed in that room of whispers.

"Get out," he said to McKay. "You've done what you had to do. Now leave. I ain't expecting to see you again until the night when the Orphans and the Pack meet again, and on the Pack's terms."

The priest approached, his black skirts rustling about him. "You are aggravating the family, son," he whispered to McKay.

"That's right," said Kid Harris. "You are aggravating the family, you are aggravating everyone. So get out. Get the fuck out."

"Sons," the priest began to whisper once more, but McKay had already turned, Kid Harris was leading the sister to the

61

row where the family sat, and the men around the coffin were lifting the wooden box, carrying the boy and the wood and the silence into the Avenue, where the black limousines waited.

"They can't understand," said McKay. I took his hand and we walked down the aisle. McKay hesitated, again staring at nothing; so I pulled at his hand to lead him away from the altar, the priest, the whispers.

"It wasn't anything personal," said McKay.

I laughed. "Everything is personal," I said.

"No," said McKay. "No. Death and honor are not personal."

We passed the row of Pack Property and one of the girls, I did not see which, spat at the floor where I stood. I walked on, but now held my back straighter and walked closer to McKay.

When we stood once more in the street, McKay said, "They don't know." I believed that I did know the reason McKay attended the wake: not to gloat, and never for pity, only because he could not walk down the Avenue with the same step if he had not knelt before the coffin.

We walked toward the Chevy. "I could drive," I said, knowing that those words would bring McKay back to me.

"Not a chance," McKay said, and he smiled.

In the Chevy I sat close to McKay. I felt that if I let him get too far away, even for a minute, I would lose him. I wanted to get rid of the black dress, of the magic charm in my pocket, anything that might cast a spell.

"What's dead is dead, and then it's not," said McKay.

"Get lost," I said, and turned up the volume of the radio.

McKay kissed me. "That's what I like to hear." He smiled.

I could not smile; I was listening to McKay. What's dead is dead. And what's dead is not dead. At the altar, by the coffin, they could not see that McKay did know something. I listened to McKay now. For me, it was only love. But not for McKay. What he wanted was honor. And I was beginning to know that there simply was no such thing.

4

PROPERTY OF

I

WE DROVE DOWN the Avenue, away from death. Finally McKay stopped the Chevy across the street from a Texaco station.

"You may get to drive this car yet," said McKay. "Can you drive a stick shift?"

Who but the Dolphin had ever been known to drive McKay's Chevy? Not one other Orphan would McKay trust with the silver-studded mag wheels, with the custom-made wood-and-chrome steering wheel. Now he was asking if I knew how to drive. There was no one on the Avenue who would not jump at a chance to drive the Chevy. As McKay opened the Chevy door, I slid over to the driver's seat and placed my fingers on the wood of the steering wheel.

"I'm leaving the engine running," said McKay through the half-open window. "You just wait here and don't touch anything. When you see me walking to you, you put the car in gear. When I open the passenger door, you step on the gas." I nodded, and looked at the waiting speedometer. "I want you to know," McKay continued, "that this is a nothing job. Don't get any ideas that I'm gonna ever involve you in any jobs that are important. Don't get any ideas just because you drive the Chevy once."

So this was the job he mentioned to the Dolphin. The heist. Nothing big, nothing fancy; only a small heist to chase away some of the shadows cast by the Christian Brothers Funeral Home.

63

I watched McKay walk away to stand on the corner across from the station. With the engine straining and the radio playing softly, it was just another wait for McKay. The time passed with cigarettes and songs. Finally the gas station attendant went into the men's room and then McKay was walking back to me. His easy pace had not altered, but McKay kept his hands in his pockets and his eyes on the cement. I wrenched the car into gear; reverse, wrong – back into first.

McKay threw open the passenger door. "Drive to the station," he said.

I stepped on the gas and steered the Chevy into a quick U-turn without the use of the brake. I left rubber on the Avenue as I pulled the Chevy into the gas station driveway and alongside the row of gas pumps.

"Easy," said McKay. I nodded as he jumped from the car.

I was not calm, but my excitement had nothing to do with the heist. Of this illegal act I had no fear. But the power of the Chevy's engine had gotten to me. I felt I had never driven before.

McKay began quickly loading large boxes into the back seat of the Chevy. Then, in seconds, he had carried a large wooden barrel from the waiting room of the station. I was calm now. I admired McKay's quick movements, and I smiled as I looked into my own dark eyes in the rearview mirror.

In minutes, McKay had completely looted the station. Just in time, for as McKay finished loading the Chevy and threw himself into the front seat, the station attendant opened the door of the men's room and stood not a hundred yards away from us. My eyes focused not upon the station attendant's face, but upon the name "Al" scrawled in gold across the breast pocket of his Texaco shirt.

"Hit it," said McKay, and I floored the Chevy. In the rearview mirror I could see Al chasing us. McKay was holding the door open; he had not had time to close it fully. He turned and watched Al chasing us, then he grabbed my shoulder.

"Get down," he said. For a few seconds I could not see, though I kept my foot on the gas, so that the pedal touched the floor.

We were already turning a corner when I heard a gun firing. I had no fear – it was too late for Al. The Texaco station had already been looted: we had the barrels, the boxes, the money was in McKay's pockets, and the wind of the Avenue was whistling over the roof of our getaway car. McKay slammed his door shut and locked it. There was no catching us now.

"Get your foot off the gas," said McKay. I didn't listen to him. I wanted to drive the Chevy now that I had the chance. "You heard me," said McKay. "Off."

McKay moved next to me, grabbed the wheel, and turned it so sharply that we skidded to the curb. I had no choice; I stepped on the brake.

"Thanks," said McKay. "Now I know the shocks are fucked."

"This car," I said. "How did you get this car so fast?"

"I know it, I know the shocks are totally fucked over."

"This car can fly."

"Yeah? Fly somebody else's car. Didn't anyone ever tell you to use the brake when you took a corner?"

He motioned me with a nod of his head, and I climbed over his knees so that he could take control of the Chevy. Although I lingered as I moved over McKay, he drew away from me, and took out the stolen bills and began to count.

"How much?" I said.

"What do you care?"

"My share," I said. "How much?"

"Get off my case," said McKay. "There is no your share."

"Fifty-fifty," I told him.

McKay paused in his addition, stopping the rustle of money.

"Eighty-twenty," he said.

"I'll take it," I said.

My share came to not quite twenty-five dollars. McKay did not smile as he counted off the bills and placed them in my hand. But this was no joke, and I hadn't expected a smile. And although the percentage was off in our partnership – it was still a partnership of sorts, even though I settled for less than I wanted.

We were silent. McKay didn't like my driving and he didn't

like my bargaining. If I moved closer to him, he would only turn away. So I stayed in my corner of the front seat and said, "At least you can let me buy you a drink." McKay nodded, and pulled the car back out into the traffic of the Avenue.

The Tin Angel Bar was Orphans' territory. Never before had I ordered a beer or a whiskey at its polished counter. The color TV screen was tinted a bluish color by the smoke which lay heavy in the air and the jukebox sounded loudly.

"If you're buying, partner," said McKay, "I'll have whiskey and water. A double, partner, since you is so wealthy."

I ordered, and watched McKay walk past the barstools to a booth where Starry and Kind sat. If Starry neither trusted nor liked Kind, she certainly was an excellent politician, a terrific actress, for they talked and gestured and laughed, and greeted McKay with smiles. I followed McKay, holding the whiskey and a rum and Coke, feeling the cold of the glasses in my hands. I sat on the bench near Kind, across from McKay.

McKay held his arm around Starry's shoulders. She covered her smile with her hand and nodded a greeting to me.

"Gotta get this damn tooth fixed," Starry said.

"You're still beautiful," said McKay.

Kind's painted eyes were cold as she watched them.

"You're still full of crap," said Starry.

"Now how can you say that to the man?" said Kind, and her eyes smiled at McKay.

Did I have to sit and listen to this? Did I really? I stood; the glasses rattled on the tabletop.

"Sit down," said McKay.

I sat. McKay's dark eyes were upon me, and I knew that although I had stood, there was nowhere I wanted to go.

"Hey," Starry said to me, as I began to sip rum and Coke, "you know that Kid Harris will be after you for the trouble you caused him. You and me both."

"What are you telling her that for?" said McKay. "You're losing faith in the Orphans and you're scaring my girl, all because you lost one fucking tooth? That ain't like you, Starry."

"Boy," said Starry, "I could never lose faith in you or in the Orphans. I'm just stating the truth. And I ain't worried none

66

about scaring her." Starry winked at me. "Seems to me," she said to McKay, "that she don't scare easy." Starry nodded and raised her glass of tequila in my direction. "You don't scare easy," she said, and she smiled.

Kind had been tapping her long painted fingernails upon the tabletop; she was letting us know she was bored.

"McKay," she said, wrapping a curl of fox-colored hair around her finger, "when you gonna give me another ride in that Chevy of yours?"

McKay smiled. Starry rolled her eyes, and I ignored them all and studied the ice that floated like a sinking ship within my glass.

"Because," Kind continued, "I sure could use a ride right now."

"I'll bet you could," said Starry.

"I gotta get to work now, don't I?" said Kind. And she aimed her painted eyes at McKay.

"Go ahead," I said to McKay as I watched the ice, "give her a ride."

"That's so sweet," said Kind, "you giving him permission."

"It won't be long," McKay said to me as he stood.

"Take your time," I said.

"I will," said McKay. He nodded to Kind. "You're damn right I'll take my time."

I stood to let Kind pass by. Then I sat down again and did not bother to watch them walk out the door.

"Told you," said Starry. "I told you about her."

"He's only giving her a ride," I said.

"If that's what you want to call it."

I didn't want her pity, but I could stand another drink. I ordered one for myself and another tequila for Starry. She offered me a cigarette, and as we smoked and drank in silence I studied her thin face in the blue-tinted light of the bar. Her golden hoop earrings made soft sounds as she moved her head in time to the jukebox music. I could see by the shaking of her hands that although it was not yet dark, this was certainly not just her second drink.

We were silent for some time. Starry kept her attention on the doorway of the Tin Angel. Whoever she was waiting for didn't enter the bar. Finally she said, "Can I trust you?"

"If you want."

"But can I trust you not to talk to McKay?"

"Now, does it look like I'm gonna be talking to McKay soon again?"

"You will," said Starry, and she held the glass of tequila so tightly it seemed impossible that the glass would not break. "He screws Kind, that's all. You can't expect him to drop her all of a sudden, can you?"

I certainly could.

"McKay screws everyone," Starry said softly.

Again we were silent; again Starry watched the door.

"Some things," she continued, "I'd rather McKay not know. Some things I don't want the Orphans or the Property to know. Of course the Dolphin, well, now he's something else again. The Dolphin knows everything. You can't hide nothing from the Dolphin. But you," Starry said, "until you prove me wrong, I'm gonna trust you."

"All right," I said. "All right, then, trust me."

"I need money."

That was the secret? "Who doesn't?" I said.

"But I need it now." Starry leaned forward across the barroom table and her voice was low and hoarse. "I need it now because the fucker didn't show. I need it now because the goddamn john didn't show, because he probably saw McKay's Chevy parked in front of the Angel, and some of them get scared away when they find out I'm with the Orphans."

I stared at Starry.

"I said the fucker didn't show and I need the money now," she whispered.

"All right," I said. "All right, just shut up, because I don't want to know, do you hear?"

I reached into my pocket for the money McKay had given me and handed her a ten. "Is this enough?" I said. "Because otherwise McKay will wonder where the money's gone." Starry nodded. "Take it," I said, "but don't tell me anything."

"If you don't want to know," said Starry, "I can't blame you. To tell you the truth," she placed the money in her shirt pocket, "I don't want to know either. Most of the time I pretend I don't. Except when I need money, then I can't help but know."

"What you do is your business," I said. Now that she had the money, I wanted Starry to leave so that I could be alone and not have to listen to her talk on.

"Just tell me," said Starry. "Why are you giving me the money?"

"Maybe I want you to owe me. Maybe I want to have something on you."

"Bullshit. If you wanted me to owe you, you'd want to know everything about me."

"I want you on my side," I said, and it was true. I now had a side, and I wanted Starry on it.

"Against Kind."

"And against the Dolphin," I said.

"No good," Starry said. "Against Kind, but not against the Dolphin. The Dolphin knows all." Starry gulped the last of her drink and with the ten dollars in her shirt pocket her hands were now steadier.

"I don't care," I said. I thought of the tattoos that gleamed in the night, of the refusal of his eye to meet mine, of his mysterious hold on McKay. "I'm against him," I said.

"Good luck but count me out."

"Sure," I said.

"I'm on your side," said Starry. "And I'll give you some advice. Don't."

"Don't what?"

"Don't become one of the Property," Starry whispered.

"I won't," I told her. "I never intended to be Property."

"And don't fall in love with McKay."

I was silent.

"You already are," she whispered across that blue barroom table.

"I already am," I said.

"Then you're already one of the Property," said Starry.

"No," I said.

Starry stood and edged her way out of the booth. "About the Dolphin," she said, "if you want to know why I can't go against him, just think who I might be going to meet with this ten dollars in my hand." She smiled a very soft smile, and I thought I had never seen her look younger.

"It will be a long time," I said, as Starry began to walk away, "before you see the words 'Property Of' on my back."

I sat alone in the booth now, in the last booth of that bar.

"Girl," Starry said to me as she threw her leather jacket around her, "the words are already written there."

The door of the Tin Angel slammed behind her and I was alone, without McKay, without Starry. I could think of nothing to do but order another drink. Then I left the table to place some dimes in the jukebox. I stood before the lights, the colors, the rows of printed song titles, and I watched the arm rise and then fall on the black discs. I watched the colors and thought: it is not so very despicable to belong.

Oh, yes, yes, I know: cities have been pillaged, countries ruined. Yes, I know the position of Property is always on its back. But still, it is not so very despicable to belong. I admit belonging, being owned is always sad. You think that is a peculiar word to apply to tragedy? You think "sad" is an inadequate word for a historical force? But I do not speak of the property of capitalism, the historical sort that is discussed at the cocktail parties of the world. The Property I speak of is the self. The self that does not belong, is not owned by itself but by others. By another.

This Property is the self which is sold because its position is on its back, because it is starving, dying of thirst, it is suffering the torments of plague, civil war, and sadness. And when the self is dying of thirst, it is not unusual for a canteen to be accepted in trade. Particularly when what is sold has never belonged to itself.

So Starry wears an emblem on her back which states that she is owned, she belongs, she is Property. And then she sells what really is no longer hers – her self. And did you want a revolution from the Property of the Orphans? Property cannot even speak to Property. A revolution when the enemy is each other, themselves, herself? Sharp eyes staring knives into even colder eyes; arms draped over the shoulders of owners. The hiss when the word "sister" is spoken. A revolution when the enemy is unknown?

Everyone agrees, of course, that it is best to belong to oneself. When this is not possible, when there is no water, when there is only hiking through the desert with small particles of sand clinging to the desert garments, there is not much choice but to sell the self in the hope that the canteen will be passed and water will finally touch the lips and the throat. Also the tongue.

There is nothing disgusting or immoral about this transaction; there is nothing despicable in selling the self under these desert conditions. There are no political or economic references I wish to make at this point. I was not Property, I was not one of them. I could not find fault with the bargaining for tequila and survival. I had nothing to do with them, or with the effects of selling the self; that action which seems to cause temporary blindness and permanent sadness, and which seems to break the heart.

The door of the Angel had slammed behind her, and the words were on her back. I could not remember what buttons I'd pushed, what songs I'd selected on the jukebox. And it really didn't matter; I only needed a lyric, some tune, any melody to force Starry and the Property from my mind. Starry's words – lies or truth; I did not want to know. I didn't want to know why she met the Dolphin tonight with ten dollars, my ten dollars, ready in her hand. And I realized, standing there before the jukebox, that I did not even know what McKay had stolen from the gas station, what rattled in the barrels, what was stored in the stolen boxes, where he was with Kind right now, why I cared. I did not need to, I did not want to know.

I erased every doubt and each suspicion with music and the thought of making love with McKay. I erased the words "Property Of."

Not me. No – not me.

I left the Tin Angel and began to walk down the Avenue. I heard McKay's Chevy pull up alongside me before I saw it.

"Get in," he said, and maybe I didn't hear him, because I kept on walking.

"Get in," said McKay, and maybe I heard him, because I

opened the door of the Chevy, and sat. We drove without words past the City Line, past St. Anne's, we drove until McKay parked the Chevy in the asphalt parking lot of an auto repair shop.

McKay carried the stolen boxes inside. Then he opened the passenger door, and I followed him through the deserted shop and up one flight of stairs.

"My place," McKay said, and he opened the wooden door.

I looked around at the small kitchen, the bed, the color TV and the stereo system, the small wooden table, and the engine that lay upon newspapers in the center of the floor.

"This place was Cantinni's," he said. "Ah, it's sort of a mess, see, Cantinni didn't exactly keep the place spotless."

"That was four years ago," I said.

McKay shrugged. "Time flies," he said.

I walked to the bed. A mattress, some pillows, a quilt. And I wondered if Kind had slept in this bed. How many others had loved McKay on this mattress? What was it Cantinni and Wanda had whispered, what words had they spoken, and did they sleep here, together, on this bed, and did they sleep here, together, on the evening before Cantinni's Corvette went into a curve it never came out of?

"This could use some sheets," I said.

And Starry. Had Starry ever slept here? Probably. Perhaps there was nothing between Starry and McKay, but she had probably slept here. I realized that I didn't mind the thought of Starry and McKay together on this bed. Not because I knew now, whether I wanted to or not, how many men Starry had been with, or that a bed, a mattress, could mean as little as ten dollars to her – but because I knew that for Starry sex with McKay would be like making love to all of the Orphans at one time. I might have been jealous of whispers to one man, but not to several.

"Don't get no ideas about Kind," said McKay. "She's nothing to me, you know."

I didn't know; but it did not seem to matter anymore.

"How can you sleep on a bed without sheets?" I said.

"Buy some," said McKay.

"It's not my apartment," I said. Not that I had any other.

Once I had come onto the Avenue there was no other home, only a house, an apartment where family had become strangers once strangers had become family. Only faces watching boot heels walk away toward the Avenue. Duties that would never be met, photograph albums covered with dust and webs and unopened. Strangers.

"Don't you know?" said McKay, as he sat on the edge of the mattress. "Don't you know yet?" He held me and nothing else seemed to matter, not even Kind. "That you ain't going nowhere?"

It was true. I had no appointments, no promises to keep. I had already been gone for a long time; first my eyes staring out of the window, then my feet, always walking away. I had lived on the Avenue even before I knew its streets.

"You ain't going nowhere," he said again.

McKay and I made love on that bed without sheets. I ignored the indentations upon the mattress left by other thighs, other hips and breasts. I ignored them all in that bed with McKay. In the morning, after McKay had left the apartment to pick up my suitcase, and then after he had reheated the coffee and left once more to meet the Orphans, I lay in that bed, the quilt wrapped around me. I drank coffee and I traced the line of my hip upon the soft mattress fabric. I closed my eyes, so that I could not see, and I traced the line the mattress had left upon my skin. I kept my eyes closed for a while, I drank the coffee before it was cold. And then I went shopping for sheets.

II

Through the plate glass of Monty's candy store I could see Gina sweeping candy wrappers off the floor. Irene sat at the far end of the counter, sipping a soda and playing a hand of rummy with Monty. I stood outside, in the cold, and carried my package close to me. I did not want Irene or Gina to smile at my purchase; I did not want Monty to wink or shake his head as he saw the sheets I carried. When I had tired of holding the brown paper package tight against my chest, when I had tired of standing and peering through the glass of the window, I began to walk back down the Avenue toward McKay's place.

In the darkening apartment I unpacked my suitcase and placed my clothes on hangers in the closet. When I turned on the color TV I saw that the serial number had been filed off. I rearranged my clothes and found a shelf in the bathroom for my make-up. I stored the empty suitcase under the bed. As it grew darker still, I closed the venetian blinds, dusted them, and switched on the stereo. Then I took a shower, changed my clothes, and watched the clock.

When McKay walked through the door it appeared that I was watching TV, listening to the radio, and reading *Sports Illustrated*. Actually, I was doing none of the above; I was merely waiting for McKay.

"Where the fuck have you been?" I said.

He didn't answer. He threw his leather jacket on the bed, took a can of Budweiser from the refrigerator, and sat down in front of the TV.

"Did you hear me?" I said.

"I'm ignoring you," said McKay.

"Go to hell," I said. I switched off the stereo, then stood before the TV, directly in McKay's line of vision, and then shut the life from the screen.

"You see, girl," said McKay, "if I don't ignore you after waiting for the Dolphin to show for two hours, if I don't ignore you now, you'll be regretting it."

"I thought you'd be back before this, that's all," I said.

"Well, I wasn't," he drawled. He drank from the can of beer.

"I wanted to go out somewhere," I said.

"I gotta wait for the Dolphin."

"Leave a message for him at Monty's."

"I have no money."

"You just had more than a hundred dollars."

"I mean, I have no money to go out."

Now McKay was silent, and I began rearranging the clothes in the closet as McKay stared at the blank TV screen. I smoked a cigarette and looked at the clock. McKay rose to get

74

another beer, and as he passed the bed he accidentally knocked the brown paper bag off the mattress.

"What's this?" McKay said. I was silent as he leaned over to retrieve the package and then as he opened the bag and took from it the two sheets and pillowcases I had bought.

McKay walked to me as I sat in a wooden chair, looking out the window and smoking a cigarette.

"It's crazy to fight like this," he said. "It's too soon to fight." He held the sheets in his hand, and I nodded, though I did not face him.

"Blue," McKay said. "I like blue. How'd you know that? How'd you know I liked blue?"

I turned to him, and McKay knelt so that his head was level with mine. I touched his dark hair and then whispered as I felt his arms around me. "Only a few hours," I said. "I don't expect you to see me if you don't want to. But tonight," I whispered, "can't we go out? I'll stay and watch TV every other night. But not tonight."

It was more than wanting to go out with McKay. It was wanting to keep him away from the Dolphin.

"Yes," said McKay. "Yes," he whispered.

McKay telephoned Monty's and left a message for the Dolphin with Gina. He said that he could be found at the Moonglow Drive-In.

"Why did you tell her where we would be?" I said.

"Hey, I been compromising," said McKay. "What do you want, blood? When I got business, I got business. I told you that; don't expect anything else."

So I followed McKay. Though I had seen the film at the Moonglow twice before, I followed McKay. He drove down the Avenue, he paid for us both, and with the cans of soda and beer rattling on the floor of the car, we parked in the last row of the almost empty lot.

McKay attached the speaker to the car window and I sat close to him. After the titles had shown across the screen and the film had begun, he turned away from my embrace and opened the Chevy door. Cold air fell upon us like a knife as McKay leaned his head out close to the frozen asphalt of the lot. He began to vomit.

I ignored him. I pretended McKay had not opened the door of the Chevy, but he continued to make those retching noises as Peter Fonda spoke sweet love to Nancy Sinatra.

"McKay," I said. "What did you tell me about being sick in this car?"

He stared at me with dark eyes. "You wanted to go out, well, now you're out." He whipped on his pink motorcycle goggles and opened one of the sodas. But sodas could not help now. I could see he was going to be sick again.

"Go to the men's room," I said. I lit a cigarette and tried to pay attention to Nancy as she pleaded with Fonda not to ride off again to terrorize towns and villages up and down the California freeway. I had heard her speak these words twice before and so I could not concentrate when it seemed I knew the dialogue better than Nancy did. The cigarette lighter of the Chevy smoked with old marijuana and popped with seeds.

McKay threw the car door open and leaned out into the cold once more. His body heaved, and then the noises in his throat quieted and his shoulders stopped their shaking.

"At last," I said, and I blew a stream of smoke between us. I had no pity.

"What you want?" said McKay.

"Honey, I want you," I said.

"You got me," said McKay.

"You'd rather be with the Dolphin," I said.

"Enough."

"Why don't you let me talk?" I said.

"Talk," said McKay.

We were silent.

"You never let me talk," I said.

"Christ," said McKay, "you and your fucking attitudes."

"I only want you to hold me," I said. I did not say I want you to forget about the Dolphin, the Orphans, and think only of me.

McKay grabbed my arm. "Am I holding you now?' he said.

"Shut up," I said. "I hate men," I told him.

McKay turned from me to study the blue of the GTO parked next to us.

"Why don't we forget this movie and go find the Dolphin,"

I said. "What's an evening without him?"

"I've had enough of your talk, and I'm sick of your attitudes," said McKay. He turned the key in the starter, he wrenched the car into gear, he forgot the speaker in the window.

"You forgot something," I said calmly. He turned the wheel sharply and the Chevy hit the speaker's metal pole. The pole sprang into the blue GTO. The speaker hung in the window no longer attached to its pole. We curled our lips and muttered to each other. Nancy spoke silently on the screen before us.

He pulled the car back into the parking space; and there was a knock at the window. McKay rolled the glass down, the speaker crashed onto the asphalt of the lot, I stared at the center of a headless orange jacket.

"Hey, man, you hit my car."

"Yeah."

"I mean, man, you hit my car!"

McKay lazily leaned his head out the window and gave a slow whistle. "You're right," he said. "Tell you what, I'm gonna try not to do it again. Now I can't promise anything, but I'm gonna try to see it don't happen a second time." Here was my man. I moved closer to him, placed my arm around his shoulder. We stared out the window together. The orange jacket disappeared, the GTO disappeared. I moved back to my side of the car. "Look," McKay told me, "I don't want no hassles. But if there's a scratch on this car, I'm gonna kill you."

"McKay," I said, "I've seen this movie before. Twice before. I'm here because I wanted to be alone with you. Without the Dolphin. To be together. Alone." He was silent. "Together," I said.

"Honey, what you want?" said McKay.

"Take me home," I said.

He started the car, he stepped on the gas. The Chevy roared through the movie parking lot, its chrome shone moonlight, the speaker was left on the cement. We sped down the Avenue, we left rubber in the driveway of a White Castle, we came to a stop in the alleyway where no neon could reach.

The short-order cook, who was ready to leave the grill at any hope of a fight, stood in the alley waiting for action. Instead he got us. He stared at the Chevy's headlights. McKay switched them off and glared at the cook. The cook, knowing McKay's name, knowing the Orphans' reputation, pulled his white hat farther down over his head and slunk back into the kitchen door of the Castle.

"You know," said McKay. "You know what I'm doing."

"I know what you're doing."

We were silent.

"What the hell are you doing?" I said.

"Get in the back seat," McKay answered.

I climbed into the back as McKay opened the Chevy door. Snow was in the midnight. McKay was beside me once more. Outside in the parking lot waitresses answered the calls of bright headlights with hamburgers wrapped in plastic-coated paper. Several Orphans loitered in the warmth of the Castle drinking coffee, talking and combing their hair.

"Girl," McKay said to me, "we got to talk. I can't lie to you."

A tap at our window and through the fog I could see the Dolphin standing there.

"Don't turn around," I said to McKay. "Stay with me," I said. McKay turned to the glass and saw the colors of the Dolphin's arms, the tattoos shimmering at the wrist and throat. McKay rolled down the window. "Why?" I said and the word was lost in cold air.

"My man," the Dolphin said, and I stared blackly at him as he leaned his head into McKay's window. I did not have to ask how the Dolphin had found us. Starry had said "The Dolphin knows all," and I knew there was no escape from him.

"I could be holding in less than a half hour if I could get a ride into the city," the Dolphin said.

Manhattan once more. The Dolphin's hold on McKay once more. "Then get one," I said.

The Dolphin didn't turn his sunglassed eyes my way. "Shut up," he said and continued staring at McKay.

"I'd like something to drink," I said.

"You're not holding now? You hung me up today and now you don't even have any shit? Don't you know I'm carrying my last hit?" McKay whispered to the Dolphin. And the red of a crown lapped at the Dolphin's knuckles, the tail of a peacock wisped at his throat.

"I'd like to be alone with you," I said to McKay. We held our territories in the back seat and watched the Dolphin stick his arm inside the Chevy and turn its wheel with his smallest finger.

"Dolphin," I said, "why don't you leave us alone."

The Dolphin ignored my words. "Leave McKay alone," I said. I moved deeper into my corner of the Chevy, as far away from the Dolphin as I could.

"If she's so stupid," the Dolphin said, his black-gloved hand turning the car wheel slowly, the blue denim jacket sleeve framing the paintings on his hand. "If she's so stupid that she don't know what's happening, she don't deserve to know."

"Give me a few minutes," McKay whispered to the Dolphin.

"You've had enough time," the Dolphin said.

McKay nodded. "Give me a minute."

"Tell her, man," the Dolphin said and he turned his face to me. Did our eyes meet through his dark glasses? I could not tell, for the Dolphin had turned his head to McKay and he nodded. "Later." The Dolphin walked slowly away from the Chevy and the window of the car was left open.

"You don't owe me anything. You don't have to tell me anything," I lied.

McKay reached out his hand to me. "I can't stop," he said. "I have to give him the ride."

I answered "Go" with eyes that Nancy Sinatra would never have given to Peter Fonda.

"It's not the Dolphin," said McKay. "He's the one who does me favors. He's going uptown for me."

Favors like the favors the Dolphin must do for Starry when she held ten dollars in her hand. Tonight's sodas and sickness. "Why do you have to go?" I said.

"What do you want from me?" He lit a cigarette and my

79

boot crushed an ancient beer can. I reached over McKay and into the front seat to switch on the headlights and call the eye of a waitress. "God damn," McKay said as he also jumped forward to turn off the glare, the call. I slid back to my side of the back seat. As he half stood, half crouched with one leg thrown over the front seat, I told McKay I wanted a soda, a pizza, a song, a cigarette, anything so that McKay would not have to tell me. Outside the Dolphin's stare was in our direction and I could see his heel pound the asphalt.

McKay tore off his leather jacket, the jacket I thought he would never remove, never forget. He shoved it onto the floor and slammed his body into the back seat. He sat in T-shirt and goggles. "Why can't you ever shut up?" he said. I only knew that I couldn't. I did not want to ask the questions, but my words took control and I had no choice. Now that I had the right to scribble McKay's name on endless matchbook covers, on endless pages of yellow paper, now that I had his name, I found I could not do as he asked. He wanted a wordless drive into Manhattan with the Dolphin, and me waiting in the White Castle or on a stool at Monty's counter. But I could not, I would not be silent.

"Open the door, McKay," I said, "but I won't leave unless we talk. You owe me nothing, you don't belong to me, I know. But I won't leave."

He fumbled at his waist, undid the gold belt buckle. "Why not wait until we're alone without the Dolphin waiting?" I said. He tied the belt around his arm – too late for me to jump out the window in silence, too late for me to stop wanting to know.

"McKay," I said. A Buick full of girls cruised by us, their heads turned, necks craned to see McKay's car. Waitresses answered light calls and the Orphans waited in the winter night. "Say something to me," I whispered.

I kicked the car seat with my heel, I stepped on black leather crumpled on the floor. McKay reached under the car seat and pulled out a pale envelope and left it on the seat, close to my touch. He pulled the belt tight as iron around his arm, the veins pale sea-blue. Our eyes. I looked into the eyes and they were mine, black and fire. McKay held the tail of

the belt out to me to grasp in silence, and through the
Chevy's open window cold night air blew through me like
white horses.

July

5

THE PRICE OF ADMISSION

I

TIME FLIES; IT also walks, crawls, occasionally it does the stroll. Like mood, time is made of air. Like mood, time firms and then disappears. So very quick; so very slow. Birth, death, revelation, orgasm, accident, trauma, the intake of one breath. Would you have sentences to try to replace hours, moons, menstrual periods, sleepless nights? Time is of air, and has little to do with words and minutes.

Some things seem to change. Jose applied for the New York City Police Department. Failing to meet height requirements, he bought a pair of Frye boots, was accepted into the training program, and was welcomed by McKay as a cop in the pocket. Starry was seen less and less on the Avenue – although some of the Orphans claimed to have sighted her in several unknown cars; she moved from Toyotas to Cadillacs with ease – and was now the Number One Property in name only. The weather grew warmer; soon it was July, and the weather was hot.

And some things seem not to change. The Dolphin never called me by name, never looked into my eye, or entered McKay's apartment when I was present. In time I forgot him, and remembered the colors of his tattoos only in certain dreams at night. I could not, could never sleep at night until I heard McKay's key turn in the lock, until I felt him close beside me. Each time he was away from me I feared I would lose him, and so during the nights I held McKay and waited until I heard his breathing deepen. Only then could I finally close my eyes and sleep. And the same conversation between us, over and over again, recurring like clockwork. From the first time I found him on the tile floor of the bathroom, fallen from his seat on the rim of the bathtub with the belt still around his arm and the spoon and the needle resting near him on the tile, we spoke the same words.

"Again?" I would say.

"Don't give *me* jive," he would answer.

"Go ahead, kill yourself," I would advise.

"I'm cool, darling," he would say. "If I even think I'm hooked, I'm gonna quit it. Trust me, darling," he would whisper.

"Again?" I would say.

The heat seemed to burn away the repetition of our dialogue. The eyes that could never be perceived by any sequential time were so dark they could melt the second hand off any clock. Time passed; it was easily erased with the blink of one eye. It was July, and the weather was hotter. The Chevy was fixed up for racing and we moved into summer.

When McKay mailed the twenty-five-dollar application fee to the track out on the Island, I planned to use the race as an excuse to get away from the Avenue for a weekend. I walked down the Avenue carrying a bag of groceries, and I noticed that any plant, any weed, that might have grown between the cracks of the sidewalk had begun to wilt. For weeks the radio had promised that the heat wave would end, but we all knew this was not true. The radio itself admitted the lie with its tired voice, with per cents, ratios, and the promise of a cold front.

New York was dying of the heat; and I planned to get us away from it all.

"Darling," said McKay as I walked into the apartment with a brown grocery bag full of sodas and beer, "the people gonna meet us at the track."

I did not want "the people," the Orphans, to follow McKay as always. I placed the bag on the wooden table. I unhooked a soda from its plastic harness and ran the cold can along my neck. The windows were open, and soot covered the window-sills. McKay sat in a chair by the window watching me, cloaked in black leather even in the heat of July. I tossed the

86

metal ring of the soda can on the table. "Fuck you," I said.

McKay smiled. I removed my July-damp clothes and wrapped a thin bathrobe around myself. McKay stared lazily as I undressed. "What do you want?" said McKay.

Did that matter? What I wanted was McKay, but even when he was with me, he wasn't with me. The only time I did not fear McKay leaving me was while he slept, and even then I stole touches and glances to ward off heart attacks and comas. Even then there were dreams.

McKay smiled. "The Orphans cannot live without me. How can I deprive them of the right to see the Chevy beat out every other car on the track?"

"Do what you want," I said, and I began to pack a small suitcase.

"Do what I want," said McKay. "I have obligations," he said, and he pointed to a six-pack of beer. I threw a can of Budweiser across the room and McKay nodded. "What service," he sneered.

He drank the beer, watching me for a while. Then he walked into the toilet, locking the door behind him. Whenever the lock of the bathroom door was turned I ceased to think, I ceased to feel, I stared into air and tried not to count seconds. I lived again only when I heard the doorknob move, only when McKay walked out of the locked room with his eyes heavy and quiet and dark.

McKay sat again in the chair and his head nodded on his shoulder. When I clicked the suitcase shut and threw it on the wooden floor he turned to stare at me.

"And another thing," he said and his words were slurred and easy. I walked into the bathroom to run the shower. McKay's works, the needle and the envelope, still lay on the porcelain of the toothbrush holder. "I'm talking to you," called McKay. "And I'm saying that you're spending too much time with Starry. Hear me now? I want you to quit that."

Although I had never told McKay what I knew about Starry – the stories of where she went in those shiny Cadillacs, or how much heroin she was using daily – she was not fooling McKay. Maybe some of the other Orphans, but not McKay.

He knew the look, the whisper, the nod. I shut the door of the bathroom; the mirror began to cloud, steam rose, and I threw my bathrobe onto the floor. McKay opened the door. He stood in the doorway in leather and steam.

"I know what she is," said McKay.

"What is she?" I said. I thought of nights alone without Starry to call on the telephone while I waited for the hours to pass, while I waited for McKay, who was out on the Avenue with the Orphans, with the Dolphin.

"A whore," said McKay. "And I don't want you with no whore."

"Those are nice words," I said, "about the Number One Property of *your* people."

"Not for long," said McKay. "She won't be Number One for much longer."

Her knuckles turning white as she grasped the bottle of tequila on the Night of the Wolf; as she waited for the Orphans' return. Starry belonged to the Orphans. And did McKay want me alone now, without even Starry's voice? Sitting alone with my fear of needles; alone in the darkened apartment with no number in my telephone book?

McKay closed the door of the bathroom. "I know she's a junkie," he said.

"You should talk," I said, and although the room was small and closed, and filled with steam, my skin felt unusually cold.

"Don't say that," he said quietly.

"All right," I whispered.

"Don't say that," he said, and McKay opened the door and grabbed the suitcase from the floor.

I shut off the shower, threw on some clothes, and tried to catch up to him as he walked down the stairs and out to the street where the Chevy waited. I ran.

"All right," I said.

McKay walked by the greeting of the auto repair shop mechanic, whom he regularly supplied with stolen goods, and slid into the Chevy. He started the engine. There was no doubt McKay would leave without me, so I opened the door, and we sat silently as the engine droned and the summer heat surrounded us.

"Maybe I get high sometimes," McKay said. "There's a difference between that and Starry dragging the Orphans' name in the dirt. There's a difference between getting high and fucking for a fix."

McKay steered the Chevy toward the highway which would lead to the end of the Island and to the track. "I won't see her as much," I said.

"You won't see her at all," said McKay.

It was not such an unreasonable demand. I had not seen Starry as much as McKay imagined. She was not often on the Avenue anymore. And although Starry never was absent from an official meeting of the Property, her time was spent in the city, hassling, hustling, searching for money and then spending it on packages of white powder. Lately we had not seen each other at all, but it was true, our voices met nightly through the telephone wires.

"Whatever you say," I told him, and McKay gave me his nod, and his smile once more.

Miles later McKay registered the Chevy. As he spoke with other drivers and mechanics, and they admired the sheen of the car, I sat in the empty stadium in the heat of late afternoon. Although the track was not far from the ocean, no wind rose, and the sawdust that coated the earth of the track was still. I watched McKay with the eyes of a stranger: the dark eyes, the easy walk, the motorcycle goggles, the leather, and the smile. It was still McKay. He was McKay, all right.

The other Orphans began to arrive; with leather and laughter they encircled the Chevy. Martin the Marine leaned over the Chevy's open hood, as Danny the Sweet danced before the Chevy's engine and waved to me. I only nodded in response, for Danny was another McKay couldn't tolerate. Yes, McKay allowed the Sweet to make runs into the city and pick up envelopes from Flash's apartment, but he hated the Sweet's never-ending smile. And so lately Danny the Sweet and I only nodded to each other as we passed on the Avenue. And although he continued to smile at me, the Sweet had stopped his offers of candy bars and advice.

Jose had officially joined the Department, but still he could not miss a race of McKay's. I watched McKay and the "cop in his pocket" stand apart from the other Orphans, and Jose smiled and nodded and drew circles in the sawdust with his boot heel as McKay talked.

Irene had brought her Viet Nam veteran boyfriend to the track. He held his arm around her as her laughter rose into the air. I smiled. Could the boyfriend, with his short, combed-back hair, have known while he sat with his pencil in some rice paddy how many of the Property had smiled at his mis-spelled words, how many times his line "I can't wait to get back to the States to fuck you" had been referred to? The boyfriend smiled as he was introduced to the leather and the looks of the Orphans in the diminishing sunlight of the afternoon. No, he did not know.

T.J. and Gina stood together. They had become more of a couple than any other Orphan and Property. T.J. held a silver-headed cane, a present from McKay, and occasionally leaned on Gina's arm for support. His wound from the Night of the Wolf had made walking difficult, and more and more he needed Gina – so much so that she had quit her job at Monty's in order to be with T.J. as much as possible. Officially, T.J. and Gina were of the Orphans, but they stood together now. T.J. was no longer an asset to the Orphans, although he remained a sort of mascot, with his silver cane and his black eye patch and his legendary wounds.

The Dolphin had not appeared at the track, but then the Dolphin rarely appeared at social gatherings. Tosh and Leona stood sullenly among the Orphans and with them were Kind and Starry. I was never glad to see Kind, to see her painted eye on McKay, on the letters of his jacket, but I had learned to ignore her smiles and her eyes. It was Starry, not Kind, I did not want to see at the track. I did not want to see Starry this far away from the city limits, for she had told me, laughingly, in the safety of the Tin Angel, that each time she left New York, each time she crossed the line, her nose began to run, her body ache, even if she carried a week's supply of heroin sewn into the lining of her jacket. She could not leave the city.

McKay left the Orphans gathered around the Chevy to come sit with me in the bleachers. He took my hand. "Darling, I know," he said.

I stared into the air. "What do you know?" I turned to McKay and saw that he did not smile at my words. "Darling," I said, and I held my arm around McKay, took the hand which held mine and placed his fingers to my lips. "You know," I whispered.

"At least the Dolphin ain't here," said McKay. "That should make you smile."

I responded to that.

"Ah, I see it does. Well, it won't make Starry smile. She would never have left the city if she knew the Dolphin wouldn't be here."

"You lied?" I said.

McKay gave me his darkest eye.

"You implied," I said.

"I won't have talk all along the Avenue about the Number One Property. The Orphans can't have so little honor as that."

I saw Kind's eye on us. "You can always draft Kind," I said.

"An idea," said McKay, laughing, and he left me so that he could return once more to the Chevy. I followed, for Starry motioned to me with a wave of her hand.

The crowds began to stream through the turnstiles, and the Orphans claimed front-row seats. Starry waited behind the Orphans for me to reach her.

"I'm hurting," Starry said. "I never thought McKay would be this far out of the city without the Dolphin to cop from. He's going to be hurting, too, McKay is. Or does he have some shit?" Starry pressed her fingers into my arm, and she held me back from joining the Orphans, who passed a reefer from one hand to the next. "Does he have some?" Starry whispered. "Can you get me something to get high with?"

"Starry," I said. "McKay is not a goddamn addict. He just gets high sometimes. He doesn't need it, he doesn't have to bring dope with him."

"Bullshit," Starry said. "You don't know."

"I do," I said. "What's more, McKay knows about you. He knows how much dope you been using."

"That's why he didn't say a word about the Dolphin not being here. He wants me to admit it. He wants to force me to resign from the Orphans." Starry bit her lip. "That fucker," she said. "McKay will screw every one of us with his honor."

"He won't force you to resign," I said.

"That wouldn't be honorable," she sneered.

I reached out to touch Starry's shoulder, but she shrugged me off. We sat with the Orphans and as Danny the Sweet passed a joint to me I watched Starry's shoulders shudder slightly. Her pale hands shook as I passed her the reefer.

"Long time no see," said the Sweet as McKay's Chevy forced a Ford to jump the track and smash into the wire meshing that protected the stands.

"A long time," I agreed, but I could not look at the Sweet as I answered him. He placed his hand on my knee.

"It's all right," said the Sweet. "It's cool," he said. "Hey, you think I feel ignored? Hey, you think I'm insulted? It's cool, I tell you."

"It's cool?" I smiled at him.

Danny kissed me very lightly; his breath was sweet as sugared cough syrup. "You know it is," he said. I sat between Starry and Danny the Sweet, and we watched McKay win.

After the races, when the moon was high, and the air cool and salty, the Orphans gathered around a campfire on the shoreline. With the prize money in his pocket and the speed of the Chevy common knowledge, McKay smiled into the air. I stayed close to McKay, and used words which made him promise that we would not spend the night in a sleeping bag, on the sand, surrounded by Orphans. He was a winner; the least he could afford was a motel room and a few hours. We sat close together in the sand and whispered. Then I saw Starry's face, the strained whiteness against the night. I nodded to McKay, and he motioned Starry to join us.

"Glad to see you could make it to the race," McKay said as he sipped from a can of beer. The dark fire of his eyes settled on Starry's profile. "You know it wouldn't look good if the Number One Property wasn't around for my victory."

"Fuck your victory," said Starry.

McKay lit a cigarette and was silent.

"McKay," Starry said, "don't ask me to do this."

"Honey," he said, "you asked for it. And I have no choice

but to protect the Orphans' name."

"From what? What are you protecting? McKay, don't ask me to give up what I have. Don't ask me to give it all up."

If McKay took the Orphans away from Starry she would belong to no one. If he took away the letters on the jacket she would belong to no one. Only the city, the needle; no one else.

"Let it wait until tomorrow," I whispered to Starry.

"She can't wait," said McKay. "Don't you see she can't wait?"

"I know you're using," said Starry. She hesitated. "I need it now," she said. "I need it right now."

McKay was silent.

"All right," she whispered. "Fix me and I'll go. Fix me and I'll go back to the city."

McKay was ready. He stood up and his shadow covered us. The sound of the Orphans rose around us, for Irene had announced her engagement to the Viet Nam boyfriend, and great hoots of laughter and cheers greeted her words.

"I want you to know it's not the dope," McKay said to Starry. "It's honor that's at stake."

Starry shook her head. "McKay," I whispered. When he spoke of honor I felt that losing him was seconds away.

"Why a hooker?" McKay continued. "Why didn't you come to me and tell me?"

"So I've turned some tricks," Starry whispered. "How the hell do you expect me to get money? I could rob a liquor store as well as you can, but that wouldn't be 'honorable' for Property to do. What am I supposed to do with no car, with no gun, with nothing but my body? If I had come to you, if I had told you I was hurting and I had a habit, what would you have done?"

McKay was silent.

"Yeah," said Starry. "Yeah, that's right. Nothing. You would've told me to shut up and done nothing. You wait," Starry said. "You wait till you have no money, till you need to cop some dope and there's no one there. Wait till you hurt so bad that you no longer care about honor. Wait. You'll be turning tricks before long. Before you even know it, you'll be turning tricks, McKay."

McKay stared into the night. The air was cold now that the wind was rising off the ocean. Tomorrow the heat would begin once more, the temperature would rise, and skins would burn. But tonight, even with the protection of fire and leather, bumps rose on the skin.

Starry was shivering in the cold. "Just fix me once," she said. "I know you got dope with you, fix me once and I'm gone for good."

McKay sat so close that his jacket covered both our shoulders. "You have it with you here?" I whispered. "Why do you have it with you?" Perhaps my whisper was so soft that McKay did not hear. He did not answer.

"Flash wants me to move in with him," Starry said to me.

My words were immediate. "You won't," I said.

"I will," she said. "Why not?"

"You change your allegiance fast," said McKay.

"Boy, you know me better than that," said Starry. "But if I'm not Property, I need something. I need protection. I might as well be with Flash, at least he can always fix me. He's got dope all the time and he'll take care of me."

"In the Chevy," said McKay. "And then that's it. I don't want to see you with the Orphans no more. I don't even want to see you on the Avenue."

McKay and Starry spoke as dreamers do, looking not at each other, but only into the air. I watched Starry's face for a tear, for anything, but she only stared in the direction of the Atlantic. The water was too dark to see, but the waves broke onto the sand like a heartbeat in the night.

I watched them walk to the Chevy. Then I looked away and wished myself in that car with McKay and Starry, holding the belt, rolling up my sleeve; together in the Chevy. I felt only jealousy. This was not the way I was jealous of Kind, or of the cars full of girls that followed the Chevy down the Avenue. I was jealous in a way I would have never been of sex, of another woman. I was jealous of the intimacy of the needle. Any fear, any sadness at Starry's exclusion disappeared. If she stayed she would be closer to McKay than I was, as close as the Dolphin. I wanted her gone.

Danny the Sweet was awakened from sleep. He was given

94

Flash's address and told to start the engine of his Pontiac immediately and drive Starry back over the City Line. The Sweet, as always, was flattered by McKay's choosing him to run an errand. With his grin in the moonlight and his boots racing so that he could comply with McKay's wishes, Danny made me want to reach out to him as he passed by winking and rolling his eyes. But McKay's eyes were their darkest and I only nodded to the Sweet and walked slowly toward the Pontiac with Starry.

"I won't be hustling no more," Starry said with slurred words. "I only did that to keep secrets from the Orphans. To protect the Orphans. Now I got Flash and no secrets." She smiled. "So now you'll be Number One Property."

"No," I said. "I never cared about that."

"Only McKay."

McKay had started the Chevy engine. He called my name and the Sweet honked the Pontiac's horn.

"You watch," Starry said. "He'll be turning tricks."

We both looked at McKay as he sat at the wheel of the Chevy. There was the salt smell of ocean, the night, and his dark eyes.

"That man?" I laughed. "Starry, honey, that man is too beautiful to have to turn tricks." And we laughed the laugh that turns to silence much too quickly.

"Don't be jealous of the needle," Starry said, and I wondered if my fears were so easy to see as that. "Don't be jealous of the needle; it's not such a very fine lover as you may think. But if you got the money, it sure is a reliable lover. It always comes."

Irene and her Viet Nam boyfriend danced in the sand and the Orphans howled and clapped hands. The Chevy engine began to strain. I left Starry at the door of the Pontiac to walk toward McKay.

"You know one thing," Starry called and I did not turn around; I only stopped in the sand. "You know I still got a telephone. You know you can call me."

I kept walking, I left tracks in the sand. The Sweet's Pontiac drove off the shore on its way to the city. I thought, after all the months, the words, the kisses, I still have not gotten what

I wanted. Yes, McKay allowed me to unpack my suitcase in his closet; but he would not admit me into his soul. And I wanted nothing less. If you say that was too much to ask, I will agree. And then I will repeat: I wanted nothing less. It seemed I could not get what I wanted. I opened the door, sat near McKay in the Chevy, and as we drove, the wheels spun sand into the night. Through the silence of the shore we could still hear the howls of the Orphans.

We drove to a seven-dollar-a-night motel and as we pulled into the parking lot McKay turned to me. "I'm going to quit it," he said. "I ain't gonna be like Starry. I can live without getting high. I can live after I cross the City Line."

I looked into his eyes and I wanted every secret of mine to be his, every secret of his to be mine. I began to know the spells; the spell was love, the spell was honor, and the easiest spell of all was what McKay now spoke of: heroin. That is why I wanted the same needle in both our arms. I thought it might be worth the price to have someone with eyes like McKay's to fix me for the first time with the magic that has no color, no odor, no chant, no song at all. Yes, it's true I wanted the needle in his vein; but it was only love.

"One more time," he said, as we walked toward the bright fluorescence of the motel. "It would be crazy to waste good dope. One more time is all," he whispered.

It was only love. And I thought I had found the easiest of spells.

"Together," I said.

"No," he said.

Six months with McKay, and being with him was lonelier than being without him. At the beginning I thought I only wanted his name, but that was not enough. Words were not enough. Not even a body, skin, whispers, not even these were enough. And so I stopped McKay in the darkness of the parking lot with arms, with whispers, and with sighs.

"Yes," I said.

"This one time," he said. "Only this one time."

Six months, six ways to fall in love, six positions of helplessness, and still all is changed and nothing is different. Do I always go to that motel with McKay? Does he always pour white powder into my vein as we stand in the toilet of the motel room as the gold-speckled ceiling showers flecks of paint on our skins? Am I always willing to pay the price of admission on that night? And is there always the same ritual; do I always roll up his sleeve and kneel before him and smile as the point of the needle touches his skin? Over and over again and always?

I confess to you now. I confess it all: I was willing. I wanted the spell, I wanted the magic; I would agree to any drug to keep him hooked. I wanted the tracks to run down McKay's arm in thin crooked lines, and I wanted to control the direction in which they ran. Through the heart. I wanted the tracks to run straight through the heart. I smiled, and ran the spoon that held the heroin across my tongue, and it was sweet. It was sweet, and it was easy, and I thought it was the price I had to pay.

The marks on my arms didn't touch the vein; there were never that many of them, only enough to try to stop the knowing. The knowing that I was trying to begin what could not be begun. The marks on my arms were only to stop a confession from ever having to be written down in black and white, in sentences and lies. It did not seem like so much at the time. It was only white powder and the blue liquid of his vein and love. That was all, powder and liquid and a heartbeat. That did not seem too high a price to pay for what I wanted. Not when what I wanted was everything. And I said the word very softly, and held McKay close, and closed my eyes.

"Yes," I said to him. "Yes."

II

I sat on the farthest stool at Monty's counter and watched McKay as he stood enclosed in the glass telephone booth. I chewed ice as a remedy against the heat. The old fan nailed to Monty's ceiling spun with a humming sound.

"Forget the ice," said Monty, "and have a drink. A real drink."

"What do you suggest?" I asked, and played with the cuff of my shirt.

"A double gin," said Monty.

"Your lips touch alcohol?"

"When the temperature rises above ninety these lips welcome a bit of gin."

"A bit?" I said. "A bit of gin? Old man."

"There's worse than drink," said Monty.

So that was it. An admission of drink for a confession of dope. It wouldn't work. I pulled the chain I wore from beneath my shirt. I held up the charm, and I smiled.

"You haven't thrown it away?" said Monty. "You surprise me."

More than not throwing the locket away, I had taken to wearing the charm constantly; even when I wore nothing else, even while I slept, I wore the tooth of a beaten man, the tooth of a dragon.

"Why haven't you thrown it away?" Monty said.

"I don't know," I said softly.

"What, now?" said Monty.

"Superstition," I said.

Monty shrugged and I looked away. McKay was dialing again, searching for the Dolphin with numbers and telephone wires. Dialing again in the glass booth.

"Not a trace of Starry on the Avenue," said Monty. There hadn't been a trace of Starry anywhere. Her name was never mentioned among the Orphans, not one of the Property had asked what had become of her. But if the wind of the Avenue blew as Monty said it did, the Orphans and the Property had all known for some time why Starry was no longer seen walking down the Avenue sidewalk, why she no longer waited in the last booth of the Tin Angel.

"She seems to be gone," I said, and Monty poured himself a glass of gin.

McKay came out of the telephone booth. He slid his boot heels along the wet sheen of the newly waxed linoleum and then skidded to a stop.

"Got it," he said. "Come with me for the ride."

"No," I said.

"No?" said McKay.

"No?" said Monty.

It was true I had taken to going everywhere McKay went, but they should not have been surprised at my answer when the destination was the Dolphin. Never would I go to the Dolphin.

Some corner kids hung around the freezer case. "Hey," said McKay. "You." He nodded to a dark-haired boy who lounged near the coldness of the freezer with a scowl and a cigarette. The corner kid walked toward us; there was no refusing an Orphan.

"He's the one," said Monty. "The kid's name is Tony and he's the one seems to have so many questions about the Orphans."

The corner kid stared silently at the floor.

"Tony," I said, "don't you got something to do?"

Tony shook his head and McKay smiled. "Leave the kid alone," McKay told me.

"McKay, he's fourteen," I said. "What do you need him for?"

"Don't you worry," said Monty. "This one is not what you call young. This one can grab a purse from an old lady in seconds. This one's outfit is never complete unless he's carrying a ball bearing in a sock to knock a fellow's eyeteeth down his throat."

"Hey, fuck off," Tony told Monty.

McKay laughed. "You know what my jacket says?"

Tony nodded and his eyes moved warily. "Sure," he said. "You the Prez."

"That true about old ladies?" said McKay.

"No," said Tony.

"That true about, what is it, a ball bearing in a sock?"

Tony smiled and McKay winked at me. "A ball bearing," he said. "In my day it was brass knuckles."

"Times change," said Monty with a shrug.

"You want to take a ride into the city with me?" McKay asked Tony.

"McKay, no," I said. "Don't take him with you."

Tony scowled at me.

"Look," said McKay. "There ain't no Orphans around and I want some company along for the ride. Also, I have heard it mentioned that Tony here might be interested in joining up with the Orphans. Ain't that right, Monty?"

Monty nodded. "That's right," he said.

Tony's eyes were wide. The other corner kids watched silently, knowing that they had lost one of their own.

I shrugged. "Do what you want," I told McKay.

McKay moved near to me. "Be at the apartment when I get home," he whispered.

"Get going," I said.

"I'll bring you something nice," said McKay.

"Something nice?" I said. I thought of the safety I felt when McKay was high. Only when he was in a dream and I held him in my arms was I not afraid he would leave me. I watched McKay walk out the doorway with Tony following silently at his boot heels. I could not hear McKay's reply.

"What you say, darling?" I called.

"He said," Tony, the chosen corner kid, said – walking past his old friends as though he had never before seen them – "something real nice."

My eyes stared into Tony's. "Something nice," I whispered. And Tony turned to follow McKay, to run and catch up to McKay and the Chevy.

I looked over at Monty. "He's too young," I said.

"He's not young," said Monty. "That boy is not young. I can spot the young ones. But that one" – Monty motioned with his head toward the empty doorway – "that one will take McKay's place someday. Even McKay can see that. So let the kid learn the tricks now; you know he'll learn them sooner or later."

We silently watched the empty doorway. Then I went behind the counter, mixed up a vanilla soda, and sat once more.

"You wear the charm," said Monty. "But hidden, of course."

I touched the chain at my neck, the locket I always wore beneath my blouse. "Do you think I want everyone to know what a fool you've made of me?"

"There never was anything wrong with a fool," said Monty.

"Is that true?" I said lazily, and I moved the clear soda in the glass around in small whirlpools with my fingertip.

Monty lifted his hand from the counter top. With a quick move he raised the sleeve of my blouse halfway up my arm, so that white muslin was pushed like petals around my elbow.

I was silent; then I brushed the cloth back into its place around my wrist.

"You're fresh today, old man."

"Long sleeves in the heat of July, darling?"

I ignored him; let the wind of the Avenue carry him the answers he wanted.

"How many times?"

I was silent and thinking only of dark eyes.

"How many times?" Monty asked again.

"Five or six," I said. "Big deal, only five or six times. What is it your business what I do?"

"So I'm wrong about McKay," said Monty. "So I've judged it all wrong. So he is a fool, after all."

"Shut up," I said. "Who the hell do you think you are to talk about McKay like that? Nobody talks about him like that."

"Not even you?"

"Old man," I said.

"Where is his honor when he gives you the heroin? Where is it then? Tell me, you don't shoot up yourself, he fixes you, doesn't he? I give any odds all of the Avenue will be talking about McKay soon enough."

What did I care about the old man's words? What could he know about McKay that I did not know? I had McKay; now he only saw the Dolphin to score dope, he only saw the Orphans on official business. I had him now; and it was me who sat in the front seat of the Chevy, me who kept the engine running, me who stashed the pale envelopes of heroin in the space between my stocking and the skin of my thigh. It was me with McKay.

"To hell with you," I said to Monty. "A few charms and

101

spells and you think you know something. To hell with you, you liar. You goddamn fool."

"I admit it all," said Monty, and I raised my glass in agreement. "Ignore me. Ignore the tracks on your arms. Ignore the talk about McKay. What do I know about Property of the Orphans?"

"Hah," I said. "I'm no Property."

"Listen to me," said Monty. "If you give up yourself, there won't be another."

"Listen to me," I said. "I'm not giving up anything. And I'm not giving up McKay."

"You can wash it all away," said Monty, and he brought out the bottle of gin and placed it on the counter. "You can wash it all away, but having seen."

"You poet," I said.

"So I'm a drunk," said Monty. "So you called it right when you called me a fool. And I tell you even this cannot stop sight."

"Close your eyes," I said.

"Close your eyes," Monty repeated. "There is no way to stop from seeing. Not even heroin."

"Five times," I began and Monty only stared at me with his winking eyes. I shrugged.

"Often at burials," said Monty.

"You gonna get into the morbid stuff now, old man?"

"Often at burials," he continued, "certain tribes perform a ritual of sewing the lids of the eyes closed tight. Who can really say why? Perhaps so that the dead cannot pass on secrets to the living. But eyes that will see cannot be sewn closed."

"I've got the charm, don't I? I have the magic of this locket," I said. "The charm McKay says you once offered to him, the magic he refused." Monty nodded and sipped gin. "Why do you lie, old man? Why do you tell McKay this is the tooth of a dragon, and then tell me it's the tooth of a beaten man?"

Monty smiled. "There is no difference," he said.

"There's a difference," I said.

"No," said Monty. "No, the two are one and the same."

102

I rose from my seat at the counter. I did not want to hear any more of his words.

Monty raised his glass to me. "It won't stop it, the heroin," he said. "You know that."

"Old man," I said as I walked to the door, and the silver locket which held the tooth of a beaten man, the tooth of a dragon, fell upon my breast, "I don't believe a word you say."

I walked out the door and into the heat of the Avenue. I placed sunglasses over my eyes to protect them against the reflected glare of sun and cement, and still my eyes burned, my head spun and I had to hesitate. You cannot sew closed eyes that will see, the fool had said. I continued down the Avenue to wait for McKay's return. The burning in my eyes felt nothing like tears, nothing like pain, and only a little like sight.

6

ACTS OF FEAR

I

THE TELEPHONE AWAKENED me. I ran to lift the receiver and silence the ring. The morning was still dark but already hot. McKay slept deeply. Through the wires I could hear the voice of Jose.

"Are you there?" he said.

"Yes, I'm here." I sat on the wooden chair near the window, my feet pulled up so that I could rest my head on my knees. The air was heavy, and full of the threat of thunder and more heat.

"McKay there?"

"Jose, he's here but he's sleeping," I said to the Orphans' man on the force.

"You better wake him," said Jose. I didn't answer; I listened to McKay's breathing. "There's going to be trouble, girl. Now you go wake him."

I held the phone receiver against my neck and watched McKay sleep. It was so early that traffic noise was only just beginning out on the Avenue.

"McKay," I said. I walked to the bed, sat, and touched his shoulder. "It's Jose," I said. "It's Jose on the phone."

McKay opened his eyes; there was silence and heat out on the Avenue. I watched McKay walk to the phone. I crossed my bare arms and rocked softly and did not listen to a word he said; I only watched McKay. Then I went to the kitchen to boil water for coffee and to fear some news of trouble with the police, with heroin, with the Dolphin.

McKay, already fully dressed in leathers, walked into the kitchen. "It's the Pack," he said.

I was relieved; I poured coffee. What did I care about the Pack?

"They've got Danny the Sweet," McKay said.

"What do you mean they've got him?" I said. What would the Pack want with Danny, when the Orphans themselves did not want him?

"I mean they got him." He drank hot coffee in gulps. McKay was readying himself to leave the apartment; he was willing to leave me alone with the words, "They've got Danny the Sweet."

"McKay," I said. "Not this time. Don't give me silence this time. The Sweet is my friend, so don't give me silence."

"You don't want to know," said McKay.

He was right; I did not want to know. But because I did not reach out to the Sweet as he passed by I had no choice.

"Damn you," I said. "Tell me."

I let McKay hold me for a moment, and then I moved away. "Darling, I don't have to tell you," he said. "You already know."

I knew; already I knew more than I wanted to. Why did I need to know more? Why did I have to know whether it was the knife or the gun?

"No," I said. "No."

McKay shrugged. He opened a kitchen cabinet, and the hinge cried out as the wood of the door moved. Alongside the cereal, the coffee, and the sugar, was McKay's gun. McKay and I never spoke of his owning a gun. He stored the twenty-two where my eye would see it at each and every breakfast, yet we refused to give each other words or denials. He placed the gun in an inside pocket cut into the silk lining of his jacket.

"McKay," I said. "No."

"In the back of the neck," said McKay. "He was shot in the back of the neck."

"You don't believe Jose for a minute, do you?" I said.

"Jose knows what the cops know. He knows the names of the dead."

"No one would bother with the Sweet. He's worthless."

McKay nodded. "It's to get to me," he said. "That idiot Sweet," McKay said softly. "They know I have no choice but to avenge an Orphan."

McKay walked from the kitchen and I followed. "You're not going," I said.

"I am," said McKay. "And you know I am. I have to go. The Pack knows that the Sweet was only worthless while he lived."

"That's not the way it is," I said.

McKay shook his head. "Don't talk to me of what it should be, girl. I'm telling it to you like it is. And it is honor now. And it is war."

"Not yet," I said. "Don't go yet. Let's get high first. Get high with me, and then go."

McKay smiled. "Not this time. Idiot that he was, he was my soldier. Not this time," McKay said, and he began dialing the phone. He was calling up the Dolphin, he was summoning the Orphans. I should have reached out my hand to place it on the lips of the Sweet as he grinned in the moonlight. But now if Danny the Sweet was lost, he was lost, and I did not want a sacrifice for a smile that was already lost. I did not want to have to wait once more, to have to count the bullets in the gun when McKay returned. I did not want to have to wait, to have to place bandages and cold compresses on scars after a battle fought over what was already lost.

I wanted McKay high, so he would be mine. I wanted him to forget the battle and let the heroin into his veins. Pure love, pure fear, pure selfishness: I did not want the losing to continue.

McKay spoke to the Dolphin. I walked over to him and whispered words of interference in his ear. "I want to get high," I told him. "I need to get high," I lied. McKay shook his head, and continued speaking through the wires to the Dolphin.

Any plan, any advice of the Dolphin's could never hold honor. It would be revenge that would belong only to the colors of the butterfly and the scar upon the cheek. And Danny the Sweet would be doubly lost.

"McKay," I said. "I want you now."

106

What could revenge do for the Sweet now? What good was honor? I would not risk losing McKay, not for the Sweet, and certainly not for honor.

"Now," I said. "Right now," I whispered. I held McKay and felt the metal of the .22 in the lining of his jacket. McKay touched my face, but he did not look at me; he was with the honor, with revenge. I slipped one hand into McKay's jeans, and with the other hand I began to work the zipper. And still he was with honor, with the Orphans, with the Dolphin. When the dark eyes finally turned to me, they were blank. I could not help but imagine that McKay did not recognize me, that he could not remember my face or the touch of my hand.

I left him talking to the Dolphin. I left him with the phone in his hand and his dark eyes blank when they looked my way. I threw a raincoat over my naked body and I grabbed the car keys off the wooden table.

"Girl, get back here," called McKay when he heard the sound of the metal. But it was too late. I was already out and in the street. I was on a course that led to the Chevy, which always waited, paint gleaming like black midnight, in the alleyway for McKay. If words couldn't stop McKay, and if no plea, no touch would make him forget honor and revenge, perhaps the gas pedal of the Chevy could make him forget.

I started the engine. My raincoat fluttered about my knees, for I had not had time to button the cloth around myself. Dawn was just beginningto break in colors and steam over the Avenue. I stepped on the gas.

I could never remember, later, if I had actually planned to go anywhere, if there had been a direction to drive toward, a somebody to see. Monty? Could it be I intended to steer the Chevy toward Monty and ask what secrets, what lies, what rumors he had heard? Starry? How could I ever have found Starry with no address, no road map, with no knowledge of Manhattan streets? Was it a desire to visit each hospital, funeral parlor, the chapels of churches, the counters of every drugstore on the Avenue until I found the Sweet? Or had I planned only to step on the gas? Nothing more than that, only to step on the gas? Only to hear the screech of tires, to know the power of the Chevy's engine, and to feel the velvet of the upholstery against my skin?

McKay was out in the street now. I had known he would follow. For that moment I had gotten him away from the Dolphin, from honor, from it all. So I stepped on the gas pedal of the car that turned heads in the street. I put into gear the Chevy that carloads of girls followed up and down the Avenue. I sat at the wheel of McKay's Chevy, the car with the shiny finish not even the auto shop mechanic would run a fingernail across. I drove.

When the side of the Chevy hit the lamppost, when I felt the tires rush onto the curb, onto the sidewalk, when the body of the Chevy screamed and ricocheted into the door of the auto repair shop garage, I was not surprised. It seemed the most natural of things. I kept my foot on the gas. I could hear the paint as it fell off the Chevy like dust. I kept my foot on the gas, and the engine roared, but the Chevy could no longer move, for its fender was tightly wedged into the door of the garage. I laid my forehead upon the cool wood of the custom-made steering wheel. My raincoat lay open; I felt the morning wind of the Avenue enter the Chevy's open window and touch me. The sun had only begun to rise, and it seemed the most natural of things that I should lay my forehead upon the steering wheel and close my eyes.

"That there the craziest fucking girl you ever saw," someone – perhaps the auto shop mechanic – said.

McKay opened the door and turned the ignition key. The engine sputtered and then died. McKay only stared at me, with the darkest of eyes he stared at me.

"Will it run?" I heard McKay say to someone on the street.

Some Avenue expert, some mechanic, some voice answered, "Shit, man, it'll run. But look at it, man, look at that car. Shit."

"Will it run?"

"Well, man, you gonna race it and that car's gonna blow or something. Man, that's fucked up. That's leaking oil like something else. You want to be safe, you'll get yourself a diagnostic test, man."

"Get out," McKay said to me. "Get out of the car," he said softly.

108

I wanted McKay to hit me, to rip my hand from its grasp on the steering wheel, to scream bloody curses into the air, but not to force me to leave the Chevy in silence.

In the early-morning light of the Avenue the strangers that are drawn to the sound of screeching tires and broken glass gathered around us. A young corner kid of ten or twelve stooped to grab the disfigured side-view mirror from out of a pool of shattered metal and glass. From the gutter, he grabbed a souvenir, a souvenir of the Chevy, a souvenir of McKay. A memento to remember the morning when the craziest fucking girl drove the '59 Chevy into a garage door and souvenirs lay in the gutter, in pieces. My shoulders began to shake.

"McKay," I said. He held my arm and helped me from the driver's seat to the Avenue sidewalk. McKay held me close to him, and the eyes of those who follow accidents were upon us.

"He's dead," said McKay. "The Sweet is dead."

"McKay," I said. I knew the Sweet was dead. I was the one who knew that, I was the one who wanted the dead to remain dead, who wanted the living to remain alive..

"That's all there is to it," said McKay. "He had no honor in life, but the Orphans give it to him in death. There is no way for you to stop that. There is no way for you to stop me."

I was silent and McKay kissed me and held my raincoat tightly closed. We watched the mechanic and some older neighborhood boys push the Chevy back into the street.

"Will you forgive me?" I whispered. I knew my words could be met only with silence. He could never forgive an act that was only an act of love and nothing more. "Will you forgive me?" I said.

McKay did not answer. Then he turned from me, and I watched him toss the .22 into the glove compartment of the Chevy, watched him pour oil into an engine that seemed to have no end to its thirst. I had to let him go. I stood in the heat, in the sun, of the Avenue, and I had to watch McKay start the engine and ride away.

The corner kid who had salvaged the side-view mirror was chased by a slightly taller dark-haired boy who grabbed the mirror for himself. It was Tony. For a moment I smiled, thinking that perhaps since that day McKay had taken him for a ride Tony had waited outside the auto repair shop, outside the apartment, waiting for a word, for a nod, for anything from McKay.

Tony held the broken metal-and-glass souvenir in his hands and walked to the corner of the Avenue where I stood. I held the raincoat tight around me. In the hot morning wind the coat moved and soft fabric touched my legs. We did not look at each other, Tony and I, we only stood on the same corner. He held the mirror in his hands and we only stood together on a corner of the Avenue, and watched McKay go.

II

For several days McKay did not return to the apartment, I remained clothed only in a bathrobe, and I consumed enough Seconals and gin so that I no longer remembered that the season was summer. After the third day I was no longer waiting for McKay. I was only waiting.

I did not even leave the apartment to buy food. I ordered a pizza delivered one night, but one bite made me ill, and so the pizza, still encased in its cardboard box, found its way into the pail of overflowing garbage. I stared at hours of television, and I kept the venetian blinds closed tight against the sun. On one six-o'clock news report I heard words about a death on the Avenue: a young man with a smile on his face and a bullet hole in his neck found in the back seat of a '57 Pontiac. The Pontiac was red and white, the mag wheels were silver-spoked. I closed my eyes.

I confess: I always thought Danny the Sweet was a fool, but I never thought he would die. He was much too young for anything like death. Even the one that might have claimed him in some delta in Indochina was avoided with a smile and a low score on every test the Army placed before him. Even the war did not want him. He was much too young even for that. He was no more than a sigh and a bullet hole and a way to trap McKay.

I had not gone to the funeral. McKay went, but I sat home alone and drank iced tea and fell asleep before the TV set. I

110

did not cry. There seemed nothing to cry for; the death he died was not his own.

Am I heartless to speak this way about the death of an old, a sweet friend? Do you think it is cancer or the heat that caused me to think only of McKay? Still only of McKay. Is it cruelty to forget the color of the Sweet's eyes so very easily? I wanted what was living, I needed what was living, do you blame me for that?

To get that I was not above reaching for straws, or for spells. And so I had sat in the front seat of the Chevy, and as I had laid my head upon the steering wheel, I had reached for the charm of the tooth encased in silver as it rested between my breasts. My fingers had stroked the silver as the wheels of the Chevy climbed over the curb; I murmured a chant against the power of the mood, though I knew I had no magic big enough, no herb strong enough to stop the direction we moved in.

McKay held me and made promises to the dead, and I was left on the Avenue with a child who held a broken mirror. I was left in an apartment, with dark silence and gin. The mood would have its way, and it would continue to move in its own direction. It would only deepen, darken and deepen.

What would you have me do? There was no way to stop what was to happen; McKay would walk toward honor if he could not drive. Even the needle, even the counting of veins, the charting of their various shades of blue upon a color chart, would not do. What would you have me do, cry or turn away? After herbs and wizards, after love and the screeching of tires, was there a way to fight soldiers who would be sheep? Should I have tape-recorded their bleating on eight-track cassettes to replay in the nights?

There was no stopping darkness and air. There seemed little choice at all but to close my eyes and continue. I turned the dial to another channel and drank more gin. I did not listen to news, to warnings; I was waiting.

One evening, as I sat before the TV, Jose walked through the unlocked door. I nodded hello.

"Girl," said Jose, "clean up this mess and put some clothes on. Jesus."

111

I lit a cigarette and stared at the TV screen. "You may be the Man now, and you may wear a badge," I said, "but you ain't got nothing on me; so don't give me orders. You want to be a guest, that's fine with me, as long as you're a silent guest."

"Get yourself together," said Jose, and I shrugged. Jose took a beer from the refrigerator. "Listen," he said. "I am hip to confidential files. Now, do you hear what I'm telling you? I have seen the police files on the Orphans, and I'm telling you I am privy to certain confidential information."

Jose was looking like an Orphan, but talking like a peace officer. I winked at him. "Big deal," I said, and I pinned some loose strands of hair back from my face.

"They gonna be busted if they meet with the Pack. Kid Harris made himself a sweet deal. The cops get the Orphans; the Pack gets the Avenue. Dwell on that for a while. Danny the Sweet's death was a trap to force McKay to search out the Pack. He's walking into a trap."

"What do you want?" I said. "I don't know anything; ask McKay."

"Now I'd be asking McKay if I knew where the fuck he was, wouldn't I?" said Jose.

Jose told me that the Orphans had been barricaded within the clubhouse for a week. They ate, slept, and planned revenge in the basement below Munda's Liquor Store. But now they were gone. The clubhouse was empty and the Orphans could not be found.

I listened to Jose's words. I believed McKay was being set up, I believed the death of the Sweet was no more than a trap. "How do I know you're not a part of the setup?" I asked.

Jose paled when I questioned his allegiance to the Orphans, to McKay. "Girl," he said, "you think what you want to think. I'm cool, but you think what you want to think. Being in the Department ain't nothing to interfere with the way I feel about the Orphans."

"You know what I hear?" I said. "Jose, I hear the cops get the best dope. You want to turn me on to some of the best dope in New York City? Maybe if you did that I could remember where McKay was," I lied.

"You get dressed or you go like you are, but you and me are going to find McKay. You and me are going to be the harbingers of the news that the Pack's planned a setup."

I smiled at Jose's scowl. But I threw on some jeans, a shirt, and a colored silk scarf around my hair. We drove up and down the quiet Avenue in Jose's Mustang convertible. We rode past the empty clubhouse. Jose turned his head at each street corner searching the darkness for an informant, for any sign.

"If McKay don't want to be found, he won't be found," I said.

"We'll try Monty," said Jose, and I shrugged. I had been in the apartment for so many days without air that now it seemed the night wind hurt my lungs and caused my head to spin. I placed sunglasses over my eyes.

Jose stared at me. "You're looking more and more like a dope fiend all the time. More and more," he said.

I rolled up the sleeve of my shirt. "Do you want to check for tracks?"

"McKay gonna ditch you if you don't watch out."

"Then maybe I can be the one to move in with Flash," I said easily, though Jose's words echoed fears of my own. Jose looked at me from the corner of his eye. "Don't give me none of your eyes," I said.

"Don't give me none of your talk," he said. "I got the power to have you incarcerated, don't you forget that. I don't want to hear my cousin, the bastard, referred to again."

Starry's presence was with us in the Mustang, but like some ancient curse, her name was never to be mentioned.

"You got me shaking with fear," I said as Jose scowled and pulled the Mustang up against the curb outside Monty's.

Jose held my arm as we walked into the candy store.

"Are you arrested?" Monty said. I smiled and opened the freezer case for a can of soda.

"What do you hear?" said Jose.

"I hear a lot," said Monty.

"Girl," said Jose, and I sat at the counter.

"Looking for McKay," I said.

"Are you?" said Monty. "Or is he?" He pointed to Jose.

113

"What am I?" said Jose. "Now what the fuck am I, a traitor?"

"Is he on the force or is he not on the force?" Monty said to me.

"Are you running numbers from this store or are you not running numbers from this store?" said Jose.

"I'm looking for him," I said. "Old man, I'm looking for McKay."

"He's on the Avenue," said Monty. "Tell the cop he might question that one." And Monty nodded his head toward the farthest end of the counter where the corner kid, Tony, sat.

"Him again," I said.

"Him again," said Monty. "McKay's protégé." We smiled at each other and watched Tony leaf through the pages of a comic book. We watched him start as Jose placed a hand upon his thin shoulder.

"Sorry to hear about the Sweet," Monty said. I shrugged. "Can't save them all," he said.

"McKay," I said. Now that I was out of the apartment and on the Avenue once more, I felt I had to find him. Secret files and a setup. I wanted to find McKay. "Do you know where he is?"

"Yes," said Monty.

"Tell me."

"The creek," said Monty. "The creek and no place else is where you'll find McKay." We stared at Jose, at his hand on Tony's shoulder.

"Tony doesn't know where McKay is," I said.

Monty smiled. "If you want to go, you might, you know. Those two will follow soon enough."

I nodded and walked quietly from the store. I needed to find McKay, to find him alone. Jose had forced me to leave the apartment and search out McKay, but now I wanted to find him. When I reached the Avenue, when the night air rushed my lungs, I began to run. My boots hit the asphalt; the silk scarf danced in air. I ran until the pain in my chest grew so deep that I could only walk quickly with my thumb out to try to hitch a ride down to the end of the Avenue where, hidden behind alleyways and trees, the creek ran.

I hitched a ride with a Dodge Dart, but I did not look at the face of the driver. I only placed my hand on the metal door lever and tried to catch my breath. The Dodge let me out a block or so away from the creek, where there was darkness and the loud unfamiliar sound of crickets and other living things. Here the only reminders of the city were the empty beer cans, the yellowed copies of the *News*, and the highway sound which echoed above the tunnels that crossed over the creek. I stood in the darkness and felt suddenly thirsty when I saw that the creek's waters had evaporated with the July heat, that the creek was only dark sand.

I climbed down a steep bank and walked along the creek's waterless course. It began at the Avenue and ended there several curves and tunnels later. As I walked my boot heels made soft crunching noises in the sand. Above there were stars. Now I thought perhaps I had been wrong to let Jose's words of a trap and the night air of the Avenue convince me to search out McKay and try to change the course of what he insisted had to be. I heard the noises of living things in the bushes that lined the creek's bank. I walked faster until I had reached the last tunnel before the creek once again met the Avenue. I stood against the concave cement wall of the tunnel and I listened to the slow sound of water dripping down a metal pipe and the occasional hum of a car engine as it passed over the tunnel on a route which led to the city. I heard voices.

I knew I should never have left the apartment, never have listened to Jose's words or tied the silk scarf around my head. I should have continued to wait in the dark. Had I thought it possible to move stars, to trick tricksters and elude the trap? I recognized one voice in an instant; it was the howl of Kid Harris. In the darkness of the tunnel a match was lit, and I could see the face of Kid Harris and the figures of fifteen or twenty of the Pack around him. I tried not to breathe.

"What I want," said Kid Harris, "is the Dolphin. And after that, McKay. The rest you leave for the cops. The rest are promised to the cops, unless you are being directly confronted with an assault."

A short dark figure whispered to the Kid. Then those two left the Pack counting knives and rattling chains and began to walk in my direction. My pulse sounded far too loud. Kid Harris nodded in my direction and I tried to melt skin into cement. He stopped before me and lit another match and I saw the gleam in his pale eye.

"We meet again," said Kid Harris. I was silent. "Don't we?" he said softly.

"Can't say that it's my pleasure," I said.

"Try saying it," said Kid Harris.

"I'm not here against you," I said. "I only want to find McKay."

"Try saying it," said Kid Harris. "Tell me it's your pleasure."

I was silent and Kid Harris drank from a bottle of what smelled like whiskey. He drained the whiskey and then broke the bottle against the cement wall of the tunnel. "Remember this?" he said as he held the glass close to my face. More and more of Kid Harris's soldiers now stood around me. Their colors were invisible but I could hear breathing and the sound of mumbled words and laughter.

"He'll kill you," I said.

Kid Harris laughed softly. "What I want to know is what you wanted to go and get mixed up with McKay for when you could have had one of the Pack."

I smiled. I thought of the Night of the Wolf, and I smiled. "Now why would I want to walk down the Avenue with a man with crippled hands?" I said.

Even some of the Pack snickered at the reference to Harris's broken hands, which were healed only as long as they were not referred to. He did not hit me so very hard the first time.

"Crippled?" said Kid Harris. "You made a mistake in your allegiance. You chose the losing side. You made a mistake and I'm going to show you why."

Kid Harris touched my face, his fingers stroked my neck. I could not remember if I had left the lights on in the apartment. And the stove, I had boiled coffee in the afternoon, had I left the burner on?

"The first mistake is always the last," said the dark soldier at Harris's side, laughing.

"Ain't that the truth," Kid Harris said softly. I could see the

116

shine of his red hair, like a fox, like a wolf, in the darkness of the night.

I wondered if Jose had already found McKay, if they were now drinking quietly in the Tin Angel Bar, discussing other tactics, forgetting the battlefield of the creek. Was it possible McKay could have forgotten? The silence of the creek seemed too much for me to bear. I held my hands over my ears.

"What is she, crazy?" said Kid Harris's soldier.

Harris may have shrugged; it was too dark for me to see. "Doesn't matter," he said.

"There's not much time," someone said, "if you want to hit McKay and the Dolphin before the Man gets here."

"The cops don't make a move till they get the signal from me. They don't even walk toward the creek till they hear two shots fired into the air," Kid Harris said. "So I got some time." He moved close to me and whispered words in my ear. But I could not make out the syllables: the silence of the creek was far too loud.

Arms held me. Although the jacket was leather, I knew the arms were not McKay's. There was darkness and he was saying words that sounded like "Don't act like you never done this before." My feet slipped and then there was the coldness of cement against my back and something was happening to my clothes. Something was happening. I heard laughter and the rattle of chains, and louder still, I heard the sound of my blouse tearing. I could not be sure if my jeans really were around my knees or if I only imagined the coldness touching my skin. I could no longer feel the difference between parts of my body which were still covered with cloth and those which were not.

My arms tried to hold him away from me, but still I was not quite sure it was my body on the cement. His hands on my breasts, if those were my breasts, if this was my body, if this was me. My arms would not stop trying to push him away, and once I felt my leg kick him, but then some other hand held my leg against the cement, and I had no feeling, no sensation in that leg, and I thought perhaps the skin might have been frozen by the coldness of cement.

He was finished now. I thought perhaps he might be

finished now, for I felt the weight lift off me. There was silence, and voices, and cement and earth. My eyes were open and staring into darkness, and there was a silence that grew louder.

"Hurry up," said a voice.

"Get rid of her," I heard the soldier at Harris's side whisper.

"Forget her," said Harris, if it was Harris. I was thirsty and something had happened, and I found I could not remember the color of the upholstery in Danny the Sweet's Pontiac. It was McKay's Chevy that was black and maroon, but I could not remember the color of the Pontiac. It was not blue, god damn it, I knew it was not blue.

I felt the nearness of Kid Harris. He stood above me, and once his boot grazed my leg. I touched my thigh and it was wet, chilled by cement.

"Shut up," Kid Harris whispered. The silence was broken only by the soft echo of footsteps in the sand.

More footsteps and the boot of Kid Harris close by. I touched my thigh again, and I was suddenly quite sure it belonged to me. This was my body on the cement. I cried out. Kid Harris kicked me, but I only screamed again, a warning to those footsteps which echoed in the sand. I covered my face with my arms to protect myself against the boot of Kid Harris.

In seconds the Orphans had attacked. Chains against cement, sand flying in the air. I could not uncover my face. His arms helped me to stand, and the silk lining of the leather jacket was placed around my shoulders. I pulled up my jeans and tied the silk scarf at my neck, and my hair fell, heavy and damp, onto it. We moved like lovers in the dark, McKay and I, unaware of the curses that surrounded us, toward the far end of the tunnel.

"McKay." It was the voice of Kid Harris.

"I want her out of here," McKay said, and I felt other arms around me. It was him again, the boy, Tony. "And I want you out of here," McKay whispered and the boy nodded, though I felt his arms tighten in an unspoken protest.

"McKay," said the voice of Kid Harris.

"I hear you," McKay's voice answered. I held the leather

118

jacket around my shoulders and walked with Tony toward the Avenue. The sound of the battle was behind us, and at the mouth of the tunnel stood the Dolphin. He gazed at the fight as he leaned against the wall of the tunnel. There was a smile at the Dolphin's lips. He reached into a pocket and flashed a switchblade; the silver glowed in the dark. For the first time the Dolphin looked at me and he nodded. Then he walked on, through the tunnel and toward the battleground. Tony and I climbed the far bank of the creek. On the Avenue Jose waited.

As Tony opened the door of Jose's Mustang his hands shook, and I whispered, "Do you like what you see? Do you like the game that's being played?"

We heard one gunshot. I waited for another, but no other sound echoed from the creek and I knew that shot had not been Harris's signal. The sound of one gun firing was McKay's answer to Kid Harris.

"Hurry up," said Jose as I sat in the front seat of the Mustang. Now I realized that McKay's jacket was around me. It had been an error of McKay's; he could not have forgotten the jacket. I wanted to run back through the smoke, past the Dolphin, so that McKay could wear the leather as he fought the Pack. But I only held the jacket around myself, and stroked the leather, and sat in silence.

"Come on. Come on," said Jose. "I'm not waiting for the Department to arrive. I can kiss the force goodbye if they see me here."

Tony slammed the door of Jose's car shut and began to run. "Fucking kid," said Jose. Tony ran down the Avenue, away from the creek. Even without hearing, I knew the sound of his deep intakes of breath; I knew the wheezing sound of fear. Jose started the engine and floored the Mustang down the Avenue. I leaned my head out the open window and strands of hair blew like whips across my face.

"Don't tell me anything," said Jose. "Don't give me any depositions." I could feel his eyes on me. "Shit," he said, "don't tell me anything."

Sirens sounded from the direction of the creek. I held the leather of the jacket between my fingers.

"Shit," said Jose.

"You know the way," I said.

"You want to go there?"

There was nowhere else to go.

"You know the way," I repeated, and Jose nodded. There was no one to drive toward but Starry.

We drove through the night in silence on the highway that led to the city. The wind was both hot and cold. On the ramp of the Queensboro Bridge I remembered the color of the Sweet's Pontiac. The color was red and white, the mag wheels were silver-spoked. We drove and there was night and wind and leather and the color of the Sweet's Pontiac. And finally there were tears. I began to cry.

7

DANCING IN THE DARK

AT BREAKFAST WE had orange juice, Hostess cupcakes, and smiles.

"I do believe," said Starry as she rolled marijuana into a thin wheat-colored joint, "every summer gets hotter."

When Jose had brought me to Starry's apartment no questions were asked. Without a word or a blink of an eye, Starry brought from her closet a shirt with sleeves too short, to replace my torn blouse, and a skirt too small at the waist, to replace my ripped, mud-stained jeans. Jose promised to leave a message at Monty's, and lined yellow paper with my scrawl on it waited at the counter for McKay. Days passed with no word from him. In the *Daily News* and on six-o'clock TV broadcasts, there were descriptions of Kid Harris and hints of the gang warfare that began with the death of Danny the Sweet, with the body found in the back seat of a Pontiac.

I lit a cigarette and tossed the match into a plate already full of ashes and ancient butts. There had not yet been a chance to talk to Starry alone. Flash was close to her always, his hand on her shoulder, his eyes seeing only her. Now Flash and his dealer sat in the bedroom, arguing over the price of dope, sniffing and tasting white powder, and passing glassine envelopes of heroin back and forth. Now that we were alone and could talk, I did not know what to say. In the days after the creek I had become afraid of words. I mistrusted anything but silence and marijuana. "Starry," I said finally, "this is no good."

"It's very good." She smiled.

Starry was thinner than I had ever seen her. Her arms were

121

covered by long sleeves, her blond hair was paler where it had been streaked with platinum tint. Her eyes were large and heavy-lidded; sometimes they appeared almost closed.

"You look like a junkie," I said, and Starry smiled. "Look in the mirror," she told me. "You're looking more strung out than me. Leastwise I know where *my* man is."

I shrugged. McKay would appear at the door sooner or later. It was only a matter of time. Somewhere on the Avenue McKay was waiting for the newspapers to forget gang warfare, for the Police Department to erase Kid Harris's fingerprints from its files. It was only a matter of time until McKay came for me.

Starry and I stared at each other. We both knew there were scars. The bruises on my face, the tracks on her arm were nothing. We did not have to see to know there were scars. And we did not, we could not, speak of violence.

Speaking would break the code, would violate the remedy for recovery. We stared at each other; we stared away. Many remedies are suggested for brutality; some recommend jasmine tea with honey, others suggest lobotomy. But I remembered that most recommend one thing as an antidote for violence: silence. The remedy, the magic, the potion, the key: silence.

I knew the prescription: take one act of violence (a rape, a knife at the throat, a fist in the small of the back, etc.), add widened eyes, possibly one short stifled scream (possibly not), the shaking of hands, and not one word. Mix up all the facts (until unsure of what was real and what was imagined, whether indeed there was an act of violence at all). Store in a cool dry place (possibly the back of the mind, somewhere near the base of the neck will do). And forget.

The "not one word" is the trick; although references are, of course, allowable. Preferably unspoken references: a twitch will do. An occasional shudder is just fine.

But silence, I knew, was the key to recovery. Better still, removal of any violence-related word from the mind. When the eyes tear, think it is pollution; smog has attacked the iris. When the hands shake there is always the possibility of earthquake. Never admit to anything; never let the words take over and make the violence live. No one will pose a question to a victim of violence when there can be no answer but a widened eye; when the magic balm of silence is at work.

Starry knew the formula. I watched her not watching me. She did not look because most of the permanent scars of violence are invisible and are only reactivated by words. Keep silence, keep silent.

Shut up and do not think. All the theorists agree: shut up and keep the words from being said. And all of the scars will remain invisible; and all of the scars will be dreams; and all of the scars will remain under the skin. Where they belong.

"Enough of McKay," Starry said, her eyes looking everywhere but into mine, "let me tell you 'bout my man."

And I smiled because we both knew that any violation of the magic of silence might cause complications, including a scream, including sight. And we knew this could be fatal.

"About your man." I laughed. "Now what about him?"

She could look at me now; we were conspirators; there would be no talk of violence, of screams, of scars.

"He treats me good," Starry said. "Flash gets me high and he's in love with me. He thinks he's in love with me."

Although Flash was a heroin connection for some of the Orphans, he himself only smoked reefer. Occasionally he got high with Starry the way I got high with McKay, only to know something of the dream and to share in the nod.

"And you?" I asked.

Starry smiled. "It makes him happy if I pretend. He knows I'm pretending, I know I'm pretending, but it makes him happy."

Flash and the dealer walked from the bedroom. The dealer placed a broad-brimmed velvet hat on his head; he nodded to Starry. As Flash and the dealer stood in the hallway, engaging in some last-minute arguments, Starry frowned. "He's a no-gooder, that one," she whispered. "Glad I don't have no dealings with him anymore. Flash takes care of it all now." She smiled.

Flash came to sit with us at the table. "Pure stuff," he whispered. I felt the way a third person feels when words are intimate and are of love and are meant for only two.

"Beautiful dope," Flash said and Starry touched his hand. "Got some news," Flash said to me. "Jose called last night and there's news on McKay." He pushed himself away from the table and leaned far back in his chair.

There was silence and I lit another cigarette. I feared news about McKay. I listened to the street voices and the sound of Manhattan summer filter up and through the open window like ashes, like soot. I was afraid of anything but silence.

"Don't be dramatic," Starry said. "Give us the news from your cousin, the peace officer."

"Well," Flash said to me, "the news is not good."

"Well, give it to us," said Starry and her eyes shone like an Orphan's for news of McKay.

"He'll be here tonight," said Flash.

Why did Flash think that was not good news? I tried to catch Starry's eye, but her vision was now focused on the door which led to the pure, to the beautiful stuff: the stuff that let her forget the Orphans with ease.

"He'll be here tonight, but he's on the run," Flash said. "The Man's after his ass, now. They looking for to nail him."

I was silent.

"For murder," Flash said.

On the couch where I had slept the past few nights was the leather jacket I used now as a pillow. Was it that McKay had been unprotected? Was it my fault?

"They'll never find him," I said.

Flash shrugged. "Whatever," he said. "He can't stay here more than one night. I can't risk getting busted." He held his hand over Starry's as her fingers tapped anxiously on the tabletop. She nodded agreement, and I understood. I would have nodded also. I for McKay; Starry for heroin. For beautiful stuff.

Through the morning and the afternoon I waited, and still there was no knock at the door. That night, after Flash and Starry had gone to bed, I waited until it was very late, and the streets were quiet and still. Then I fell asleep with my head upon the leather jacket. When there was a knock at the door I didn't move. In this apartment silence greeted every knock. Flash stood at the door, looking through the peephole into the hallway. No lights were turned on. In the bedroom Starry dreamed.

"Who there?" Flash whispered. I felt cramps in my legs from sleeping on the thin width of the couch, but I did not move.

There was a muffled answer from the hallway. As Flash opened the door a thin stream of light filtered into the apartment. I could see the outline of Flash's bare back and the darkness of another figure. It was McKay. But still I was silent, still I did not move.

"I'm in need," I heard his voice say. The voice did not sound like McKay's.

There was darkness again as Flash closed the door and bolted the locks.

"Are you holding?" said McKay's voice. "I haven't gotten off in two days. Are you holding?"

I heard Flash whisper reassuringly. "Man, you know you can count on Flash."

There was some noise in the bathroom; running water and voices. I waited. Finally he walked to the couch, to me. He kneeled on the floor and rested his head close to mine. I reached out my arm.

I moved closer toward the back of the couch so that McKay could lie with me. Already, even as he spoke, he was dreaming.

"I took care of it all," he whispered and I held a finger to his lips to stop the words. "I took care of everything," he said. There was darkness, shadows. I had to touch McKay to make sure he was really with me.

McKay slept deeply. I dreamed and woke throughout the night. In the morning I waited for McKay's eyes to open. Starry and Flash already sat in the kitchen; there was the odor of coffee and of marijuana. Starry nodded at McKay; this was their first meeting since McKay had forced Starry to leave the Orphans. Starry smiled. "So it comes to this?"

McKay wore the leather jacket of the Orphans once more. He lit a cigarette and jangled the Chevy's keys in his fingers. "To what, girl?" McKay said softly. "To what?"

"It's too early in the day to be uptight," Flash said. "Have some reefer." I accepted a joint and shared it with Starry. Her eyes were on the President of the Orphans.

"Them Pack boys gonna need a new President, I hear," said Flash.

"That's right," McKay said. "But then, the Orphans got to find themselves a new idiot and a new . . ." Starry's eyes were on McKay and he did not finish the sentence.

Starry's knuckles were white as she held a coffee cup tightly. Her eyes continued to stare.

"War?" Flash said.

"War," said McKay, shrugging. "There's always war. We can get by. We did when Cantinni was wasted, we will now."

"I know a place where you can stay," Starry told me. She touched my hand and then wrote down an address on a matchbook cover. Beyond the limits of the city: Long Beach. Irene.

I showed the matchbook to McKay. "Irene?" said McKay. He nodded his head.

"Irene hasn't been on the Avenue for months," I said.

"That's 'cause she's out on the Island with Viet Nam. They got, can you dig it, married." Starry began to laugh and I joined her. The Chevy's car keys were rattled impatiently.

"Married?" I said and we laughed.

"To Viet Nam," Starry said. We laughed again.

"Hey," McKay said to me. "Enough." I held my hand over my mouth.

"She could do it," Starry said. "All of Viet Nam."

"Enough," McKay said. Starry and I could not look at one another for fear of smiles.

"My cousin, the peace officer, says you should keep low for a while. Says it wouldn't hurt to disappear from the Avenue."

McKay nodded. "Just give me enough shit for a couple of days," he said. There were no more smiles. I lit a cigarette and watched Flash and McKay walk from the room.

"He has got it bad," Starry whispered. "Don't you see he got it bad?"

"You're wrong," I said. "He's the same as he always was."

"Don't you think I know when I see a dope fiend? He'd eat shit to get high."

126

"No," I said.

Starry stared after Flash and McKay. She brushed stray wisps of platinum hair from her face. "I don't hold no grudges against the man," she said. " 'Specially not a man whose hands shake when he lights a match."

"Bullshit," I said.

"Bullshit," she said. "All right, bullshit. See what you want to see. It's your business. It's your man."

McKay walked into the living room and held open the door. I walked to him. "Hey," Starry called. "Hey, President. Where's your main man? How come you're here without your main man?"

"Shut up," Flash said.

Starry smiled. "It's the Dolphin that makes the connections, how come you hustling for yourself?"

"Starry," I said.

McKay walked toward her and I stood by the open door. "Were you talking to me?" he said. There was a faint smile on Starry's lips.

"She didn't say nothing," said Flash.

"That's right, President," McKay said to Starry. "The Dolphin goes where I want him to go. The Dolphin makes a connection when I want him to make a connection."

Starry smiled. "Sure," she said. "President," she whispered.

McKay walked out of the apartment, his boot heels sounding loudly on wood. I could hear the downstairs door of the apartment building slam. I followed him; I ran. I did not have time to say goodbye or grab my cigarettes from the table or stare into Starry's eyes. McKay waited in the Chevy. We began to drive. The Chevy was covered with grease and dust, it no longer shone. But on the highway it moved like air.

We did not speak. We drove out on the Island, toward Irene's Long Beach address.. After a while McKay pulled the Chevy off the highway; we stopped at a diner in Levittown. In neon, the diner advised us to eat, but as we sat in the red plastic booth and McKay kept his eyes focused on the traffic of Hempstead Turnpike, I was not hungry. I turned the leaves of the jukebox that hung on the wall.

127

"Do we talk?" I said. I did not want to know much; a word or a paragraph would do.

"Nothing to say," said McKay. He was demanding a conspiracy of silence; the memory of the night at the creek lay heavy in the air. White porcelain dinner dishes were set before us, and outside trucks and trailers rolled by.

"All of what has happened and we don't say a word?" I said. McKay glared at me as he ate scrambled eggs. I was going against magic; I knew that. I felt for the locket I wore; I touched the silver.

"What happened to me," I began, holding the locket in my fingers.

"Shut up," said McKay.

"What happened to me that night," I said, "by the creek was that I was raped." I closed my eyes. I opened my eyes. I had said it; I had violated our pact. I had gone against silence.

McKay picked up his plate and slammed it down on the tabletop. "Shut up," he said.

The eyes of truck drivers and of the white-coated short-order cook were upon us now.

"And Kid Harris is dead," I said. Small pieces of egg had spilled from McKay's plate and now dusted the tabletop.

"That's right," said McKay. "That's goddamn right Kid Harris is dead. He paid for the Sweet's death. He paid for what he did to you."

"For what he did to me?" I said. "And for the 'idiot's' death?"

"That's right," said McKay, and his eyes avoided mine.

"Bullshit," I whispered. "Not for either one of us. Only for honor. For your goddamn Orphans and your goddamn honor and nothing else."

"You want to know?" said McKay. "You really want to know? I'll tell you. I'll tell you it all, if you really want to know." He was talking softly now, talking softly and sipping coffee and I had gone too far. I had pushed him too far. I wanted to go back into the silence. I had only wanted a few words; I had never asked to be told it all.

"Forget it," I said.

"I held the gun," McKay said. "I pointed it at him, at Kid Harris."

"Forget it," I said.

"And then he turned," said McKay.

I rose from the table and walked from the diner toward the Chevy. Through the plate-glass window of the diner I could see McKay pay the cashier. McKay walked to the Chevy and sat in the driver's seat. He turned on the ignition and steered the Chevy back toward the highway. We did not look at each other.

"Did you hear me?" McKay said. "I said he turned."

I lit a cigarette. "So he turned, so he turned," I said. "Big deal, so he turned. So I don't care. I don't care if he's dead."

McKay's eyes were on the highway lanes. We drove into the town where Irene lived with Viet Nam, where gulls gathered in summer and winter. The noise of boardwalk rides and amusements was in the air. McKay parked the Chevy in front of a dirty-pink stucco apartment building whose address matched the one Starry had given me. We sat for a long time in the Chevy. I smoked several cigarettes while McKay left the Chevy to walk on the boardwalk. I listened to the gulls and to the radio.

McKay did not return to the car until the sky was as pink as the stucco apartment building. I had fallen asleep. A cigarette had burned itself down to ash in my hand.

McKay sat on the curb across from Irene's apartment building. I left the Chevy and sat near him; our feet were side by side in the gutter. I did not say a word.

"I shot him in the back," McKay said.

His voice was so soft I could barely hear the words, so soft that I could not recognize it as McKay's. Gulls flew over the Ferris wheel, over the waves. In a third-story window I thought I saw Irene dancing to some song, some radio, her arms around a figure that might be Viet Nam.

"You did not," I said.

"The Dolphin saw it. The Dolphin was right there and he saw it."

I held my arms around McKay and whispered sounds that were not quite words in his ear. His dark eyes were closed and he held one hand to his head. Above us, and over the waves, the sky was scarlet and navy blue; it was beginning to be night. Kid Harris had won with one simple movement: he turned as his pale eyes stared into the barrel of the .22. He forced McKay to strike him not between the eyes, but, instead, between the shoulder blades.

"I fucking shot the bastard in the back," said McKay.

I forgot the touch of Kid Harris's hand on me. I forgot the smile of Danny the Sweet. I thought of honor, only of honor and McKay. McKay rested his head at the curve of my neck. I could feel the flutter of his eyelashes as he tried to stop his eyes from closing. And finally there was silence. It seemed I could not live with the silence and I could not live without it. I watched reflections from apartment windows. And I shut my mouth, shut my pain, my sight, my vision. I tried to forget what I knew. Boots were in the gutter and the July night stars were out. I wanted to know, and I did not want to know. I wanted to see, and I did not want to see.

To see or not to see, to know or not to know. Is there ever a choice? You answer whatever you like, but I say no; there is no choice. There is the battle, there is confusion; there is no choice.

Why did I insist, why did I demand to be told what I did not want to be told? Perhaps for the same reason McKay pulled the trigger although Kid Harris had already turned. Because it was too late, because the motion was already fixed by magic or the environment, by nothing, by everything. Reasons were too much to ask for; only lies, or possibilities.

And so, for no reason, my enemy was dead. My enemy fell when the bullet hit Kid Harris in the back. One accident in the dark, one error of perception and the movement of one foot and my enemy, Honor, was dead.

For McKay honor had been the world. For me it had only been a word, and there is no fiercer enemy than a word. A word that can be written down in pages and punctuated with quotation marks and commas and spelled out in contracts and poems and sighs, in old whispers and song lyrics, in promises and vows. And the word I thought had always kept McKay from me had now died in the waterless creek in the darkness of one July night. It died with blood that ran into the sand as Kid Harris lay with silent pale eyes.

But for McKay, it had been the world. One word had been all reason, and now it lay at the bottom of the creek. Because of that I wanted a resurrection. I would have agreed to the use of any herb, poisonous or not; I would have mixed the potion in the blackest iron cauldron myself. Without one word McKay was without the world. And too far away from me.

So for no reason my enemy was dead. I may have smiled or sighed but there was no celebration. I did not hire horsemen to circle the Avenue calling out victory. My enemy had tricked me from the very start. What I thought was alive was long dead, and there is no victory when the enemy was a corpse long long before the battle had ever begun. Even if that enemy is a word.

We sat together beneath the shadows. It was night, and I thought that if I listened very closely I might hear the sound of the carousel. I listened, but I could hear only the waves and the gulls. I whispered sounds into McKay's ear. I moved my lips, but the sound of the waves and of the gulls would have made it impossible to hear words anyway.

II

At first Viet Nam was disturbed. He paced the living-room carpet and mumbled and looked at us only from the corner of his eye. He elbowed Irene into the kitchen where he raised his voice and slammed dishes. At first he was disturbed.

After a few days of McKay's dark silence, after several afternoons of Irene and me drinking beer and watching *The Days of Our Lives* and *Truth or Consequences* – after he realized he was stuck with us, Viet Nam stopped slamming dishes and doors. He stopped pacing. He even stopped his nocturnal walks through the apartment while McKay and I were making love on the floor where we were camped out. Viet Nam now only shrugged his shoulders and did his best to ignore the presence of Irene's two guests.

I helped Irene clean the apartment. I watched her wedding

131

ring flash as she washed dishes, drank beer, or mixed flour and sugar into cakes. I read magazines and watched McKay as his silence deepened. Irene had grown even heavier, and the hair curlers she wore were combed out only when we occasionally walked to the boardwalk to play pinball or to watch the riders on the merry-go-round. Although she was officially removed from the Avenue and from the Orphans, Irene's allegiance was still to McKay and to the past. She talked endlessly of ancient meetings and parties, and of those who had long ago left the Orphans through death or desertion. Daily the four of us sat in the hot summer apartment with ocean wind, hearing Irene's remembrances or Viet Nam's repeated tales of his war and peacetime glories.

One night no wind or fan could cool the apartment, and Irene's dinner was disturbed when McKay stabbed a steak knife into the wood of the table. He did so as Viet Nam repeated the highlights of taking a village of old people and children, of burning huts with safety matches till they glowed like firewood. The steak knife stood upright in the wood; the tabletop was now slashed and splintery.

"Fuck it, man," said Viet Nam as McKay leaned back in his chair. "You're a fucking guest here."

McKay stared at the ceiling and Irene urged silence with her large eyes, gazing first at Viet Nam and then at McKay. "Would you tell this asshole if I have to hear the same fucking story about his goddamn war once more I'll kill him?" said McKay. "I'll kill him."

"You are a guest," said Viet Nam. "You would be out on the streets, with your dope and your whore, if it wasn't for Irene. Who," said Viet Nam, his face flushed, his hands shaking, "do you think you are?"

"Honey," said Irene and her eyes were large.

"Honey, shit," said Viet Nam, and he tossed a plate to the floor. The porcelain clattered and broke upon the wooden floor. "Who do you think you are," he continued, "to ruin this fucking dinner that Irene here has worked so hard to fix? Who? That's what I really want to know, who does he think he is?"

I walked away from the table.

"Where do you think you're going?" Viet Nam called after me. "This is the dinner hour," he said. "This is the fucking dinner hour."

I sat on the couch and lit a joint. I inhaled. I believed McKay would kill him; I believed murder was like air to him now. I could see Irene believed it also; she reached out her hand to Viet Nam but he waved her away.

"Irene," McKay said. "Do you want to tell him that I'm going to kill him?"

"He's going to kill you," Irene said.

McKay nodded. "Thanks," he said to Irene.

"McKay," I said. Murder might be like air but Viet Nam was not worth the inconvenience murder brought. "Why bother?" I said.

"I don't know," McKay said.

Viet Nam glared at Irene. She had taken orders from the President of the Orphans. I nodded toward the door. McKay and I jumped nightly from the boardwalk to walk along the dark beach. We walked, always, far from the sound of the boardwalk amusements, and McKay would kneel in the sand holding the pale envelope, and I would stare into the dark ocean water that in the morning would again be blue as eyes.

I knew McKay did not walk the beach only at night. Once, when I was with Irene, I had seen him crouched in the darkness underneath the boardwalk, rolling up his sleeve while before him the sand shone white with sun. But I walked with McKay only at night, for then I could stare into the dark as he placed the needle in his vein. Then I did not have to look.

We walked in the direction we always did, but I knew we could not go on the way we did. We could not stay at Irene's forever, not when McKay was running low on heroin and Flash feared being busted and the Dolphin seemed to have disappeared. I waited on the boardwalk while McKay jumped, and then I followed. McKay stood waiting to catch me if I should fall the way Tammy Leone had done the summer before; she had broken her neck. I jumped, then I placed my arm through McKay's and we walked toward the water.

There were stars in the sky. I stopped once to remove my

leather sandals so that my toes could feel the sand. When McKay sat down on the damp sand at the shoreline I walked on, keeping inches away from the tide as it moved coldly closer. Soon McKay walked beside me once more.

"I've got to go back to the Avenue," McKay said. "I'm carrying the last of it and I got to find the Dolphin, and I got to make some connection."

A wind rose off the ocean and we returned to the board-walk to sit under its shelter.

"Where is the Dolphin?" I said.

"He's making me wait," said McKay. "He's showing me who needs who."

"You don't need him," I said. But the Dolphin had the heroin and the Dolphin's eyes had seen McKay fire the .22, had seen the bullet enter the body between the shoulder blades. My words were lies.

Feet passed on the wooden walk above us. McKay nodded into a dream. I feared water rats and the police, but I could not bring myself to wake him. Hours later we both woke in darkness. The garbage pails that lined the beach were cloaked in mist and the ocean water was dark gray. There was drizzle and fog and cold, but I smiled, glad that we had not spent another night on the shag carpeting in the pink stucco apartment building with Irene and Viet Nam.

We climbed back up the boardwalk and bought coffee at a food stand. I held both steaming plastic coffee containers as McKay was sick over the boardwalk railing. His eyes looked into mine and I nodded and watched him walk away to stand behind the Ferris wheel and shoot up. He smiled as he walked back to me. We leaned over the railing and drank coffee and watched the fog move off the water and edge toward the shore.

I held my arm around his waist. Above us gulls flew in circles. We drank coffee and then we walked on. Morning was breaking as we reached the pink apartment building. I held him back at the stairs. "McKay," I said.

"No talk," he said. "I don't want any talk."

"It was an accident."

"Accident."

"You couldn't know he would turn."

"Accident," McKay said.

"You're still you," I said.

"Am I?" He smiled.

"Yes," I lied.

"You're stupid or you lie," he said. "And get rid of that. Get rid of that," he said, pointing to the silver locket.

"This is nothing," I said. I did not look at him.

"Then why do you wear it?" I did not answer, only followed him through the door of Irene's apartment. I wore the locket for good luck, though it seemed to bring none. I was not sure why I wore it, I only knew I did not want to give up the charm. So I was silent. So McKay was silent. We sat together in the darkened apartment.

Outside, in the hallway, there was a squeak from the board of a wooden stair. "Shit," McKay said and searched wildly through the lining and pockets of his jacket for the .22. We had long feared some peace officer's knock at the door. I moved close against the hard back of the couch and thought the word "murder." It was only a word, but the sound of the wooden stair was real.

"Shit," McKay said again. He stood first by the window, checking the street for patrol cars or uniforms; then he went to stand by the door.

Viet Nam walked from the bedroom wearing only shorts and a pair of heavy lace-up combat boots. He saw me sitting on the couch and scowled. Perhaps when we had not returned at night he had thought we were gone for good. Then Viet Nam saw McKay, holding the gun, and standing tense as wire at the wooden door.

"What the fuck," said Viet Nam loudly. He walked toward McKay, his combat boots leaving indentations in the shag rug. "Jesus Christ," he said.

McKay did not move. His eyes stared at the wood of the door, at the metal doorknob. Then he moved only his arm, reaching out and pointing the gun at Viet Nam. "If you take one more step or say one more word," McKay said softly, "I'll kill you."

Viet Nam backed off, and McKay lowered the gun. I had

not thought of the acts that had occurred as criminal. I had feared silence and heroin and the Dolphin and even McKay, but I had never thought of the Law. I had never thought the words "crime" and "criminal." They had never seemed to apply. Certainly not to McKay. What had McKay to do with crime? Murder, honor, yes; but crime?

The doorknob moved very slightly. I thought of shoot-outs and jails and what I would wear to a trial (I had no outfit that would do: no hat, no gloves; what would I wear?). McKay shut off the light and we waited in darkness. Viet Nam breathed heavily. Irene stood, now, in the doorway of the bedroom, in hair curlers and a robe and the shadow of a grin. Irene was enjoying the silence, the wait, the shadow of illegal acts – she was remembering the Orphans.

Slowly the door began to open and McKay followed the spill of hallway light with the sight of the .22. The large shadow of a man loomed in the doorway. The shadow hesitated and McKay reached out, grabbed the neck of the intruder in the crook of his arm, and held the gun against the shadow's head. There was the sound of loud breathing, but no sirens and no blue colors of any peace officers.

"Brother," the shadow gasped. "Brother."

McKay loosened his grip and threw the shadow against the wall so that they now faced each other. There was a glimmer of colors. Irene's face paled. McKay threw the gun to the floor. Even in the dark we knew the Dolphin.

"Brother," the Dolphin said once more.

"Fucking Christ," said Viet Nam. He stared at the skin paintings which covered the Dolphin. "I want you out of here. I want you all out."

"Brother, you are nervous," said the Dolphin as he switched on the light.

"Nervous?" said McKay. "Where the hell have you been? The Man's after my ass, Flash won't sell me shit, and you're saying I'm nervous?"

"Nervous." The Dolphin smiled.

"Nervous, shit," said McKay.

"I said nervous," said the Dolphin..

There was silence. I did not want to hear what would be

136

said, and I did not want to see McKay admit his defeat.

"Nervous since the night at the creek," said the Dolphin. He was using what he knew and he would not let McKay forget. The Dolphin was not about to let it be, to let the silence be.

"Yeah," said McKay. "Yeah, all right. I'm edgy, what do you expect, I'm edgy."

"Trust me," said the Dolphin.

"McKay," I said.

"I trust you," McKay answered. He had no other answer, he had no choice. The Dolphin, who had stood by McKay's side in the waterless creek, knew that McKay had no choice. He smiled.

"I got what you need," the Dolphin said. He held an envelope of white powder in the air.

I walked out with McKay. We left Irene standing in the doorway and followed the Dolphin. In the street the Chevy waited, but its shine had been scraped away by sand and salt and night air.

"We all got secrets to keep," said the Dolphin as he started the Chevy. McKay sat in the back seat and closed his eyes. I sat next to him and opened a window. The Dolphin drove. I leaned my head out of the window and counted clouds. "Trust me," the Dolphin had said. All the way back to the Avenue I counted clouds and was silent. I could not look at the butterfly which moved like ice, or at McKay. I turned away.

8

GOING DOWN

I

OFTEN MCKAY DID not return from the Avenue at night. I let it be until the whispers about Kind grew too loud, and then I looked for them. I looked for them at Monty's, I peered into the darkness of the Tin Angel, I questioned each Orphan who sat drinking beer in the clubhouse beneath Munda's Liquor Store. I walked into the apartment. Her painted eyes glowed wild and jade in the dark.

"I've been looking all over the Avenue for you," I said. "And now I've found you."

McKay's jacket lay on the floor, the leather covered the wooden boards. There was darkness and heat and the sound of metal as my key hit the tabletop. There was movement in the bed.

"I'll get her out of here," he said.

"Don't get her out of here."

"I'll get her out of here."

"No, no, don't let me interrupt you."

"Look, don't start up with me."

"Don't start up with you?" I said. "Why didn't you tell me that before?" I would not have listened, but still I said, "Why didn't you tell me that at the beginning."

I switched on the light. Kind held a sheet around her. She smiled. I smiled back. We were coy as daggers. I walked to the bed and pulled the sheet from her hands. "I paid for this," I said.

"I want you to forget about this," McKay said to me. "I

want you to forget about this because it doesn't mean anything."

"And what does?" I said. My voice was sharp, my mascara was heavy as lead. I was tired from searching for McKay, and I knew there was no market for used sheets. So I sat in the chair by the window and looked into the Avenue and waited for an answer.

"Well," I said when McKay only shrugged, "what matters, then? What the fuck matters?"

"I don't know," he said. "O.K.? O.K.? I fucking well do not know, all right?"

"Terrific," I said. "Terrific."

"I'll tell you what matters," Kind said.

"Shut up," McKay said.

"The Orphans matter, that's what matters. And I'll tell you something else," she said to me.

McKay threw an ashtray across the room; ashes and cigarette butts scattered on the floor. "Shut up," he said.

Kind tossed her head like a fox, and like a fox, she was silent. I stared at her. I was not jealous. Since we had returned from the beach to the Avenue I knew McKay was often absent at Orphan meetings. When he did not return to the apartment at night, I knew he was with someone else. When the Dolphin telephoned demanding to know where his "President" was, I said I did not know. But I knew. I knew McKay was after eyes other than mine, eyes that had not seen his hands shake or his head nod. And he was after eyes other than the Dolphin's, eyes that had not seen Kid Harris turn in the waterless creek. He was after eyes that believed in the letters of the jacket, that believed in McKay.

I was not jealous, because he was mine. No matter how many nights he spent with Kind, McKay was mine. He belonged to the Dolphin, and he belonged to me. Kind read the golden letters the way McKay wanted them to be read, but the Dolphin and I saw them as McKay did – as a lie. So I was not jealous; it was too late now. I knew too much; he knew too much. And he belonged to me. Kind's eyes were green. She saw what I could no longer see, and she was angry.

"You're crazy," she said to me. "You're fucking crazy," she said. She sat without the sheet covering her, and, although the summer sun had shone for months, her body was white. "I'm balling your man, you hear me? He's been cheating on you and you just sit there."

I shrugged. What did she know? Did the difference between being dumb and being smart have anything at all to do with knowing? Me, I knew: I knew Kind had been after the title of Number One Property, I knew McKay had been cheating on me. And I knew more than that: I knew McKay was a junkie. This was not an easy thing to know.

At first when he says he's holding the dope for someone, he is believed. I believed it, you would believe it, everyone believes it. Later when his eyes are heavy-lidded and dark it is most probably a sty or the effect of too much gin and tonic. Surely. The needle is a friend's; the works do not belong to him, they are a talisman to ward off evil spirits or they belong to the diabetic who lives in the next apartment. He doesn't even know how the needle got into his vein; it was a frame-up, someone implanted it there as he slept.

This was not an easy thing to know; and I knew it. After all the tracks, after pawnshops began to display in their windows the electrical appliances that were once found in our apartment, I knew McKay had a habit.

So where were my smarts? How could I know so much and be so dumb? Why didn't I walk out the door, or strangle Kind with the arm of a leather jacket, toss the heroin out the window, and kiss McKay goodbye? Come on. Did you expect me to do any of that?

Once I knew nothing about McKay and now I knew everything about him. This seemed as good a reason as any for not walking out the door. There are so many ways to stop the knowing, and I tried them all. I tried silence, I tried heroin, I tried calling it love. And then I stopped trying to call my dumbness any one of ten thousand names.

I submitted to the direction of the mood. I gave up reasons that were worthless when contemplating air. Reasons I gave back to the dust. It was the mood, and I was in it. No matter what I knew, it was my place to be dumb. And I was.

And when Kind said, "Don't you care?" any answer would have been a lie.

"You're crazy," Kind said.

"Get out," McKay said to her.

"You promised," Kind said. "He promised me," she told me.

McKay walked away from the bed. He lit a cigarette and smiled.

"Number One Property," Kind said. "You promised."

"He's taken to lying," I said.

"Hey," McKay said.

"He's taken to implying," I said.

"He's the President Of," she said. McKay laughed deeply; he exhaled. He stood naked in darkness and smoke was heavy in the air.

"Forget that shit," he said.

"McKay," I said. Knowing it was one thing, saying it another. "McKay," I said.

"All right. All right," he said.

I smiled and shook my head. "Bastard," I said and he shrugged.

"You're crazy. You're both crazy," she said.

No, we were not that; we were only conspirators. And so we smiled. Conspirators in knowledge, in silence, in love; and so we smiled.

"Fuck you," said Kind. "Fuck you and fuck the Orphans."

McKay winked as well as he could, but his eyes were heavy and dark. As Kind stood and began to dress, McKay sat on the bed once more. He leaned far back into the pillows and closed his eyes.

He still cared – even now. I watched Kind dress, I watched McKay, his head in the pillows, his eyes closed.

"Some President," Kind whispered. I saw the muscles in McKay's face tighten. He was absent from official meetings. Rumors about him had begun on the Avenue. The muscles in his face grew tighter.

"I know," Kind said to me. Her voice was angry. She was furious that we shrugged off what she had wanted for so long. "I know why you're not jealous," she said. "It's because he

141

can't get it up, isn't that it? Isn't that why you're not jealous?"

What did she want from love with a junkie? Or did she not know about McKay and heroin? Had the wind of the Avenue not yet carried that message to her and had she been too busy imagining herself as the Number One Property to run her fingers over the tracks in his arms or to count the veins?

"Kind," I said. McKay's eyes were still closed and Kind stood before a mirror, tossing her head like a fox and streaking eyeliner over her lids. "Go. Just go."

"I'm going," Kind said. "You can believe I'm going. And you can believe everyone on the Avenue, all of the Avenue, will know what I know." They did already, and so McKay didn't blink an eye and I walked into the kitchen and ran the water in the sink, and touched the coldness to my face and neck. "Did you hear me?" Kind said.

I heard her. What did she expect? An argument? I would give her none; I had none to give.

"I'm telling everything I know," I heard Kind's voice say as she slammed shut the door of the apartment. What could she tell? What could she know?

That McKay was a junkie, that he could no longer act the way a President should act, that he whispered in his sleep, that the Orphans no longer mattered to him, that he was a lousy lover, a liar? And that I was a fool, crazy, too dumb and in love even to be jealous? Was that what she knew and would tell? So let her know that, and let her tell that.

Too dumb and in love. I ran the cold water. It seemed the more I knew, the dumber I was. Now I knew McKay had a bad habit, I even knew which were his favorite veins. I knew what was most important: the Orphans and Honor were now dead for McKay. I knew that although heads still turned on the Avenue when McKay passed by, the Pack was not afraid of the President of the Orphans, who themselves talked about McKay at Presidentless meetings.

I knew more and more all the time. The Chevy remained parked waiting for its shine and its carburetor to be renewed, and I gave up marijuana and eye make-up and magazines so that McKay could have more money for dope. I was dumb and in love.

I walked back to McKay and sat near him. No apologies were offered; none were needed.

"I need money," he said.

"Who doesn't?" I said. But he hadn't enough money to buy bullets for the .22, or enough to fill the Chevy's gas tank. And he needed more and more dope: all the time, he needed more and more magic to close his eyes.

"The Dolphin will give you credit," I said.

"Hah," said McKay. "The Dolphin will give me shit."

Flash would not deal to McKay; he was afraid of the Dolphin, afraid of his cousin Jose. And so the Dolphin now controlled two secrets: heroin and the waterless creek. It was true, he did not seem to believe in credit.

"I got to do something," said McKay and he turned so that he lay on his stomach, so that his head was buried in pillows, so that I saw only his back.

I stroked his skin and said, "I can call Starry."

"Flash won't cop for me," said McKay.

"Not about dope," I said. "I won't call her about dope."

McKay turned and looked at me. "What you mean when you say what you're saying, do you want to tell me what that's supposed to mean?"

"I mean Starry knows how to get money," I said, and I lit a cigarette and waited for his response.

"Jesus Christ," he said. "Forget it. Jesus Christ, I ain't that low."

I had not known if he was or not. I still did not, and I wanted to know if he needed dope bad enough to consider allowing me to turn tricks.

"Is there another way?" I said. "Is there some other way to get money?"

"Yes," said McKay. "There must be."

"Yeah, you gonna become a bank president? Or maybe you can just race that Chevy, you only need a few hundred to fix it up. How, you tell me, how are you going to get money?"

McKay was silent. I walked to the phone, still wondering if he would really allow me to contact Starry. I dialed; he was silent.

Before Starry could answer, before McKay could respond,

143

there was a knock at the door. I threw the receiver back into its cradle.

I answered the door: the Dolphin. "Ah," I said, "it's you."

"Ah," he answered, and his tattoos shone with sweat and color. "It's me."

"He's busy," I said. I thought McKay might be asleep; I thought he might not be asleep. I knew he did not want to see the Dolphin.

"He's always busy lately," said the Dolphin. I could not tell if the Dolphin looked at me through his dark sunglasses. Had that been a reference to Kind, to dope, to what? "Could it be he's avoiding me?" the Dolphin said.

"What do I know," I said.

"Too much," said the Dolphin, and he walked past me into the apartment. "You know too much."

McKay sat in bed. He had clothed himself in jeans and the leather jacket of the Orphans while I had talked in the doorway with the Dolphin.

"You giving me troubles, now," the Dolphin said. "Now, why you want to go and give me troubles for?"

McKay shrugged. "I don't know what you mean, brother."

"Brother," said the Dolphin, "you better get in line."

"You want me in line?"

"I don't care if you're straight or not," said the Dolphin. "All I want is the Avenue taken care of."

"Who says the Avenue is yours?"

The Dolphin smiled. "You know it is," he said.

If McKay wanted credit, this was not the way to get it. McKay shrugged. "Get off my case," he said.

"I'll do more than that." The Dolphin smiled. "I'll close your case permanently."

"Really?" said McKay. "Really?"

I looked at McKay and frowned. He had enough trouble, why ask for more? What Starry had once said was true: there was no going against the Dolphin. He knew all. He did, why deny it? The Dolphin knew the secrets of the Avenue and which wind, north or south, carried each one.

"I don't give a shit about your honor or your junk," said the Dolphin. "You're either President or you're not. And," the Dolphin said, as he held a pale envelope in the air, "I'll crush you if I have to."

McKay was silent. He turned away. "What do you want?" he said.

The Dolphin waited and then he said, "Your resignation."

No Chevy, no Orphans, no money, no junk. I leaned against the cold plaster wall. My face was warm and I felt sick; I was silent and I watched them.

"If I say no?" said McKay.

"If you say no," the Dolphin said. He removed his sunglasses; the butterfly's wing circled one eye, and his gaze was pale and cold. "If you say no, then I would say your chances are no better than Cantinni's were."

Had he said what I thought he said? Had he implied what I thought he implied? How far would he take a lie, how far the truth, and what had he said? I stared at McKay and in the iris of his eye there was movement.

"Cantinni?" he said.

"President Of." The Dolphin smiled. 'Brother."

"You threatening murder?"

"Political assassination." The butterfly moved slightly, and the peacock's feathers seemed to open and fan out beneath the Dolphin's neck. "But then, I'm not threatening anything," he said.

"Brother," said McKay. "Brother."

"Resign," I said. "Give him the fucking jacket and resign."

"Who is the President?" McKay asked.

"Jesus Christ, give it up," I said.

"There was nothing?" he asked.

Even this, this one answer, the Dolphin would not give. He smiled.

"No," McKay said. "No, I will not."

The Dolphin shrugged. "Do what you want," he said, and he turned to the door.

All three of us smiled at those words. Those ridiculous words. McKay laughed. "Brother," he said.

"Brother," answered the Dolphin.

They nodded at each other and the Dolphin walked to the door. He opened the latch, the wood moved, and then he hesitated. I could see McKay was in pain, he was hurting, he was dope sick. But he was silent, and only the beads of sweat on his forehead betrayed him.

"Why didn't you tell me?" McKay said.

I didn't want to hear. Yet I stood there and watched them and listened to McKay ask why he was never told there was no President of the Orphans, there was and never had been any honor. Only paintings that told no story, only the Dolphin, only a lie.

"Why didn't you tell me?" he asked.

The Dolphin smiled once more. There was almost a gentleness between the two, now that there were no secrets, no lies. "You never asked," the Dolphin said, and McKay nodded. He could do no more than nod.

The Dolphin left us; he shut the door. McKay smiled; he smiled into the air. He reached out for a pack of cigarettes which lay on the wooden floor and I went to him to light the match. I had to go to him to light the match, for as the Dolphin shut the door, McKay's hands began to shake.

At last, McKay had to reach out and hand the cigarette to me to kill in the ashtray I retrieved from across the room. From the place on the wooden boards where it had landed when it had been thrown. I watched him silently grasp one hand in the other, bend the fingers backward. But it was too late: his hands had begun to shake.

II

He told me to hide anything that might be dangerous: knives, the .22, forks, rubbing alcohol, the telephone. He ate Seconals and watched quiz shows on TV. The tremors in his hands were terrible to see, and so I looked away.

There was no money and no chance of any. McKay was too sick without a fix to pull a heist and the Chevy was impounded by the auto repair mechanic in the garage below us as collateral on two months' back rent. The stereo system had already been sold to T.J. and Gina, but we decided against hocking the TV. We needed more to look at than the

146

walls and each other and the shaking of his hands.

We also needed cigarettes and food that would satisfy McKay's craving for sweets. I left him sitting in bed, covered by a quilt and questioning the answers of *Jeopardy*. I walked to Monty's where I could still get credit. At the candy store I could charge packs of cigarettes and sodas.

I walked down the Avenue. When I reached Monty's there was a gathering of Orphans at the doorway. I walked on by, brushing shoulders with Tosh, elbowing my way through Kind and Leona. I avoided their eyes and was silent.

Inside the candy store the air was dark and cool, laced with the odor of malt and tobacco. I sat at the counter and rested my purse full of razor blades and steak knives on the linoleum. Afraid of outgoing calls to the city, to a connection, I had hidden the phone in a dresser drawer, the rubbing alcohol in the vegetable bin of the refrigerator, and I carried with me anything else that might be dangerous to McKay.

"Credit?" I said to Monty. When he nodded I ordered a soda, several packs of cigarettes, a half dozen Mr. Goodbars, and cans of Coke. I wanted to leave the store right away and get back to McKay, but I did not want to pass the Orphans again. So I sipped a vanilla Coke and smoked several cigarettes.

I watched Tosh, Leona, Kind, the Marine, and the rest through the plate-glass window, waiting for them to leave. Monty leaned his elbows on the counter top. "What do you know?" I said distractedly, my eye on the Orphans.

Monty shrugged. "I know McKay's got a habit he can't fix with Coca-Cola," he said.

I smiled. "What else is new?"

We were silent for a while. The store was empty except for an occasional customer buying ice cream or a copy of the *Daily News*. The bells above the door jangled softly. Tosh and the Orphans walked in, filling the candy store with silence and leather.

"Oh shit," I said softly.

Monty moved away, retreating to the far end of the counter. Tosh sat on the stool nearest me, and the other Orphans and Property stood behind us. The candy store was very narrow and the backs of the Orphans rubbed up against airplane models and teddy bears.

"Sister," said Tosh.

"Didn't know we were related," I said. I wondered how much was known. What Kind knew could not hurt McKay; what the Dolphin knew could.

"Well," Tosh said, running a hand over his shaven head, "if you're still with McKay I guess we ain't related."

They knew something. "I'm still with him," I said.

"Then you're against the Orphans," he said.

"And with a junkie," Kind said.

There was silence.

"I'm still with the President of the Orphans."

"Wrong," said Tosh.

"You're sitting next to the President of the Orphans right now," said Leona.

I looked at Tosh and he smiled. "Bullshit," I said, but I thought, "Of course." Of course the Dolphin would choose Tosh, a soldier who was used to taking orders and who would never let honor or words get in the way. Tosh would protect the Avenue for the Dolphin and never ask questions. "Bullshit you're the President," I said.

"Tell McKay," Tosh said.

"You tell him," I said.

Tosh hesitated. He looked at the other Orphans for support. "Oh yeah?"

The Dolphin was no fool. I had to smile.

"Yeah," I said. "You want McKay to know you think you're President of the Orphans, you tell him."

I reached for the brown paper bag which held the last of my credit (I figured McKay and I owed Monty thirty-five dollars' worth of sugar and tobacco now) and threw the Coke and cigarettes into my purse alongside the steak knives and razor blades. I could tell they knew nothing about McKay and the creek; they suspected nothing about the Dolphin and Cantinni's murder. But they knew enough.

Monty was winking at me. I thought of the silver locket I wore and wondered if that was why; or if the movement of the old man's lids was merely an intertwining of eyelashes. I rose

148

from the counter. Kind stood in front of me so that I would have to push by her to leave the narrow candy store.

"Kind," I said, "don't give me any shit."

"You already got all the shit you could ever need." She smiled. I smiled too. We were sweet as cyanide and calm as electric wire. Her neck touched the paw of a teddy bear as she moved aside.

"Sister," I said.

"Sister," she answered.

The Orphans parted, leaving a thin aisle for me to walk through. I was on the Avenue, once more walking on the hot cement. I didn't look back.

I walked for a while, for some reason thinking not of McKay or of Kind, but of Danny the Sweet. I was no longer afraid to think of the Sweet. I wanted to think of him and not of Kind's eyes or the tracks on McKay's arm. I smiled and walked on. The cans of soda in my purse made sloshing noises as they hit against the knives and other dangerous metals.

I stopped at a corner to wait for a light; someone was following me. I turned my head to glance over my shoulder but behind me the Avenue was still. I was nervous; I cracked my knuckles and stood first on one foot and then the other. When the light turned green I looked left, I looked right, I looked behind me. And then I ran.

Behind me I heard the sound of boot heels on cement. A block before the auto repair shop and the apartment where McKay waited I turned into an alleyway. It was cool and dark in the narrow shelter of gray and red bricks. I leaned against the wall and breathed deeply. I saw black leather. I held my breath and watched the entrance to the alleyway where a black jacket sleeve hesitated. I bit my thumb. A figure moved into the entrance of the alley; his shadow blotted out the sun. He walked toward me and I thought of the darkness in the creek and the touch of Kid Harris. He hesitated, and I saw that the leather jacket was too large for him who wore it, that the cuffs fell to the knuckles. I saw that the black leather covered Tony.

"God damn you," I said. My heartbeat grew slower, my pulse calmed. Ivy that had once been green climbed up the brick walls around us. "God damn you, kid," I said.

I knew Tony had often followed McKay around on the Avenue, but I didn't want him following me.

"I want to see McKay," he said.

I lit a cigarette and, what the hell, I offered Tony one. What did I care about lungs that were only fourteen years old?

"Forget it," I said.

"Don't give me loose talk," said Tony. But I wouldn't buy any jive toughness from a kid who was too short and thin to find the correct-size leathers.

"Hey, I said forget it, boy," I told him. "McKay is sick. And he's not seeing anyone."

"He'll be a lot sicker," Tony said and began to walk away.

Not bad, I thought, not a bad line for a kid.

"All right," I said. "All right, tell me what you know."

Tony turned to face me. "There's a meeting tonight. I hear they vote against him tonight."

"All right," I said. I walked out into the sunlit Avenue.

Tony followed. "All right?" he said.

I stopped before the Esso station. We stood with our feet in streams of gasoline and oil.

"All fucking right," I said. "I'll tell him."

"If there's trouble, I want to be there, see?" Tony said.

"You punk," I said. We moved from the gas-station driveway to allow an impatient Firebird entry. I wanted to smile, but knew he would put the moves on me to bring him along if I did. "I'll tell him you were the one who found out about the meeting."

Tony scowled. "Yeah?" he said.

"Yeah."

I left him standing on the street. When I opened the door of the apartment McKay was asleep. The empty Seconal bottle lay by his side and his face was covered with a film of sweat. The TV droned on with no audience: Monty Hall was giving trips around the world to human asparagus, Cadillacs to life-size chickens. I turned off the volume.

"McKay," I said. If I could I would take the leather jacket with the letters "President Of" and throw it onto the Avenue to be fought over and pulled apart by souvenir collectors. I couldn't. And I knew McKay couldn't do anything but attend the Official Monthly Meeting of the Orphans. "McKay," I said, "they meet tonight."

He opened his eyes. "Fuck it," he said. He rose and dressed quickly. For a minute I saw the President of the Orphans. "I got to get off first," he said.

"I have Darvon."

"Darvon, shit. Starry's always holding."

"Flash only cops enough for her. He's not dealing, so forget it." I was tired. I sat on the bed and opened a can of Coke.

McKay rummaged through my purse and found the Darvon. He ate several. "I ain't fucking prepared," he said. "What time tonight?"

"What do you care?"

"Hey, what do you care if I care?"

We became silent and watched a wordless news broadcast on TV

"Who's my replacement?" he said finally.

"Tosh," I said. McKay threw back his head and laughed hoarsely. "Tell them about Cantinni," I said. "Tell them the Dolphin murdered Cantinni. That'll get Tosh nervous." Why was I giving him advice on the how-to's of reinstating himself as President? I shut up even before he said, "Shut up. There's no proof about that."

"There's no proof that you shot Kid Harris in the back."

He scowled. "I saw it. And that's the proof."

I shrugged; it was his war.

"I'm going to steal the Chevy," McKay said.

"Yeah?"

"Yeah."

"I'll help," I said. And McKay smiled.

We walked down to the closed garage. McKay jarred the lock open with his switchblade. As we silently pushed the Chevy into the street I felt McKay struggle with the weight of the car. He was not in shape to meet the Orphans; he was wasted. The Darvons had slowed his speech and movements. I ran back past barrels of auto parts and rows of tires McKay himself might have stolen and stealthily closed the garage door.

"Stealing my own fucking car," McKay said as he started

151

the engine and steered the Chevy out into the Avenue. The Chevy roared past the White Castle and the Esso station, past the gray stone chapel of St. Anne's. In a schoolyard corner kids shot baskets, and outside apartment buildings men in white sleeveless undershirts sat on stoops drinking beer. I looked for tremors in McKay's hands, but they held steady to the wheel.

Motorcycles idled outside the Tin Angel Bar and radio music sang into the air of the Avenue. As the sun moved lower in the sky the streets glowed with pink iridescence; the crackle of nighttime neon was beginning. We drove nearer and nearer to the liquor store.

"McKay," I said as he parked the Chevy in the parking lot of a 7-Eleven Food Store around the corner from the clubhouse.

"Will you get some wine?" he said.

"McKay," I said. I wanted to tell him that his retaining the office of President of the Orphans meant nothing to me.

"Get some wine," he said. "And check out the situation."

I walked around the corner. The Orphan's cars were parked in the alley near Munda's. In the liquor store the night clerk sat leafing through the pages of a magazine. When I picked up a bottle of Thunderbird wine and walked to the register he quickly threw the magazine under the counter.

"I.D.," he said. The clerk's face was white and thin. His fingers tapped on the counter, anxious to be rid of me and back to the magazine.

"I.D. your mother," I said. "This is for McKay. He wants it on his account."

The clerk nodded at the mention of McKay's name. He packaged the bottle of wine in a brown paper bag. In the Chevy McKay sat smoking a cigarette and staring into the air.

"It's cool," I said. As cool as it could be.

McKay opened the wine and drank with the bottle still covered with brown paper.

"Darvon and Thunderbird?" I said.

"Hey," he said. I shrugged my shoulders. It was easier to get credit at a liquor store than with a dealer of junk.

152

When he had finished half the bottle the Avenue was dark. "Stay here," he said.

He opened the door and began to walk. I opened my door and stepped over empty and crushed Slurpee cups. I followed him. He knew that I would and he reached behind him and offered me his hand. I accepted and entwined my fingers with his.

Light and smoke drifted from the open basement windows of the clubhouse. We walked down the stairs and McKay opened the door.

I stood behind him as he went into the basement. Though it was warm in the clubhouse, I held my arms around myself as if I were cold, and I followed him. Silence greeted us. Smoke and silence and the eyes of Mick Jagger glaring from a poster

McKay's pink motorcycle goggles glittered under the basement's electric lights. "Brothers," he said. The silence continued. I sat down on an orange crate near the door. I thought of leaving, I thought of a million reasons and none why McKay would want to attend the Official Monthly Meeting. I lit a cigarette and crossed my legs.

Tosh sat in a large chair. Behind him stood the Dolphin. The colors of the tattoos cast a reflection upon Tosh's shaven head.

"Brothers," McKay said once more. He nodded to the Property. "Sisters."

"McKay," Tosh said. He hesitated, running his tongue over his lips as if tasting for the words he wanted to use. "McKay," he said, "get your ass outa here."

"Yeah?" McKay said. He struck a match on his fingernail, lit a cigarette, and snuffed the match with his thumb. He inhaled. "Yeah?"

Even though his hands shook, the way he lit a match could silence a room; the way he inhaled smoke could force dozens of eyes to widen. McKay. I smiled. I knew why I had followed him to the clubhouse: to see him light one match.

The Dolphin moved from where he stood and faced McKay in the center of the room.

"McKay," he said. "Just in time."

153

McKay smiled. He threw the cigarette to the floor and crushed it with his boot heel.

"Just in time," said the Dolphin. "We need the jacket, you see. We need the jacket of the President of the Orphans."

They stared at each other and fought with their eyes. In the center of one pair was the waterless creek; in the center of the other the betrayal of Cantinni.

"Brother," said McKay. "You gonna have to take it. You want this fucking jacket, you gonna have to take it." He smiled again.

The Dolphin signaled the Orphans, and Tosh and the Marine walked toward McKay. Each held a leather sleeve; each held one of McKay's arms. McKay looked at Tosh, then at Martin the Marine. He smiled and then he moved quickly, wrenching one arm free and catching Tosh's jaw with his fist.

When they held McKay on the floor, I turned away. I did not watch as they slipped the jacket from him and left him lying on the cement with blood on his face and the pink motorcycle goggles shattered.

When there was silence once more I looked: Tosh held the leather jacket above him in the air and McKay lay clothed only in jeans and a T-shirt. His arms could now be seen: they were scarred and covered with abscesses and I felt as if I had never before seen that part of his body.

Tosh cloaked himself in McKay's jacket and sat rubbing at his jaw. McKay lay motionless. I had known he could not fight them all, but still I held my hand to my mouth, and I bit far into the skin of my palm.

The Dolphin stood above McKay. He reached into a pocket and then held two pale envelopes in the air. "Severance pay," he said. The Dolphin threw the envelopes of heroin on the floor. McKay reached for them and tucked them into his boot. Then he stood up, nodded to the Dolphin, to the Orphans and to the Property. "Brothers," he said. "Sisters."

He walked toward the clubhouse door. I wondered if he had forgotten me. Then he walked out the door and his boot heels sounded farther and farther away.

I did not move. I tasted blood. There were tooth marks on my palm and blood trickled across my skin. The room was silent. Tosh delicately touched the leather of the jacket he wore. The Dolphin stood behind him once more. And then I thought of the envelopes and then I thought of the other President of the Orphans, Cantinni. And again of the envelopes.

"What's in them?" I asked.

The Dolphin smiled. I thought of arsenic, of strychnine. "Poison," I said.

"Not necessarily," said the Dolphin.

"Poison," I said.

"Heroin," he said.

"Heroin? A gift of heroin?"

"Enough for two fixes, or for one."

"A gift?" I said.

"Ain't nothing," the Dolphin said, "for an honorable man who finds out there is no honor."

Nothing but suicide. Nothing but the dance with the ghostly white powder. I ran from the basement, the Dolphin's laughter in my ear, his words forcing me to run faster. The Chevy was still parked in the 7-Eleven lot. McKay could not be far away.

I ran back to Munda's Liquor Store and the clubhouse. In the alley the Orphans' cars were still parked. And there I stopped: he lay beside the cement wall. The needle was still in his arm. I crouched and rocked back and forth on my heels, holding my arms around my knees. I thought if I did not keep my head down I would be sick. My throat made strange noises. He looked very cold lying there on the cement in nothing but jeans and a T-shirt. His body was raised slightly away from the cement. His chest moved. The skin was a pale bluish color, and when I reached to touch him he was cold. But still his chest moved and the liquid in his veins still flowed.

The night clerk from Munda's Liquor Store saw us when he began to unload empty crates in the alleyway.

"It was an accident," I whispered as the night clerk ran to dial for an ambulance.

I watched McKay breathe until I heard sirens on the Avenue, Then I closed my eyes. Boot heels and stretcher wheels were close by. When the attendants circled around us

155

the moon was high and there was a hot night wind. I raised my head and watched them lift McKay to the stretcher. I was glad to see that they placed the oxygen mask over his face very gently.

"It was an accident," I said as I watched them take him away.

January

9
DOING TIME

I

FOR SIX MONTHS I did what women do: I waited. This is
what women are taught to be good at. It's said that a woman's
life is merely preparation for the primal nine-month wait.
Whatever the reason, they do it well. Sometimes they drink or
bite their fingernails down to the wrist. They count stars and
initials and wait: for something to happen, for something to
pass, to change, to begin, to end. In wide cotton blouses
beside empty cradles there is the wait for a child; in black and
veils there is the wait for death. In bathrobes and with painted
eyes, with the counting of stars and the turning of glossy
magazine pages, there is the wait for him, for the man. There
is always the wait for him.

How do women occupy themselves during the wait and
why, in fact, do they wait? Interesting questions to which
interesting answers have been formulated at the cocktail
parties of the world, in the conference and lecture halls of the
universe. The interpretation now served up has never been
certified, clarified, or cooked in butter and garlic. No
apologies; the cooking metaphor cannot be escaped. They
bake; they clean; they watch TV and talk; they sleep at night
or they are forced to the Seconal bottle; they kiss their
children, or they beat them; they wish that they had never had
children to clutter up the waiting, or they wish they had
children to fill the waiting. They walk; they drink coffee; they
drink gallons of gin or of wine; they place their heads in the
ovens or under the hair driers; they call fifty men into their

159

bedroom at one time, or they never turn their eyes to men. They watch second hands and suns and moons; they find ways to fill the waiting.

And the reason they wait is that they do not know they have a choice. The reason they wait is that they do it so well; because it is what they are expected to do.

A commonplace occurrence, an expected side effect while waiting is the act of crying. It is very common, while waiting, to drop tears in the lettuce leaves or between the lines of a letter. And although experts occasionally must be called in to remove hot teardrops from within the burners of the stove, or to unclog a sob from the motor of the dishwasher, the act of crying is nothing unusual. It is very common.

And do women complain of all this waiting? Sometimes; sometimes some of them complain. Some of them are allowed to complain, allowed to pull at their hair, to wail, or to list their complaints in lipstick or ink upon the wall. Those that do this do it well. Some complain, but most do not.

Either way, they wait. Usually, they wait for men. Men who are in offices or in jail. They wait for men to go away; they wait for them to come home. They wait for men to live; and it's true, many of them wait for men to die. They also do this well; even if the waiting takes a lifetime, they do it well.

Mostly, they wait to stop waiting. I stayed on the Avenue without him in the late summer, while McKay kicked a heroin habit in a six-by-eight cell on Rikers Island. The Chevy, towed from the 7-Eleven lot by the auto repair mechanic, paid my rent. And in the early fall, while McKay played dominoes and awaited trial, I began to work behind the counter at Monty's. By the time McKay was sent to Omen House, a rehabilitation center on Jones Street, I had already perfected the formula of the chocolate egg cream.

McKay did not write letters of more than one line. Any news was filtered through Jose, who officially had nothing to do with the Orphans or the Avenue, but who had asked the court to send McKay someplace softer than a jailhouse. Once or twice a week Jose would come to the darkened apartment. He talked continuously while we drank scotch and smoked reefer and made love. I did not feel I was cheating on McKay;

160

I only felt I was waiting. And while Jose babbled in the living room, in the kitchen, in bed, I imagined McKay's eyes and silence. Jose sometimes comforted me, for an hour or two. But when he left, when he walked out the door and took with him his badge and his stories, I was lonelier than ever. So I wrote letters.

Alone in the apartment or standing behind the counter at Monty's with one shoe off and the corner kids demanding sodas or cigarettes, I wrote letters. While Monty counted change in the register or after Jose had closed the door and the lock of the apartment had been bolted, I wrote letters. I did not write of death or suicide, of dope or the Orphans; I wrote only of love and the changes in the weather. I received no answers; only one-line messages signed with McKay's name.

I saw the Orphans, but did not approach them. They ignored me, erased me as they had erased Starry. I visited Irene at her apartment on days when Viet Nam worked late and I did not have to listen to his snickering questions about McKay. Starry and Flash rarely came to the Avenue, but when they did, we would meet at the Tin Angel for drinks and jukebox music. But mostly, aside from Jose's visits and the habit of walking daily to work with Tony, I was alone. I was alone and I waited, for changes in the weather and for McKay.

When the air of the Avenue had grown very cold and ice had frozen upon the cement sidewalks, I discovered at the bottom of the auto repair shop mailbox a thick envelope addressed to me. McKay's handwriting had scrawled out our Avenue address. I did not want to open it.

I carried the unopened letter with me as I walked from the dark oil-spattered auto shop. Across the Avenue the attendants at the Esso station wore thick, hooded sweatshirts. Tony was waiting for me in the driveway, where he waited for me every day. He walked silently at my side to Monty's. It was not that Tony liked me; he had no use for me. But he was McKay's protégé, McKay had written one of his one-line messages to Tony asking him to keep an eye on me, and that forced Tony to walk with me to the candy store each day. And although Tony scowled and lit a cigarette when I tried to talk

161

to him, I knew he was not with me only to act as a protector. He simply had no one else to walk with. Tony was not of the Orphans, and McKay had drawn him away from the corner kids. How could Tony walk with the gang that sniffed glue in schoolyards when he already knew how to roll a joint quicker and tighter than anyone on the Avenue, when he had already popped heroin?

The morning was early and still dark. Tony stopped at a red light and struck a match to a Camel. I did not like him much, but I had no one else to walk with.

When we reached Monty's Tony held the door open for me, and we walked past the stacks of morning newspapers that lay tied in bundles on the cold cement.

"Always such a pleasure to see you two charmers in the morning," Monty said.

Tony and I raised eyebrows. "He's hit the bottle already," Tony said.

As Tony carried the print-smelling copies of the *Daily News* inside and I hung my winter coat on a hook, Monty retreated to the dusty back room. With a countergirl he could trust with the cash register, Monty was free to drink away each day. He was rarely seen behind the counter anymore; instead he rested on a faded chintz couch amid the dust and newspapers of the back room.

I served coffee, newspapers, cigarettes, and muffins to the early-morning rush of truck drivers and school kids. Tony sat in the telephone booth, turning the pages of a *Superman* comic and smoking cigarettes. When the store had emptied, I poured coffee for myself and sat on a stool. I held a letter in the air. Tony raised his eyes from the comic and watched me.

"McKay?" he said, and I nodded. "You gonna read it?"

Again I nodded, and slit the envelope open with a knife. I was used to one-line messages; the thickness of the envelope made me uncomfortable. I feared the contents. I cut my finger on the sharp edge of the envelope when I reached in and drew out the letter. Inside the one sheet of lined loose-leaf paper was money; bills fell onto the counter.

Tony dropped the comic on the floor and stood behind me. I began to count, but when I saw two hundred-dollar bills, I stopped. "A lot of money," I said softly.

I handed it to Tony for counting, and unfolded the loose-leaf paper.

Darling,

   Like Baby Perez is always saying, "The day is dawning." A weekend pass this Saturday – if I do good I'm out on parole. Meet me under the Arch at ten. Be there. Don't hang me up or make me wait. Just be there. Baby Perez has advised I say nothing in this letter – everything can and will be used against me. I heard you're figuring to invest your money – I advise Chevrolet stock. You might even buy back now what was once sold. Take my advice. And be there.

Sincerely,
McKay

I lit a cigarette. Tony was holding the money and staring at me. "What does he say?"

"He says to buy the Chevy back."

Tony smiled now. "He's something. He's something. He's going to start to race again."

I didn't think that was what McKay had in mind. It wasn't hard to guess how the money McKay sent had been earned. Baby Perez was probably someone with connections to money; no socialite or jet-setter could be found at Rikers or in Omen House. Something illegal, something profitable.

I untied the white kitchen apron I wore and reached for my coat.

"What you doing?" Tony said.

"What you care?" I said.

We stared at each other. Tony scowled, disappointed by any exclusion from plans concerning McKay.

"The city," I said finally. I planned to stay overnight at Starry's. Once McKay was back on the Avenue, his disapproval, his dark glare would keep me away from her.

"I'll drive you," Tony said.

"Bullshit you'll drive me. With what car? With what license?"

"The Chevy. We'll get the Chevy."

I shook my head. I would not drive in the Chevy without McKay. I stood before a wall mirror, combed my hair, and watched the reflection of the silver locket I wore. "Monty," I called. The response was a mumbled echo from the back room. "Monty, I have to go." Still he did not answer me. I walked to the cash register and rang a no sale; the noise of the drawer opening and the ringing of the register brought Monty to the doorway between the back room and the store. Monty held a finger in the air.

"Stealing?" he said.

"I have to go."

"Desertion."

"McKay's got a pass," I said.

"Don't think I'm supporting McKay or any of his habits when he gets out just because you're working here."

"Who asked you to do anything?"

"Well, don't ask me to do anything."

"O.K.," I said. "O.K." We glared at each other.

"Do you need an advance?" Monty asked.

"I could use some money."

Monty waved his arm in the air. "Take a ten," he said without looking at me.

I dipped my hand into the register. "Just one ten," he warned.

"I'll pay you back," I told him as I tied a silk scarf around my head and threw my navy-blue winter coat around my shoulders.

"Go on with you," Monty muttered. "And at least do me the favor of ridding me of that." He pointed at Tony.

I placed gloves over my fingers, and fingers over the doorknob. I looked back at Monty. He had picked up an old dishrag and was mopping the already clean counter top. I hesitated.

"Go on with you. Go on with you," he chanted. With a move of his arm he waved my hesitation away.

I bolted out the door into the cold street and down the Avenue toward the subway station. Tony followed me. "You're not coming with me," I said to his shadow.

164

He followed me silently, walking with me down the cement steps and onto the platform. Tony stood against the wall and smoked a cigarette. "You have the money?" I asked him. He nodded. "Use it," I said.

"Me?"

"I ain't talking to nobody else. You can pay the mechanic off as well as me."

"Yeah," he said. "Yeah, yeah."

"Just pay him off and leave the Chevy. Wait there for McKay," I warned.

A train rattled down the track toward us. The air was smoky cold. When the train stopped, I walked into the car; the door slammed shut, and I watched Tony continue to stand on the platform. Finally I looked away, and then as the train began to move, I closed my eyes, counting the stops that would take me to Starry.

I walked in and out of subway cars and then into the air like a sleepwalker, dreaming of the next day's meeting with McKay. I went into a shop. Loud radio music blasted out of speakers attached to the store awnings, posters with low prices on them covered the plate glass. I walked in crowded aisles picking up a toothbrush, two pairs of panties, a thin black turtleneck sweater, and some cheap lilac perfume.

I knocked at Starry's door and then waved my hand at the peephole. Flash let me in.

"Sister," he said. "How goes it?"

"It goes well. McKay goes free."

"No shit? Starry," he called into the kitchen, "McKay's been sprung. In the process?" he asked me, and I nodded. "McKay's in the process of being sprung.

"Big deal," Starry's voice called from the kitchen.

I laughed. "Starry, be nice."

Starry came into the living room. "I could never be that," she said.

I threw my paper bag full of cheap merchandise onto the floor and sat on the couch. Starry was tiny still, but no eye would mistake her for a child now, with her platinum hair and not-so-fine lines around her huge eyes.

Flash sat down and rolled a joint. "What's this I hear about you and my cousin?" he said.

"You hear trash."

"Could be trash, 'cause I heard it from my cousin himself."

"It was a way to pass the time."

"Please," Starry said. "I can think of a million better ways."

"He's my cousin, I know," said Flash. "But a cop?"

"Get off my case," I said.

Starry threw her hands in the air, palms facing me. "Off," she said.

We passed a joint among us. When that was done, we smoked another.

"Baby Perez," I said.

"Yeah," Flash said.

"You know him?" I asked.

"I know of him," said Flash. "He deals in powders. Cocaine and speed."

"And what of him?" I said.

"One evil baby, that man is," said Flash.

I believed now that, had I examined the bills, I might have detected the dust of amphetamine or cocaine.

"As long as it's not heroin," I said.

"And some smack," Flash said. "I hear he deals some smack."

"Shit," I whispered. Another, a newer contact to heroin.

We smoked reefer and watched TV through the afternoon. In the early evening the dealer came to the door. Flash went into the dark hallway to talk business and score some smack for Starry and I could only glimpse the dealer's pale green eyes looking lazily into the apartment.

"Did he kick?" Starry whispered to me.

"McKay?" I said.

"McKay, does he still have a habit?"

"No, how could he connect to any dope in the slammer?"

"So he did it," she said. He had had no choice but to quit heroin; what had Starry expected?

"I won't," she whispered. "I know I won't be able to."

"Do you want to?" I whispered, watching the dealer's

broad-brimmed hat and Flash's hands moving in a bargaining gesture.

Starry laughed hoarsely. "No," she said. "I can't."

"Get busted, That'll solve your problem."

Starry's eyes widened. "I'm not getting busted," she said. She placed a hand on her flat stomach. "What I'm getting is worse than busted."

We looked at each other. From the hallway came the sound of mumbled voices and laughter.

"What do you mean?" I said.

"I have to get rid of it. It. It. I have to get rid of it." Starry's whisper rose in pitch.

"Starry," I said. "What do you do?"

"Come on," she whispered with her eye aimed toward the doorway. "I do what I've done before. But him," she nodded toward Flash. "He's never been through this before. He'll try to stop me. He'll try and force me to keep some fucking screaming junkie baby in this apartment. I can't tell him I need an abortion, and I don't have a goddamn cent of my own."

"If I had any money," I began.

"What about this Perez?" she said, her voice urgent. "He's rich. I hear he's got control of the crystal in two boroughs and he's rich."

I shook my head. "He's a friend of McKay's."

"No," she said. "No, I don't want anything to do with McKay, you hear?"

"All right," I whispered as Flash closed the door on the dealer and walked back into the apartment. There was a spring in his step and his smile was broad. "Got it," he said as he sat down close to Starry and put his arm around her shoulders.

Starry smiled weakly and kissed Flash's cheek. "Good work," she said.

"What you looking at, girl?" Flash chided me. I would not have believed it: Starry was pretending, yes, but it was the pretense that goes along with love. I did not answer. They said good night to me and walked arm in arm, the glassine envelopes in Starry's hand, into the bedroom. That night I could not sleep. I turned constantly on the couch, walked the

167

length of the living room, opened the refrigerator door and examined cheese and orange juice. When the sun rose, I dressed in the black turtleneck I had bought with Monty's advance money and sat alone at the kitchen table drinking coffee and reading the ingredients of a cereal package.

I counted minutes, not wanting to be late, not wanting to keep McKay waiting. Before eight o'clock I scrawled a note across the rough texture of a paper towel, touched lilac to my neck and throat, stood at the door of the silent apartment for a while, and then I walked out into the street. I rode buses that morning; I did not want to go underground.

By the time I had ordered toast and butter and a large Coke in a pancake house on West Fourth Street, it was nine-thirty. I left my breakfast untouched and walked toward Washington Square. Around me there was snow, and sleepers blanketed with overcoats lay upon cement benches. I waited under the Arch.

At ten o'clock I lit a cigarette; at ten-fifteen another. I stood directly under the Arch, thinking that McKay would not see me if I stood to the right or to the left. An hour passed. I shifted my weight from one foot to the other and waited. I felt him near before I saw him. When I turned, sun fell into my eyes, and I had to shade my sight with my hand.

McKay stood before me. He smiled. I whispered his name. Dressed in a black military coat and a leather cap, he smoked a cigarette and stood with a woolen scarf wrapped around his neck, his hands in his pockets. Snow fell, and my feet and hands felt numb. His hair no longer fell long about his shoulders, and his pink motorcycle goggles were gone.

McKay walked toward me, and it seemed I could not look into his eyes. There were months between us, and the ground we stood upon was not the Avenue, and I was not yet sure he was not a stranger. I held my arms around him; cold air and overcoat material came between us. I closed my eyes and held my face against his; we held each other for a long time, and I listened to him whisper. The air was very cold; my hands and feet were numb. The snow continued to fall, and, though I had waited, I did not yet want to look into his eyes.

Baby Perez, McKay told me, had women in every borough of
New York. One of them rented an apartment on MacDougal
Street with income from IBM dividends. I hesitated at the
door of the apartment building. But McKay promised
privacy, and there really was nowhere else to go. So I followed
him through the door.

The curtains were drawn. No electricity shone, yet the
apartment was bright: sunlight filtered in through the covered
windows, and the living room was decorated in white. I sat on
a white couch and unzipped my boots. I could no longer feel
my feet. Baby Perez stood behind a bar mixing drinks. His
face was sallow, his hair long and wild. He wore a dark
mustache and beard, and pierced through one ear was a small
gold hoop.

I stared at the black-and-white silk shirt. "Who is this
Perez?" I whispered to McKay.

"Who is Perez?" Perez said. "Baby Perez is a gypsy, and
good at whatever he does."

McKay laughed and told me that Perez's lawyer had
pleaded a habit to get him six months at Omen House rather
than several years upstate. Perez, however, was and always
had been clean. He was a dealer, not a user, and had
people working for him in Brooklyn and the Bronx. The
only clients he dealt with personally were – Perez now
interrupted – "rock stars and rich bitches." Once again
McKay laughed.

"The money you sent?" I said.

"An advance," McKay said, and he smiled at Perez. "We're
going into business."

Perez smiled at me. Some of his teeth were gold. I was not
impressed.

"What business?"

"Darling," McKay said.

"We going to take the Avenue by storm," Perez said.

"You don't know the Dolphin," I said.

Perez shrugged. "A fish."

"You don't know."

"But I do," McKay said, and I was silent. "We're going to take over. Perez becomes the connection for the entire Avenue, and we take over."

"We have to go through this again?" I said to McKay.

"Again and again," he said.

"Do what you want."

"Do what I want." He laughed softly.

Perez handed me a double scotch and water, and McKay walked to the bar and returned sipping from a bottle of Chivas Regal. We drank the afternoon away.

"I've got business to attend to," Perez said finally. He was indeed a hustler: a weekend pass and all Perez could think of was dealing. He tossed a key to McKay and said, "Later."

"Later," McKay said, and Perez sauntered out of the apartment. McKay and I were left silent and alone amid the white décor. I sipped scotch until I could feel the warmth down to my feet and then I turned to McKay.

"You're insane," I said to him.

"Tell me about it." He laughed.

But I would not tell him about it. I would not mention death, the Dolphin, or the needle. I shook my head and refused.

"I'm no frigging idiot," McKay said softly. "I know the Dolphin's tricks, but I'm going to get him."

"Honor," I said.

"Honor, like hell," said McKay. "Just a little no-good nastiness."

"You couldn't fight the Dolphin before."

"Bullshit. I didn't know how pure that junk he gave me was."

"McKay," I said. He lied; I knew he lied. In the alley behind the Orphans' clubhouse, McKay had committed suicide. I had touched the coldness of his body, had heard the labored breathing.

"Don't give me any crap," McKay warned, and I let it be for a while. We kissed like strangers and drank more scotch.

"You're straight?" I asked and McKay sighed. "Are you going to be straight?"

"I'm going to be smart."

"Oh shit," I said. More war and more dope, and more waiting.

"Let's drop it," McKay said. "Let's drop any talk of the Avenue."

McKay walked across the room and turned on a stereo. I counted the ribs of my turtleneck sweater. When he returned to sit near me, he said, "So, what's the story with the Orphans?" He looked unconcerned, lit a cigarette.

"I don't see much. I don't hear much."

"What do you know?" he insisted. "Who do you see?"

"I've seen Tosh."

"He wears my jacket?"

I hesitated. "He wears your jacket."

McKay cursed.

"Tony's around. He's putting the money down on the Chevy now. He thinks you're going to race again."

"What makes you think I won't when all this is over?" McKay said. "In the spring, maybe in the spring."

When all what was over? Did McKay believe there would be an end to a war he would not allow to end?

"Irene," I said. "And Starry."

"Starry, what do you need her for?"

I told McKay about Starry, hoping that if he heard her troubles, how bad her habit was, and that she hadn't enough money for an abortion, he would feel easier about our friendship. But he only scowled.

"Cut that girl loose, you hear? I don't want you with trash."

My seeing Starry, even hearing her name, brought back the Orphans, brought back honor, and memories McKay did not want, and so I was silent.

After a time McKay said, "And Jose?"

"What do you mean, Jose?" I said, turning my head and fumbling with the liquor bottle.

"Fucking a cop?" he said. "No discretion."

"You left me alone. What did you expect?"

"More," he said.

I had expected McKay to know better. I touched his shoulder. "We're better with silence," I said, and he smiled.

171

We went into the bedroom. As we did I was afraid that between the sheets in an unknown bed in this white apartment I would suddenly realize that this was not McKay at all, that the man I made love with had simply stolen McKay's smile and eyes and was only a pretender. When we passed by a gilded mirror that hung in the hallway I did not recognize McKay's reflection.

"Your hair," I could not help but say.

McKay ran one hand over his head. "Me and Tosh could be twins now." He laughed.

"Never," I said.

"It's this behaviorism shit they do at Omen House. You fuck up, and they shave your head to let you know if anyone is boss it sure as shit ain't you."

In the bedroom the curtains were drawn. McKay reached his hand out to switch on the light. I stopped him.

"In the dark?" he said. I was silent. "You can have it any way you want it," McKay said. I touched my finger to his lips and felt the curve of a smile.

I undressed in the dark, dropping my clothes in a heap on the thick white carpet.

"About Jose," I said as I lay in bed and watched McKay unbutton his shirt. Should I say that each time I lay with someone else I only imagining McKay? Would he believe me if I said I was always waiting for him?

"I don't want to know," he said, and he sat on the edge of the mattress to remove his boots, and then his jeans.

"McKay."

"Listen. Is it still going on?"

"No," I said. I would call Jose the next day and inform him that McKay would soon be free from Omen House.

McKay nodded. "Then there's nothing to know."

That was not true, but I did not say a word. He was touching me, and he seemed less and less a stranger and so I did not say another word. For six months I had waited for McKay, for six months I had not made love, I had only tried with another body not to be alone. The touch of a hand moving down my back, the rhythm of our breathing, and I felt, finally, after six months of waiting,

172

that I could again move as a lover.

I forgot the Avenue. I forgot its addresses and faces. Kid Harris and the Dolphin had never been. Starry was miles away. And there was no particular way I wanted it; I only wanted McKay. I wanted him inside me. I wanted not to be waiting and alone. When I lay on my side, I felt the cold silver of the locket between my breasts and was for a moment reminded of the power and spells of the Avenue. I tasted the liquor on McKay's tongue, and I forgot once more. I wanted him to move faster; I did not want to wait. I moved my legs around McKay's; I touched my finger to his skin; I felt his whisper, but I did not hear any words. After he came, we lay close; my legs were around him still; I listened to the silence of the room. I did not feel cold any longer; and although I tasted scotch I did not feel drunk. My thighs were wet, and I lay in silence; I still felt as if I was waiting.

"McKay," I said. He did not answer. He may have been asleep. I did not know if he dreamed of the Orphans; his breathing was deep. Lying in the white apartment, listening to silence, I did not think he dreamed of me. I tried to sleep. I counted, made lists, recalled song lyrics and correct spellings. Each time I fell into a dream, I woke. Each time I woke, I heard a clock, hidden somewhere in the bedroom, tick louder. I could not sleep.

In the morning, I watched McKay until he opened his eyes. When he smiled I did not fear the beat of a clock quite so much. With McKay awake, I did not want to leave the bed, but I knew he had Perez to meet. He had to sign in to Omen House. I dressed and went into the kitchen to boil water.

I was standing with a white coffee percolator in my hand when McKay followed and told me we had no time for breakfast.

"No time?"

"Fifteen minutes," he said.

"Not enough."

"There'll be time," McKay said. "I'm out for good in two weeks, and then there'll be time."

In two weeks there would be more meetings with Perez; there would be the Dolphin and the Avenue to be dealt with;

there would be dope; there would be the Chevy; and there would most certainly not be enough time.

"I don't believe you," I said.

"Believe me," he said.

What could I do? I said I believed him. I followed McKay from the apartment; he locked the door and then slipped the key underneath so that it rested on the thick living-room carpet. We went outside and stopped at a corner. McKay held a lit cigarette inside one coat pocket to warm his hand; his other hand held mine.

"Last night," he said. "About last night."

"Last night?" I said.

The Sunday traffic was light, but the few cars skidded gently on the icy streets. Near us a newspaper vendor was selling thick, heavy papers. McKay backed into a shop doorway. He signaled me to move with him. We stood very close.

"Was it good for you?" he said.

He had never asked me before and I regretted that he asked me now. It was better, yes, than before, because making love with a junkie was hardly anything at all. Last night had been better, but not good.

"Yes," I said, and McKay smiled.

"It's gonna get better. Everything is gonna get better."

"Is it?"

"Yes," McKay said. "There's a shitload of money in cocaine."

Cocaine, cocaine – one white powder was the same as another.

"You gonna meet rock stars and rich girls," I said.

"You wait," McKay said. "You wait and see."

I saw Baby Perez walking down Jones Street toward us. "You don't have to go back to the Avenue," I said.

"Yeah, I do."

Perez glided on ice toward us.

"You like cocaine?" I said to McKay.

He shrugged. "It's fine, but not the best."

"You've been doing cocaine while you're in the House?"

"Doing it?" McKay said. "I been selling it."

I meant to laugh, but no sound came from my throat. "You got a way about you," I said.

McKay's eyes spotted Perez. "Two weeks," McKay said. "Wait two more weeks."

I looked into McKay's eyes, eyes so dark they could almost make me forget I would be waiting as long as I was with him. With McKay I would wait for something that would never, could never come.

I smiled, and then watched McKay walk away from me. He and Perez shook hands and disappeared together through the doorway of Omen House. I waited until I could no longer see them, and then turned toward the subway station.

10

PLANS AND MORE OF THEM

I

IF MCKAY HAD attempted to call, he would have discovered the phone had been left off the hook; I did not check the mailbox for letters; and carrier pigeons landing on our window ledge would have found their beaks up against glass, chipped paint would have caught between their talons, and feathers would have fallen past the auto repair shop garage door to coat the icy Avenue.

I was thinking, and did not wish to be disturbed.

I had already telephoned Jose to call off whatever had been between us. He was not distressed. Jose had a badge and connections to the best marijuana in New York City; he would never have to spend a night alone; he would never have to search far for an ear to listen to his babblings. But he gave me a warning: Baby Perez was a no-gooder, and McKay was asking for trouble. Jose himself was finished with McKay. He advised me to do the same.

I listened to Jose, but I really did not wish to be disturbed. I listened instead to the fall of snow. I drank wine, watched TV. When the doorbell rang it would be only Tony with questions about McKay and the Orphans which I could not, or did not want to, answer. For two weeks I sat alone thinking how much I did not want to be alone. When the apartment was too quiet, I turned up the volume of the TV and listened to laugh tracks and commercials.

He suddenly arrived very late one night. Oddly, I had forgotten the date of his release. It seemed that he had never been gone, that I had never been alone.

McKay stood in the open doorway. "McKay," I said.

"Were you expecting anyone else?" he said.

"Only you," I said, but I had expected no one. I expected to be alone.

McKay shut the door and walked immediately to the phone. I had expected as much; I had expected to be alone. He placed his hand over the mouthpiece of the telephone. "Trying to get the old guard together."

Could he believe such a thing as an old guard existed? After T.J. and Gina excused themselves from Orphan activity, after Jose refused any assistance, after Viet Nam refused to grant Irene access to the phone, McKay called for a drink.

I found a bottle of Gordon's gin Jose had received as a Christmas present from a liquor store on his beat and poured two glasses full of gin.

"Zero," McKay said. He stood with his hand on the telephone. The heavy winter coat he wore fell to below his knees. He removed his leather cap and threw it to the floor. "Zero," he repeated.

I allowed myself to hope that perhaps the fight against honor would be stillborn.

"Perez will know what to do," he said finally.

"McKay," I said, "if you don't know, how the hell will Perez know?"

He ignored my words and dialed again. But he came to sit with me on the bed as he spoke with Perez. McKay moved his hand under my blouse. His fingers played with the silver locket and I did not listen to a word he said. When he hung up the receiver he said, "We're going to enlist the Pack." And then he was dialing again, ordering Tony to arrange a meeting with the Pack.

I moved away from him. "You're fucked up," I said, when he had finished speaking. Would the Pack rush to the aid of the one who had pulled the trigger, whose .22 had sent a bullet between the shoulder blades of their President?

"You say that to me again, and you'll be weeping."

"You're fucked up," I repeated.

177

McKay drank gin, and then more. "Did you hear what I said?" he asked softly.

I nodded.

"Look," McKay said, "the new Pack Prez don't care for old revenge. The dude's so happy to be President of the Pack I'm surprised I ain't received any complimentary gifts for wasting Kid Harris."

"When do you meet with the Pack?"

McKay hesitated; then he said, "Tonight."

"Tonight," I said and silently recited Jose's telephone number. McKay's eyes were their darkest; around them were the lines of sleeplessness. He had no one else to call on the phone, no one else to summon.

"I'm going with you," I told him.

"Dangerous," he said as he lit a cigarette..

I understood that, but I did not care because, as always, I believed it was more dangerous to be without McKay, more dangerous to be alone.

"The Chevy is ready," I said. "It's no beauty, but it's yours again." McKay smiled. From a dresser drawer I retrieved two keys: one for the garage door of the auto shop, the other the Chevy's.

We walked arm in arm into the night. Waiting in the street while he entered the garage, I heard the strain of the engine, then saw the headlights shine through the garage door. Before we picked up Tony, we drove down the Avenue once more, parking at the subway station to wait for Perez. There was little traffic, only an occasional patrol car driving slowly by. The side streets were dark, and around the street lamps were halos indicating snow.

"The hotshot doesn't have a car?"

"He's got a car," McKay said. "He's got several cars. But the subway is the way to make sure you ain't being followed."

"What crap," I said.

"You can't take a little intrigue?"

I thought I would like to have a list of every rock star Perez considered a customer, would like to view the statistics on how many "rich bitches" had fallen for his line. I didn't believe the numbers would be high.

Perez came up the cement subway stairs, then stood in the reflected light of a single street lamp, lighting a cigarette and exhaling smoke into the cold night air. On his head of wild hair Perez wore a suede Western hat, and around his shoulders was draped a maroon velvet cape whose neck was trimmed with muskrat fur. His corduroy slacks were tucked into high brown boots.

Perez nodded familiarly to a patrol car as it passed by him for the second time. McKay shifted gears and we pulled up at the curb beside Perez, who opened the back door of the Chevy and got in.

"Brother, brother, brother," he said to McKay. "I do not like waiting on anyone, even if it's you, McKay. I got deals to make; I got business to attend to."

"Sure," McKay said to the man of business.

Perez removed his hat and lit a reefer. He passed the joint to me. I took it and inhaled, but McKay waved it away. He drove down the Avenue, stopping at the Tin Angel Bar.

"What's this here?" Perez said.

"Picking up one of my soldiers," McKay said.

I finished the joint while we waited in the Chevy. The front and rear windows of the car were foggy with heat and smoke. "Very good dope," I said. Perez's marijuana was even better than Jose's "New York City's Finest."

"Of course," said Baby Perez. "That's my line."

A figure cloaked in black leather walked from the shadows of the Tin Angel's doorway. He opened the back door and sat down next to Perez.

"Jesus fucking Christ," said Perez. "This kid is your soldier?"

"That's right," said McKay.

"This deal looks shittier all the time. Your one soldier could use a baby-sitter," said Perez.

"Eat it," Tony said quietly.

"Tony," McKay warned. But I saw him smile at the words of his protégé.

Perez leaned forward. "Pardon me," he said to McKay, "but what did he say to Perez?" He leaned back again, and sat very close to Tony. "What did this dipshit say?"

179

"I think you heard me," Tony said.

Perez relaxed. He lit a black Russian cigarette with a silver lighter. "I think I did," he said. "And I think you should know I'm going to kill you."

"Hey, hey," McKay said. He was no longer amused by Tony's loose talk, or by Perez's threats. "There's business to take care of."

"Business," Perez agreed. "Always business first."

We drove north on the Avenue, past St. Anne's. McKay parked the Chevy in front of the blacktop basketball court. The four of us left the car and walked onto the ice of the court. No horde of school kids jumped up into the air wearing T-shirts embossed with team numbers; no one was dribbling up and down the court; there were no priests blowing whistles and shouting foul. Instead, beneath the basket, four young men stood. As we walked toward them, Perez's velvet cape swirled around his knees. McKay's black leather cap was tilted over one dark eye, Tony's black leather jacket reflected starlight. The four stood quietly watching us. When we reached them, McKay said, "Brothers."

Their eyes moved warily as wolves' as they motioned McKay to join them. Tony and I stood outside a circle consisting of McKay, Perez, and two of the strangers. One of them was short and dark and wore the letters

PRESIDENT OF
THE PACK

on the back of his jacket. The two other Pack soldiers stood guard over Tony and me.

"What the fuck?" one of them said. "This is McKay's army?"

Tony lit a cigarette with a match struck on his thumbnail in the style of McKay. The Pack guards eyed Tony's finesse with approval, but I noticed that he now sucked on a thumb which he had singed.

"What I want," I heard McKay say, "is this and only this." He stood with his hands in the pockets of his long wool coat.

"I want the Dolphin."

"I'm hip to that," said the President of the Pack. "Lots of folks would like to pop the Dolphin."

"I don't like this setup," said one of the guards.

I didn't blame him. We stood on Orphan territory, and I was certain that the wind had already carried the news of McKay's release all along the Avenue. One of the Pack guards drew a fifth of whiskey from his pocket. He drank and then passed the bottle to the other guard.

"What do you say?" Tony said to the guard.

"I say if you want a drink, show me your I.D., kid," said the guard, laughing.

"Who I'm with is my I.D.," Tony said, and the guard grudgingly passed him the whiskey.

"Perez here gets full control of the Avenue traffic, and nobody deals dope without checking it out with him first."

Perez lit another black cigarette. As the Pack looked him over I finally recognized the new President of the Pack. I had seen him once and only once before, I had seen him through the darkness of the creek as he stood at Kid Harris's side. My throat felt dry. The President turned to Perez and fingered the velvet material of his cape. Then he looked up at McKay.

"Full control of all dope dealing?" the President said. "This fag?"

Perez exhaled smoke into the Pack President's face.

"I don't know," Perez said. "On this Avenue you don't see much action. All you see is jive-ass talkers."

"Who you calling jive-ass?" the President asked. I drank from the fifth of whiskey. "This Avenue is out of your territory," continued the number-one soldier of the Pack.

"I'm expanding my business," Perez said. "And I don't have time for talking trash. You're interested in a deal or you're not."

"Wait a minute. Wait a minute," said the President. He lit a cigarette. "Who says I ain't interested?"

"What you do with Tosh is not my business," McKay said softly. "What is my business is the jacket. I get the jacket he wears."

"Solid."

"All I want," McKay said, "is the jacket."

"Perez gets all the Avenue business, but what you get?" the President asked. "McKay, what you into?"

"I'm into whatever the fuck I want to be into."

The President shrugged. "Tony," I whispered. "I got to get out of here. I'm freezing." I was no longer cold; the whiskey had fixed that. But I had to leave before the President of the Pack recognized me. I would not be able to stand his smile.

"Don't get panicky," said Tony.

"Who the hell is panicky?"

Tony leaned his head close to mine. "Don't mess up McKay's plans," he said.

The Pack guard motioned us to move farther apart.

I thought I might be able to wait a while longer if I could stop myself from thinking of the night at the creek. I stared at the asphalt and recited the alphabet. When I reached W for the third time, the President of the Pack and McKay were shaking hands.

"All you got to do," Perez said to the Pack leader, "is not think. Well do the thinking; we'll make the plans. All you got to do is follow orders, and the Avenue is yours."

The four of them now walked toward Tony, me, and the two Pack guards. Now I saw the President's face clearly, now I could remember the touch of his hands as he held me on the bottom of the creek. I thought I might be sick.

"Who's the lady?" he asked.

"The lady?" said McKay. "I don't think who the lady is should interest you. What should interest you is being ready for tomorrow night."

The President moved his face close to mine. Once more I began a silent recitation of the alphabet. I knew from his smile that he had recognized me, and I looked away and wanted silence. I waited for McKay to rescue me. McKay placed his hand on the President's shoulder; the Pack guards tensed.

"The lady is mine," McKay said.

I looked up; McKay and I looked into each other's eyes with the stare of strangers. Or of lovers. I silently spelled the letters of his name. McKay.

182

He held his arm tightly around my waist, and I placed my hands inside his coat pocket and entwined my fingers with his, as if within our palms we held the night of the creek in silence.

And yes, all right, I admit to fear.

You've been waiting, I know. And so, all right, finally I admit to fear. Did you imagine that black leather, and midnights and the mist of finely burnt hashish oil, could overpower a spell so strong as fear? In the mood I was in fear was a most intricate, a most delicate sort of magic.

Sometimes I did not know fear for what it was. I thought the racing of the heart might be the first stages of cardiac arrest; palpitations could easily be caused by an excess of tobacco; the dry mouth could be eased by a beer. No one on the Avenue lived without fear. And no one admitted to it.

What of McKay? His eyes were half closed, and the side of his face moved slightly with a twitch at his cheek. Did he or I know how well acquainted he was with fear? I think not. He was the most wonderful, the greatest pretender of the Avenue. His eyes were the darkest, his walk the easiest. You've seen that even when he lay with closed eyes in a cold alley of the Avenue, to lift one eyelid was to find a fierce gaze. So great was his pretense that I even imagined myself safe. I chalked up violence, murder, and rape to the whim of the fates, and, when I stood with McKay, I believed myself free of fear. And from doubt. So I stayed by him and recited the alphabet and imagined myself free from fear. I could think McKay a fool, insane, or cruel; I could never think him a coward. He would rush into the thick of any battle; he would walk the darkest streets in the midnight hour; he would chance the risks of crime and war: if I believed him to be without fear, I could disguise my own. So I believed.

Perez and Tony sat in front of the Chevy. "Assholes," Perez said of the Pack. "Assholes. What this Avenue is good for is a market for dope. And they fight over it and fight over it for nothing."

I sat in the back seat, very close to McKay, moving my fingers in a circular motion at the base of his neck. McKay leaned his head back and then forward, but the knots I felt would not be exorcised. But if I was with McKay, what was

183

there possibly to fear? Anything I feared had happened already.

Perez turned to face McKay. "From now on," he said, "it's all yours. If you need more capital, I'll lay it on you. But the action is all yours, and if you're busted, I don't know you."

McKay smiled into the air. Tony turned the key in the starter; exhaust rose from the tail pipe. The night was very dark, very still; the windows of the Chevy were foggy. We had reached the bottom, hadn't we? If the mood moved us somewhere new it could only be higher. We could only go higher, but, still, each time I rode in the Chevy and each time I caught sight of the dark flare of McKay's eyes, something clicked, something like the trigger of a shotgun aimed at the cortex of the brain. Something that made my eyes widen, that made my lungs grow tight, my heartbeat race. Always at these times, I would steal a glance at McKay. I could not see any of his life signs alter; my fingers on his pulse could never discern any change.

Tony shifted gears and looked at McKay through the rearview mirror. "How does it feel to be home?" he said to his President.

As I ran my fingers down and across the base of his neck, McKay leaned his head back into the deep maroon upholstery. He answered only with a very slight movement of his shoulders.

II

"All right," I said. "Don't tell me your fucking plans." I stood behind the counter at Monty's. Hamburgers were frying on the grill and McKay sat on one stool with his legs kicked out to cover two more seats.

"Don't worry," he said.

"Who's worried?" I said.

McKay watched the doorway. There was the threat that the Orphans knew McKay was now back on the Avenue.

I leaned close to him; my silver locket hit the linoleum

counter. "Honey," I whispered in his ear, "I don't give a shit what your plans are."

McKay smiled at my lie. "Just do what I tell you," he said. "I never did like you thinking too much."

I had followed the instructions he had given me: called Leona and told her I was through with McKay, asked her questions about Jose's romantic past, led her – and by now, everyone – to think that I was mad for Jose. Perhaps even he had heard, without suspecting that the words I spoke to Leona had been devised by McKay.

"I don't like it," I muttered as I flipped over a hamburger and splattered my white apron with grease.

"Did I ask for your opinion?" McKay said.

I threw one hamburger on a roll, the roll on a plate, the plate before McKay.

"It's better for you if you don't know anything," he said.

Monty lumbered out from the back room, bringing with him the odor of gin and cigars. "Ah," he said. "The no-gooder is home once more."

"Old man," McKay said, smiling.

"I want you to know," Monty said, "that of late I have decided to rid this store of bums."

"Oh, yeah?" McKay said. "Look, you old fart . . ."

Monty did not allow McKay to finish. "Do you want me to fire her?" he said.

"You don't have to fire her," McKay said. "Because she quits."

"She does, does she?" I said.

"She'll be leaving when I fire her and not before," Monty said.

"Do you want to put money down on that?" McKay said. "Do you want to bet?"

"Do you both want to fuck off?" I said; I untied my apron and threw it across the counter. I sat down on the stool closest to the door; if they continued their argument by threatening each other with my job, I would leave. They both turned to smile at me. I lit a cigarette and stared at them. Smoke billowed from the grill.

"Something's burning," Monty called.

185

"That's right," I said. I swung my legs and the stool swiveled slightly.

Monty walked to the grill and flipped the charred remains of beef into a garbage pail.

"I don't want to fight with you, old man," McKay said finally. "Fact is, I got an offer to make you."

"You?" Monty said. "Don't make me any offers."

I kicked my shoes off and reached for a copy of the *Enquirer*.

"Let me ask you one question," McKay said. "All right, then," Monty said. He winked at McKay, though I was sure he did not want to. "Ask me one question. Go on with you, ask me."

McKay smiled lazily. There was silence; I looked up from the *Enquirer* to see them staring at each other. "Well, ask him," I said. I was curious; McKay was not one to ask questions.

"Well," McKay said slowly, "what I want to know is how much you might charge me to rent this dust heap of a store for one night."

"McKay, you're one small-time punk if you think I can be bought," Monty said.

"I'm a small-time punk?" McKay said. He reached into his jeans pocket, drew out a billfold, and began counting. When he had counted out one hundred dollars Monty stopped him.

"Now where would you be getting that?" he said.

"How much to rent this joint?" McKay said.

Monty was silent. He reached under the counter and his hand reappeared holding a bottle of gin, from which he poured himself a Coca-Cola glassful.

"You yourself told me everything has a price, old man," McKay said.

"The old man's a mass of contradictions, didn't you know?" I called.

"What do you say?" McKay asked. "Do we have a deal?"

"Not so fast," Monty said.

"It's got to be fast."

"How much is your offer?" Monty said finally.

"A hundred bills."

"Hah," Monty said, disdainfully.

"One twenty-five."

"One seventy-five or nothing."

"You bastard."

"No less."

"You're a hard man," I called to Monty.

"I'm a drunk," he said, shrugging.

"You're that too," I said.

"And collateral," Monty said to McKay.

"What do you mean, collateral?"

"A herd of junkies in here could well mean broken windows and a filthy mess to clean up afterward."

"What do you mean junkies?" McKay said. "I'm straight."

"You're straight. You're straight. I don't care what you say you are, son. Collateral."

"You pay her wages, don't you?" McKay said and he pointed to me. "Something gets fucked over in the store, take it out of her wages."

"Not a chance," I said. Let McKay's plans be his own. I would not become an indentured countergirl at Monty's to pay for broken windows.

"All right, the Chevy," McKay said grudgingly.

"That car's worth nothing to me," Monty said.

"That Chevy is the finest Motown metal ever put together. Ain't worth nothing?" McKay shook his head in disbelief at Monty's appraisal.

"Well then, the Chevy," Monty said.

They shook hands to seal the bargain.

"When?" I said to McKay.

"Tonight," he answered. "After closing."

Closing was at ten o'clock. There was little time if McKay wanted to get to the Dolphin before the entire Avenue knew each detail of his plan.

"McKay," I said.

"Don't worry," he said. "It's going to be easy. It will be easy . . ." McKay began.

'Keep the rough stuff to a minimum," Monty interrupted.

". . . As pie," McKay said.

"There'll be sweeping up to do tomorrow," Monty said to me.

"Not for her," McKay said. "Because after tonight, she quits."

"How many times do I have to tell you, McKay, it's none of your business."

McKay turned to glare at me. "It is my business. You are my business. And whether you like it or not you just quit work in this dump." He kicked a stool with his heel so that it spun wildly.

Who in her right mind would want to work at Monty's? And if I wanted anything, it was to be McKay's business. But I was not. I was far down on the list – after cocaine, heroin, revenge, and the Orphans.

"I got news for you," I said to McKay. "I want to be making my own money." That too was true. I did not want to exist the way Starry did, with not enough money of her own to take a bus downtown.

"You want money? You want money?" McKay shouted. By now a few customers had come into the store. Magazines rustled, Monty rang up sales on the cash register. McKay threw his billfold on the counter. "What do you call this if you don't call it money?" he said.

"I call it yours," I said.

McKay threw a coin on the linoleum. The silver rolled down the counter top, spun with a metallic sound, and then fell before me. A dime.

"You want money, there's money," McKay said. "There's money to call Starry."

Why Starry? Why did he even mention her name?

Monty finished with his customers and came back to McKay and his billfold of cash. McKay held his hand over the money. "Tell her she's fired," he said to Monty.

Monty looked at me. His eyelashes and gin caused his gaze to waver. "Darling," he said to me. "It's a hundred and seventy-five dollars."

"I know," I said.

"It's fucking a lot of gin," McKay said.

"You tell me what you want," Monty said.

"What I want?" I said. I laughed. Well, I wanted to quit, and I wanted to stay, and I didn't believe doing either one would make a damn bit of difference. "Take the money," I said. McKay removed his hand from the counter; the green bills fluttered like wings.

"I believe," Monty said as he picked the money gently off the counter top and placed it in the cabinet under a metal sink, "you are making the grandest mistake yet, McKay."

McKay did not answer.

"I believe . . ." Monty began.

"Oh, who gives a damn what you believe, you goddamn rummy," McKay said softly. He turned to me. "Call Starry," he said.

"What if I don't?" I said. McKay laughed quietly. "What if I say no?" I asked.

"What if?" he said. "What if doesn't matter, because you will."

He was right. I would do what he told me to do and no ifs existed. I walked to the telephone booth and sat down. "What do you want me to say?" I asked.

McKay came over to the door of the booth. "That's the way," he said, smiling. "Now you're my girl!"

I looked up at McKay and waited for his instructions.

"She won't talk to me," McKay said, "unless you let her know how really important it is to her."

"What is? What is important to her?"

"The deal I can make her." McKay smiled.

I was going to betray her. I was going to betray Starry, and I could not stop myself.

"You tell her," McKay said, "that I'm going to get her an abortion, and she's going to get me a fish."

Starry feared the Dolphin more than not being able to cop a fix. Once she had told me she would never go against him. Now, she would probably have no choice. I had told McKay of her troubles, and in doing so, I had betrayed her.

"You're a bastard," I said softly. I was too tired to shout or even to care.

"That's right," McKay said.

When Starry answered I told her what McKay wanted me to tell her: that he had a deal to offer her; that if she could make excuses to Flash and get away from Manhattan for one

189

night McKay would arrange an abortion. More than that: he would pay.

"You told him?" Starry said.

"That's the deal," I said.

"What I got to do, sell my soul? What's his angle?"

"The Dolphin," I said.

"Let me talk to her," McKay said. He stood in the doorway of the booth so that I sat in darkness, covered by his shadow.

"Wait," I said. "Wait a minute."

McKay grabbed the receiver from my hand.

"Starry, I need you," he said. "And what's more, you need me."

The Avenue was worthless. And McKay knew it. But he wanted it anyway. Once he had it, he would gain nothing, have nothing.

"Arrange to meet the Dolphin at Monty's. Tell him you're setting me up with the help of the inside connection who's dying to get rid of me so she can go off with Jose." McKay looked at me. "And tell him all you want is two spoons of smack in return. You'll trade me for heroin, because the Dolphin would never believe you were handing him a free gift. Even a gift you despised as much as you do me." McKay laughed.

When I heard him laugh, when I saw that his head was thrown back in laughter and that his lips had curled back over his white teeth, I felt as though the telephone booth was too small and dark for me to stay in any longer.

"Let me by," I said. I stood and tried to move past McKay, but he stood in my way. I had done what he wanted, had done what he willed, but he would not move an inch. He stood with eyes dark as night skies and blocked my way. I tried to push past him, but he held one arm around my waist.

"McKay," I whispered.

He continued to talk to Starry, but I no longer listened. I felt weak, and my forehead burned.

Finally I heard McKay tell Starry to find a pencil with which to write something down. "I'll wait," he said into the receiver, which he then moved into the crook of his neck. He moved one hand gently across my face; his other arm was tight around my waist. I felt terribly weak; I imagined fainting.

"Don't fight me," McKay said very softly. His arm held me tighter, and I felt weaker still. We stood very close together in the phone booth. There seemed nowhere to move. And while Starry hunted through the kitchen drawers of her apartment for a pencil and paper, I moved my arms around McKay's neck and I rested my face close to his.

11

REUNIONS

I

I WAS DRESSED in a counter apron of white. Through the plate-glass window the night was dark and full of ice. The radio had predicted snow, weather reports warned of treacherous driving, of accidents and hidden patches of ice. I drank a cup of sugarless coffee and watched the hands of the clock hanging above the doorway that led to the back room of the candy store.

I counted seconds. I unbuttoned the two top buttons of my white silk blouse and then I rebuttoned it to the collar. I watched the movement of the veins in my wrists. I drank more coffee. Monty had left the store at nine-thirty without saying a word. There had not even been a look of reproach. He had simply and quietly left the store carrying the hundred seventy-five dollars and a bottle of gin. Traffic on the Avenue was slow and no customers had entered for almost an hour. A wind was rising; signs and neon shook with the air. I walked to the door. Outside Tony crouched motionless in the doorway. I opened the door very slightly; cold air rushed into the store.

"Don't do that," Tony said. His voice broke. He was jittery. He lit a cigarette against the wind and stood, looking into the darkness of the Avenue.

"It's quiet," I said.

"Not for long," said Tony.

"You're gonna freeze, standing out here."

"I do what I'm told," he said.

He had been ordered to watch for the Orphans and for the

police, and he would do so, no matter what the thermometer said. I too followed orders, and so I closed the door and retreated behind the counter. I drank more coffee and watched the guard at the door warily eye the shadows of the Avenue.

Finally, just before closing time, Tony opened the door, and Starry entered the store. I looked down at the floor, then faced her as she walked toward me. I did not know what lie she had used to escape from Flash's guarding eyes, and I did not want to know. Starry was covered by an ancient raccoon coat whose shoulders padded her own. Her face was pale; the skin shone white with cold, but her eyes glowed bright and blue.

She reached behind the counter for a pack of Tareytons. "Starry," I said. I wasn't sure she would speak to me. I didn't even want to speak to myself.

"Back on the Avenue," she mused.

"I talk too much," I apologized. "I didn't know he would involve you."

"Well," she said, lighting a cigarette. "I always was one for a good fight. This particular fight, I don't much care who wins. But what the hell, I'll watch."

"So the Dolphin believes I'm betraying McKay?"

"Why shouldn't he?" Starry said. "If you were smart, you would."

I shook my head.

"I got to say," Starry continued, "that if McKay don't make good tonight we're all screwed. I don't mind going against the Dolphin if McKay's going to finish him off. But one fuck-up, and we got the Dolphin after us."

"I'm not worried," I said. I bit my thumb. "McKay has got it all together."

"Maybe."

I poured some coffee for Starry. Then I said, "Murder. Will it be murder?"

"Well, I pray to Christ it'll be murder," Starry said. "Then all this will be finished."

I couldn't imagine the Avenue without war. The hour was ten. I turned off the current that spelled out Monty's name in neon. Crosses and double crosses. I held the silver charm

193

between my fingers. The Dolphin believed Starry and I were setting up McKay; Starry for heroin and revenge, and I out of desire of Jose, the babbling peace officer. When McKay arrived to pick me up after work, the Dolphin would be waiting for him; murder would be waiting in the candy store.

A green truck pulled up at the curb before Monty's. "What the hell," I said, "a Sears truck?" Perhaps Monty had decided to disrupt McKay's plan, I thought, by reporting a malfunctioning freezer.

"Unlock the outside door of the back room," Starry ordered me. "Go on," she said.

I walked through the dust, newspapers, and empty liquor bottles that littered Monty's haven. A mouse darted away from my step. I unlocked the back door. When I returned to the counter, Starry sat calmly drinking coffee, smoking a cigarette, turning the pages of *Glamour*.

"We'll see action tonight," she said. Minutes more passed, and the hairs on my arm stood as if charged with electricity, but Starry only sipped coffee and cream. I tapped my fingernails on the counter top in a wild beat. "Relax," Starry said to me. I could not, but I bit my thumb and was silent. I was lighting a cigarette with a safety match when the door opened. The wind of the Avenue entered the candy store, and the match was blown out before my cigarette was lit.

Tosh walked in first. He wore McKay's black leather jacket. Then followed Martin the Marine, dressed in denims, his long loose arms shaking as if he were trying to dispel a cramp. Behind these two Orphans came the Dolphin. In the doorway stood the owner of the Avenue. Snow had begun to fall and the Dolphin's painted hands brushed snowflakes off the tattoos that covered his arms and neck.

"Ladies," the Dolphin greeted us.

For a moment I felt, as we greeted the Dolphin with nods, that we really were about to betray McKay. My skin crawled. Why had I agreed to become a part of the setup, to play the role of traitoress? Had there been a way to refuse him, to say no to McKay?

The Dolphin tossed a plastic bag of white powder onto the counter before Starry. Her eyes became saucers. There were enough fixes within that half load so that Starry's hands shook, and her tongue licked lightly at her bottom lip. She reached out.

"Not yet," the Dolphin warned.

Her hand stopped in mid-air.

"You got nearly two spoons there, honey, and when I get McKay," the Dolphin said, "then you get the junk." He smiled, then turned to me. I was afraid I would blurt out a warning. I did not want to speak. "And you," the Dolphin said to me, "you get to be with your new lover-man."

I was silent. If I even attempted to say Jose's name I might burst into hysterical laughter.

"What time is McKay meeting you?" the Dolphin asked.

"He'll be here in fifteen minutes," Starry answered.

"The girl can't speak for herself?"

"What do you think?" Starry said. "You think this is easy for her, betraying McKay?"

I looked admiringly at Starry; she could lie smooth as skin. The Dolphin shrugged. I poured coffee for the three Orphans. We waited in silence. The coffee remained untouched, grew cold. Outside the wind grew wilder.

"Storm," I said to Starry.

"What's she mean by that?" Tosh said nervously.

"She means there's bad weather," said Starry.

"What you mean, bad *weather*?" Tosh insisted. The President of the Orphans was searching for a code of treachery.

"Shut up," the Dolphin said softly.

Tosh tapped his shoes on the tile floor. Each gust of wind on the Avenue sent his eyes to the doorway. Outside Tony crouched in the snow.

"What's that kid doing out there?" Tosh demanded.

"Yeah, what about the kid?" the usually silent Marine asked.

"Oh, Christ," said Starry. "It's only that punk corner kid. Ain't he got a crush on you, honey?" she said to me.

I nodded. If Tony had a crush on anyone, it was, most certainly, not on me.

Starry laughed. "He follows her everywhere."

"I don't like that kid out there," Tosh said.

"Shut up," the Dolphin said.

There was silence once more. I removed my white apron and began to count the change in the cash register as I did every night at closing. And then headlights shone through the plate glass. McKay's Chevy stopped under a single blue street lamp. Around the headlights snow floated coldly in circles. We listened to the engine coughing to a stop, saw the headlights grow dim and then dark. The Dolphin remained motionless.

A shadow fell across the moon-bright snow outside the doorway, then McKay opened the door of Monty's, sounding the bells that hung above the molding.

"Brother," the Dolphin said softly.

McKay and the Dolphin were face to face once more. I walked behind McKay and locked the door. Each was thinking I locked the other in.

Tosh and the Marine edged forward. Tosh was holding a gun.

"Ah," McKay said. "The President of the Orphans needs the protection of a Saturday-night special."

Tosh stammered. "Who you saying needs protection?" he said finally.

McKay dismissed Tosh with a wave of his hand. He turned his attention to the Dolphin. "My brother," he said softly.

Sitting very still, Starry slowly reached out her hand and deftly concealed the half load of heroin in her purse.

"You, McKay," the Dolphin said, "are a coward."

McKay threw back his head and began to laugh. Four of the Pack now stood unobserved at the rear of the store.

"Behind you," McKay said quickly.

Tosh and the Marine jumped. The Saturday-night special fell loudly upon the tile. The Dolphin only turned his head very slightly so that the feathers of the peacock at his neck seemed to rise.

"And I'll say it again," the Dolphin said. "McKay, you are a coward."

"Coward?" McKay said. He walked over to Tosh and ripped the jacket off him. With quick movements of his knife

McKay stripped the word "Orphans" from the black leather. "Coward?" he said again, and cloaked himself in the jacket that had for so long been his.

The Dolphin smiled at Starry and then at me. "Of course," he said. "Who could trust you two whores?"

Starry shrugged. I silently agreed with the Dolphin's words.

"First you shoot Kid Harris in the back," the Dolphin said, and there was no reaction from the Pack; "and then you betray a brother. McKay."

There was silence.

"Where's your honor, man?" the Dolphin asked.

The Dolphin's reference was nothing to the rest of us. But as McKay heard the Dolphin's words, he shuddered. As if fighting those words, McKay picked a stack of comics off the floor and threw them across the counter, spilling a row of sugar bowls.

"We'll call a peace," Tosh stammered. "You know, we'll call a truce and then have a council between us all."

McKay laughed. He pulled at the cuffs of the leather jacket, which was already molding itself to the shape of his body. "No," he said. "No, we won't. Because the Avenue now belongs to the Pack. I give the Avenue to them."

"The Avenue is mine," the Dolphin said. "It always was; it always is."

"Wait a minute," Tosh said to the Dolphin.

"Shut up," the Dolphin said.

"I got a flash for you," McKay said. "It ain't yours no more."

"Don't you know," the Dolphin whispered with words meant only for McKay, "you are fighting for nothing."

McKay's smile was ice. "Oh, I know," he said. "Oh, how I know, brother." McKay handed me a brown paper bag. "Open that," he said to me. I felt the outlines of a bottle. It was indeed a small green bottle that I handed to McKay. The liquid inside moved like a small sea.

"What the hell?" Tosh said. We had all of us expected the stiletto or the .22.

Tosh and the Marine shifted their weight from one foot to the other. The Pack was tense and waiting.

"McKay," the Dolphin said. He stood still as iron, and yet the paintings on his skin seemed to move. The butterfly shuddered and curled its wings around the Dolphin's cold eye.

McKay raised the green bottle as if in a toast. "For teaching me everything I know," he said to the Dolphin. The bottle was raised in the air. The laughter that sounded from McKay's throat was deep and seemed not to come from him at all. I did not think his laughter could be such a dark sound.

"It's acid," someone said. "It's lye."

I stood close enough to McKay to feel his breathing deepen. I knew, without touching him, that he was shaking. McKay moved his hand quick as light. The lye was in the air. Like dreamers, we in the candy store watched McKay; like dreamers, we listened to the Dolphin cry out. Then he clawed at his eyes. McKay winced and touched one hand to the left side of his own face and smiled. He signaled the Pack, and then there were shouts and the sound of knuckles and boots. In the dim fluorescent light, the Dolphin knelt before McKay on the tile floor. I stood by McKay and watched the Dolphin's tattooed hands tear at his burning eyes.

"McKay," I heard Starry say. "My God, why didn't you just shoot him through the head?"

Tosh and the Marine lay motionless on the floor; arms had been broken, skin cut, shouts and protest had been beaten into silence. The Pack began to carry the two half-conscious Orphans into the stolen Sears truck; they would be driven to the Brooklyn marshlands where they would wake with the taste of blood in their mouths and the knowledge that the Avenue was lost.

Starry sat on a counter stool. She raised her small thin legs so that the Dolphin would not touch her as he crawled blindly on the tile floor. He moaned and pawed gently at his eyes. He had been blinded by the lye, and now even the tattoos he had painted on his skin to disguise scars were disfigured.

I held my arm around McKay, but McKay only stared. He held one hand to his face. I kissed him then, I kissed him for a long time. I wanted to kiss him for so long that when I moved my lips away from his I would again see an empty candy store. But when I moved away from him, Starry still sat at the counter, the Dolphin still lay upon the floor.

I whispered McKay's name, but he did not answer my voice, as he had not answered my kiss. I covered the hand he held to his face with my own, and then my fingers felt what was now unprotected by McKay's palm: the liquid heat of blood on his skin. Only a few drops of the lye McKay had thrown into the Dolphin's eyes had fallen onto his own face, but those few drops had eaten through his skin like maggots.

I ran to the sink, stopping to rummage in my coat pocket for a silk scarf. I ran the scarf under cold water. Then I held the silk to McKay's skin and bathed the flesh that had been touched with lye. There was a small but very deep hole in his left cheek. McKay didn't move, he did not speak. And only when I could no longer look at his wound, did I notice the curve of McKay's lip. Outside on the Avenue the wind was dying, but still snow fell deeper and deeper, and I saw now that McKay smiled.

II

McKay and Baby Perez had arranged to meet at midnight in the parking lot of the High I-Cue Pool Hall. Perez would then drive Starry to the abortionist in the South Bronx who, Perez claimed, had received a degree from Albert Einstein Medical College. The High I-Cue was located in Pack territory. Perez would wait till twelve-thirty and no later; if McKay did not arrive, he would know the Avenue still belonged to the Dolphin.

We sped over the ice, so as not to be late; each time we were caught by a red light, each time McKay hit the brakes, the Chevy skidded wildly. McKay held the silk kerchief to the wound on his cheek; he steered the car with one hand. In the back seat Starry had accidentally dropped a lit match into the upholstery as she attempted to light a cigarette. "Jesus fucking Christ," she muttered.

The time was minutes before midnight. I moved close to McKay and lifted my hand to touch his face. "Let me see," I said.

He jerked his head away from me. "No," was all he said.

We pulled into the near-empty parking lot of the pool hall. McKay turned off the ignition and rolled his window down.

"I'm cold," I said. In the back seat Starry was mumbling and lighting matches.

"Shut up," McKay said to her.

'You shut up," she said.

"He's late," I said of Perez.

McKay did not answer me.

"I say, he's late," I repeated.

We waited for some time in silence. Then the headlights of a small sports car shone on the Avenue. Perez parked a red MG convertible close to the Chevy. His velvet cape scattered snowflakes around his boots as he walked toward McKay's window.

"Hey, hey, hey," Perez said. "Everything is everything, and we have got it to-gether."

"I'm cold," I whispered.

"Shut up," McKay said.

"No trouble?" Perez asked.

"None," said McKay.

Perez studied McKay's face. "You got cut," he said, and McKay shrugged. "As long as the other dude's looking worse." He laughed. McKay was silent. "The other dude does look worse, doesn't he? The Dolphin is taken care of?"

"The Dolphin is taken care of," McKay said. "The Avenue is now yours to deal whatever you want."

"Solid," Perez said. He peered into the back seat. "This is the chick?"

"Fuck you," Starry said. "Who is this joker?" she asked.

"This joker don't take no trash," Perez said. "So cut the babbling and let's get it on."

"I'm not ready," Starry said.

"Well, you better be ready," Perez said.

"A couple of minutes won't kill you," McKay said.

"Shit, man," Perez said. "This guy's a doctor, and a doctor keeps to his appointment schedule."

"A doctor, my ass," McKay said. "We got a last trans-action to settle."

Perez agreed to wait. He returned to the sports car. His head moved to the rhythm of the radio.

McKay turned. "Give me the shit," he said to Starry.

"I don't know what you mean, McKay."

"I want that spoonful," McKay said.

"McKay," Starry said. "I don't have it, I thought you took it. One of the fuckers from the Pack must have lifted it."

McKay opened his door. He left the car and opened the back door. "Get out," he said.

"Hey, boy, it's cold out there," Starry protested.

I left the Chevy and walked around to where McKay stood. I held my winter coat around my shoulders and the air rushed through the material of my blouse like cold needles. I held his arm. "McKay," I said. "Don't. You don't have to."

"Get out," he said to Starry.

"Honey, if you're in pain, if your face is hurting bad, I got Darvon and codeine."

McKay did not answer me.

"We can go to an emergency ward, maybe they'll give you Demerol. You just say you were holding a bottle of cleaning fluid and your hand slipped."

Starry slid slowly out of the back of the Chevy. Her eyes seemed to be studying possible paths of escape. She needed McKay and Perez if she wanted the ride to the South Bronx. But she also wanted to hold on to the heroin I knew she carried in her purse. "McKay," she said as we stood in the snow, "what you want with heroin? You can get all the money you need dealing coke for Perez. And you're straight, you ain't got no habit."

"Give me the spoon," McKay said, grabbing her arm.

"You're going to do it again," I said. "You're god damn going to do it again."

"What do you want? What the hell do you want from me?" McKay said.

"I want to go home," I said. "McKay, I just want to go home." He had the Avenue now; he was free to walk and deal on any street corner. The Dolphin was taken care of, and McKay had proven that he was through with honor, and that he was no longer anyone's fool. What did he want?

201

Starry handed him the plastic bag; McKay studied the junk. "Almost two spoons," he mused.

"Fuck you," Starry said.

"And the works," McKay said. "Give me your works."

Starry handed him a dull-edged needle and a tarnished metal spoon.

"Give me enough for a fix," she said. "Give me enough to get off. I don't want to get sick."

"One of the Pack must have lifted the dope?" McKay sneered.

"Give it to her," I said. Starry was trembling.

"Let's go inside," McKay said. "Let's all of us go inside."

I held Starry's arm, and we followed McKay into the pool hall. We passed the green felt tables and continued toward the rear, to a narrow hallway outside the toilet door.

"You wait out here," I said to McKay.

"And trust her with the junk?" McKay laughed. "Not a chance." He opened the door; the three of us entered the fluorescent-lit toilet; our reflections moved in the mirror which hung above a stained porcelain sink. McKay locked the door; he removed his belt.

"Don't bother with that," Starry said. From her purse she produced a rubber tube and a clamp. She wound the tube around her arm and clamped it tightly. "What do you say?" she demanded of McKay. McKay began to fix the heroin. "Just like the good old days," Starry sneered.

I did not want to be there with them. "I'm going to wait outside," I said.

"No, you won't," McKay said. He no longer bothered to hold the scarf to his face. The hole in his skin was raw and deep.

"Well, you sure ain't gonna be no beauty no more," Starry said to McKay. She tossed her raccoon coat to the floor, and sat upon it. The clamp was tight around the rubber tubing; her veins rose pale and blue.

"Come on," she said to McKay. "Come on," she urged.

McKay walked toward her. Starry still wore a woolen hat pulled over her hair. She stared up at McKay and he knelt. When the heroin entered her, Starry sighed, as if in the act of love.

McKay stood over the sink and fixed more dope. The water ran. McKay stared at me and nodded.

"McKay," I said. The night seemed too long; the night seemed to last forever.

"Come here," he said. I shook my head. "Hey." McKay smiled. "Get over here."

I stood with my back against the wall. "Go ahead and kill yourself," I said. "Go ahead and start it all again, but I'm having nothing to do with it."

"You know," McKay said, "you're no fun anymore. You just ain't no fun." Starry sat slumped over on the tiles; she watched us until she could no longer keep her eyes open. "When was the last time you got high?" McKay said.

"I don't know," I said. I bit my thumb and began to count the tiles of the soundproof ceiling.

"It's about time," he said. "It's about time you did."

Each time before when we got high together I had been the one to ask McKay permission. Only a few times had he allowed me heroin. And even then, he always avoided my veins.

"Why?" I said.

"I want you with me," he said.

"I'm with you," I said.

McKay shook his head. "I want you high with me."

For me, heroin had always been the way to connect with McKay, and now it was he who wanted to connect. He held me and whispered, "Please."

I began to shake, "Don't say that," I said.

"What?" McKay whispered.

"Don't say please to me."

We were so far apart there was no other way to make a connection, and so I moved away from him and rolled up my sleeve.

It seemed I could not say no.

Before McKay could form words into questions I had already said yes. Each demand, any request – none could I ever deny. I could not say no.

I did not want to be involved in war with the Orphans; I did not want heroin; but I could not help myself – I still wanted

203

McKay. And I believed the way to have him was to say yes. So I said yes to lies, and to the needle; so I agreed when I did not agree, so I wanted what I did not want.

More terrifying than the effects of beatings or murder were thoughts of the effects of the word no. Would McKay leave me, would I be left alone, would I realize later that yes had been the correct answer all along, and didn't McKay know more than I did anyway? Who was I to say no to him, especially when he needed me? When he needed me to say yes.

It was heroin that was the mood we moved in, but I did not want the heroin to move in me. I could not be twice owned: not by McKay and heroin both. Yet, I was scarring my arm for him with tracks the way others had scarred their legs by carving McKay's initials encircled by hearts. But I did not think it was heroin that McKay shot into my vein; I believed it was love; it was need; it was want. How could I say no? Both of us needed magic to make connections: I needed charms; he needed dust. What, finally, was the difference between the two? We were in need, and it was so difficult to make a connection that, when one was offered, I could not refuse. I dared not refuse. I held out my arm and I nodded yes.

But on my tongue there was a different word.

"That's it," he whispered. I closed my eyes and heard him whisper again, "Yes, that's it." But it did not seem as if he spoke to me, and so I did not answer.

I felt the belt being tightly wrapped around my arm; I felt my breathing deepen.

"You're going to skin-pop it, yeah?" I said to McKay.

He did not answer me. He stood by the sink, holding a lit match under the spoon.

"McKay?" I said.

"You'll see how much better it is," he said.

Of course, I knew how much stronger, better the rush of mainlining was. But I did not want it; I did not want to be that high. "You'll see," McKay said. He held my arm now, he placed his lips to the vein that throbbed at the inside of my elbow.

And I was certain, as I touched my hand to McKay's face, and I was certain as he pulled the belt tighter still around my arm, that he needed me. McKay needed me with him and I did not think I would be able to say no; I did not think I would be able to speak.

I felt the rush immediately, felt the warmth and sweetness of the heroin throughout my body, as if white powder had replaced all of the blood that flowed through my veins.

It was good.

"That's better, isn't it?" I heard McKay say, and I nodded.

He loosened the belt and then removed it from around my arm. I felt very easy and slow; I leaned against the wall for support. I watched McKay's back. He was at the sink again. In his mouth he held the tail end of the belt, which was now wrapped around his arm. He pulled it with his teeth until it was taut as wire.

Starry stood up. She threw the raccoon coat about her shoulders. "I'll tell you something," she whispered to me. I looked into her pale eyes and the pupils were tiny as moth's eyes. "He's changed. He's really changed, you know what I mean?"

"He's in shock," I whispered. I could not tell if my words were intelligible. I knew I was slurring syllables.

"Honey," Starry said, "we're all in shock."

"Are we?" I said. I wanted to sleep. I wanted to leave, because I felt if I did not leave I would have to lie on the tile floor and cover myself with a winter coat and dream.

"You are wasted," Starry said. "You are stone wasted," she whispered, it seemed, in my ear. "Why you want to mess with this shit?"

"Ssh," I said to her. I did not want to speak.

Finally McKay was finished. He cloaked himself once more in the black leather he had removed when he fixed himself.

"You ready?" he said softly.

"Who is waiting on who?" Starry said, opening the door and walking into the hallway. "It's goodbye to the Avenue for me," Starry called behind her. "Thank the Lord, it is goodbye."

"Let's go," McKay said to me. He held one arm around my shoulder. I leaned close against him and rested my head upon his chest. We followed Starry through the pool hall, past sharpshooters aiming cues, and into the street. My knees felt weak, and the air seemed incredibly cold.

"The Arctic," I said, and I shivered even though McKay held me close as we walked.

Starry stopped before she reached the MG. She stood on the ice, in the night; her eyes were closed. I had to be sick.

"McKay," I whispered. I moved away from his arm; I knelt by the side of the Chevy. I felt ice at my knees; I bent my head. I could feel McKay was still beside me. "Go away," I said.

"I won't," he answered.

"God damn it, go away," I said. I wanted to be sick alone. I vomited several times; I did not think I would have the strength to stand; but I stood. McKay opened the Chevy's doors; he sat behind the wheel and rested his head on the upholstery. Starry was now in the red MG, which was ringed with a cloud of marijuana smoke that had filtered through the open car windows into the night. I stood alone in the parking lot of the High I-Cue Pool Hall and looked at Starry. Perez had started his engine. When Starry noticed that I stared at her she rolled her window up. She did not smile; she did not wave. There were no words of goodbye between us. She only rolled her window up and shook her head.

Perez drove away; the sports car's black exhaust and the odor of marijuana lingered in the air. She would not be back – she had no reason to come back. I watched the taillights disappear on the Avenue; and then I realized I was cold. I realized just how cold I was. I got into the Chevy and closed the door. I could not tell if McKay knew I was with him now or not. His eyes were closed; his head nodded far down on his shoulder.

I whispered his name once, but I did not call him again. I waited for McKay to open his eyes. He swallowed and rubbed at his nose. He lit a cigarette for himself and one for me. My fingers were like rubber. I dropped the cigarette on the floor of the car; I leaned down and found the burning tobacco.

"Let's go home," McKay said. We finished our cigarettes, and then McKay started the engine. I fought to keep my eyes open, but the lids were so heavy I could not help but rest my head back and close my eyes. I did not know McKay was watching me until he reached out his hand to touch my shoulder. I jumped slightly at his touch; I opened my eyes wide to see his dark stare upon me. His hand rested gently on my shoulder, but I moved away from him. I had to open the window and breathe in night air, for I feared I might be sick once more.

12

STARTING OUT

I

"I JUST DON'T trust that cocksucker," McKay said as we drove in the Chevy down the Avenue toward the clubhouse of the Orphans.

"You're just nervous," I said.

"The hell I am," McKay said. He rubbed at his nose and lit a cigarette as we waited for a red light to turn. The burn on his face had healed, but a thin scar now lined his left cheek.

"O.K.," I said. "O.K. You're not nervous."

In three days McKay had finished the two spoons of heroin stolen from the Dolphin, and now he was to begin dealing for Baby Perez.

"McKay," I said. "Perez will be there."

"Yeah, yeah," McKay said. "And if he's not?"

"He'll be at the clubhouse," I said. If Perez failed to show at the appointed time and place, McKay would be strung out with no money and no dope. "You're gonna be a working man, finally," I said.

"Bullshit," McKay said.

"You're gonna be working for Perez," I said.

McKay laughed. "So now I can list my occupation as 'pusher'?"

"It's a start," I said.

McKay detoured at the White Castle to pick up some Cokes. We sat in the Chevy with the headlights switched on.

"Well," McKay said, after he had ordered from the waitress who appeared at the car window. "I better have an occupation that makes money, with two habits to support."

"What two habits?" I said as the waitress reappeared with two large plastic cups.

"Yours and mine," McKay answered. I was silent while he paid for the Cokes, rolled up the windows, and restarted the Chevy.

When we had rolled out of the White Castle driveway and were once again on the Avenue, I said, "You're crazy. I don't have a habit."

McKay laughed. He steered the Chevy with one hand and drank with the other. When he shifted gears, drops of Coke fell onto my leg.

"Fuck you, I don't," I said. I could count the number of times I had mainlined. So I had been chipping, so big deal.

"All right," McKay said. "All right, all right."

"I mean it," I said.

A Ford Falcon full of girls stopped beside us at a red light; the girls were staring at McKay.

"And I said, all right," McKay said.

The light turned green; McKay lit a cigarette. The car next to us did not move and the girls still stared at McKay.

"The light changed," I said.

"I know it," McKay said, ripping the Chevy into gear.

The Falcon followed us. I knew there were giggles and sighs in that car.

"Do you get high every day?" McKay asked. I drained my Coke, threw the cup on the floor, and didn't answer. It was true: I got high every day on something, but only because there was nothing else to do, and only because McKay was always high and I knew he wanted me with him. "Well, is that normal?" McKay sneered. "You going to tell me you're straight?"

"Drop dead," I said.

The Chevy was too fast for the Ford to keep up; we lost it at a bend in the Avenue. McKay parked in front of Munda's City Line Liquor Store. "That makes you happy," I said. "It really makes you happy to think I'm a junkie like you."

"Watch it," McKay said.

But I knew it did; of course it made him happy. I could be

satisfied with marijuana and a Budweiser, but McKay smiled when I sat with him at the kitchen table measuring out heroin from a glassine bag.

"No junkie ever thinks they're a junkie," McKay said shortly.

I had heard that Omen House platitude enough times. "And no asshole ever thinks they're an asshole," I said. I left the Chevy, slammed the door shut and stared into the liquor-store window. When I turned, McKay still sat in the driver's seat of the Chevy, both his hands grasping the wheel tightly. I thought perhaps he might be right: in faking love there was the danger of falling into it; was there the same danger in faking a habit? McKay opened the Chevy door; he stood on the sidewalk in black leather.

"Don't start up with me," he warned.

"Do you know what you can do?" I said.

"Now, watch yourself."

"You can keep your heroin. Keep it," I said. "I don't fucking need it."

"Get over here," McKay said as Perez pulled up to the curb in a '62 Corvette with New Jersey plates. "Get over here, because if you make a scene or if you embarrass me, I'll kill you."

Perez walked over the ice. He was wearing a suit of burgundy velvet. He greeted McKay with a handshake. In his other hand he carried a large leather briefcase. McKay held my arm tightly. We walked past the liquor store, and then down the cement steps that led to the clubhouse. McKay opened the padlocked door with a key I did not know he still had. We went into the basement and McKay switched on the light. Perez placed his briefcase on the floor.

Perez cased the room. "If only," he said, "I could communicate to you in the Gypsy tongue of Romany; for that is a language with words to describe this place."

"A dump," I said.

Perez nodded. "A dump," he agreed.

The clubhouse was indeed a mess: one window had been broken into, by the Pack or by some corner kids; snow, which had been blown inside by the Avenue wind, had melted and now flooded the floor where the mattresses lay. The odor of mildew was everywhere. Cans and bottles were littered about; posters had been ripped from the wall, and Mick Jagger now stared down at us from the wall with only one eye.

I walked across the room surveying the wreckage. "Just lovely," I said.

"Shut up," McKay said. "Just shut up." He began to pick up cans and newspapers from the floor. I sat down on an orange crate. Perez pulled up another and also sat.

"Mildew on velvet, you can never get that off," he confided to me.

I did not know if McKay had forgotten that Perez and I sat in the clubhouse, for he ignored us; he continued to clean.

"Let's get down to business," Perez said finally. McKay dropped a load of wet newspapers and magazines in a corner. "First of all," Perez said. "You come to me; I don't come to you. From now on we meet in the Bronx; none of this commuting shit for me."

"All right," McKay agreed. He leaned on the table, around which the soldiers of the Orphans had once held council meetings.

"I expect to make a two-hundred-per-cent profit at all times," Perez said. He looked at me. "It's the Gypsy in me. You be cool with me and I'll be cool with you," he said to McKay.

McKay lit a cigarette; his hands shook slightly. He needed a fix, and I wanted to divert Perez's stare from McKay's unsteady hands.

"That briefcase alligator?" I said.

"No, no. Crocodile," he said. .

"Hear that, McKay?" I said. "Crocodile."

McKay grabbed my arm. "You either shut up . . ." he said.

"Or what?" I said. I was not afraid of McKay's threats.

"Dig yourself," Perez said. "All the chick said is 'It's crocodile.'" Perez smiled. "Ah," he said. "That mean something special between you two?"

The code of lovers? It amused me to think Perez believed so. Any words between McKay and me could begin an argument – no code was necessary, any words would do.

"You are one edgy dude," Perez said. "You are one edgy dude for a man who's kicked his jones. And you are straight, right?"

"Shit, yes," said McKay, stomping his cigarette out on the clubhouse floor.

"You don't mind if I see your arms?" Perez said.

McKay backed away.

"What about Starry?" I asked. "Was Starry all right when you drove her to the doctor's?" If he looked at McKay's arms the tracks would betray a habit begun when McKay had not been out of Omen House more than a week.

"She's a bitch, but the dude said she's a fairly healthy bitch," Perez said. As he answered me, he continued to look at McKay. "Your arm," he insisted. "Just for the sake of business, you understand."

"See, I'm only gonna get off on the weekends, then I can be straight and deal during the week."

"Only on the weekends." Perez laughed.

"We did some partying to celebrate the end of the Dolphin," McKay said. "But I got it under control."

"Don't be shining me on," Perez warned. "Because I will not have a junkie dealing for me. A junkie dealing is a junkie stealing. You know what I mean?"

McKay nodded. "I know what you mean," he said.

Perez rested his briefcase on the tabletop. When the case was clicked open, three separate compartments appeared. "Cocaine, amphetamine, heroin," said Perez.

"Nice," McKay said.

"You bet your ass it's nice. And nicer still when this case is returned to me and it's filled with money."

McKay eyed the white powders. "I don't need the brief-case," he said; he removed the leather jacket and showed Perez the pockets sewn into the inner lining.

Perez appraised the secret pockets. "Very hip," he said. "You got a tailor that does that?"

McKay laughed as he began to store the plastic bags in his jacket. "No, I ain't got no tailor."

Perez shrugged. "I guess I don't care what you got, as long as you don't got the mind to beat me. You know what I

212

mean?" Perez smiled. "Because I mean I'll kill you if you pull any double crosses. Business, you understand."

"Sure, sure," McKay said. He held the bag of heroin to the light. "Looks good."

"Is good," Perez answered.

"I want to know what I'm selling," McKay said.

Perez nodded, and McKay motioned me to hand him the tiny silver spoon I carried in my pocket. He snorted a bit of heroin; he waited for a while; and then McKay said, "Very ace."

"So then, it's solid," Perez said. They shook hands once more. "Same time next week, only you'll be coming to me, you hear?"

McKay cloaked himself in the black leather jacket lined with dope; we left the clubhouse, leaving Perez figuring out some equations on a piece of legal-size paper balanced on his briefcase.

"Later," Perez called out. Once on the Avenue McKay took my hand.

"We could make it, you know," McKay said. "We could make it if you could only learn when to shut up and when to talk."

"I didn't do good in there?" I said.

"You did good," he had to agree.

I thought we might make it if we left heroin and the Avenue behind; but once we were in the Chevy McKay was already talking about dealing.

"First I'm gonna take what's mine," he said as we drove back down the Avenue, past the White Castle, past Monty's and St. Anne's. "Then I'm gonna cut the rest of the shit with sugar and make a fortune."

"McKay," I said as we pulled up at a pump at the Esso station across from our apartment, "what happens when Perez checks you for tracks?"

McKay told the attendant to fill the tank. "What happens is he won't find shit. I'll shoot it under my tongue or behind my knees; Perez will never know."

I looked at McKay and sighed.

"Don't look at me and sigh," McKay said.

The back door of the Chevy opened, and Tony got in the car. "Brother," the kid said.

"Just who I be looking for," McKay said. "You ever bag dope?" he asked. When Tony shook his head, McKay said, "We got to cut the shit and then bag it into dimes."

"The whole Avenue knows you're the main man now," Tony said.

McKay had taken over the Dolphin's position as the Avenue's dealer. Soon our telephone would be ringing; in the night our door would be knocked upon and tense voices would whisper and deals would be made. "The whole Avenue knows where to come when they're in need."

McKay smiled. He paid for the gas and steered the Chevy across the Avenue. The three of us went upstairs. "Got to get some locks on this here door," McKay said. It was now common Avenue knowledge that our apartment would be the place to find dope. McKay emptied the contents of his jacket on the wooden floor.

"Holy shit," Tony said.

McKay laid down newspapers, and from the dresser drawer he produced glassine envelopes, a scale, and a pound of sugar. I went into the kitchen, thinking of making dinner, thinking of banging pots and pans and running the water so loudly as to block out their talk. I looked in the cupboard and refrigerator – there was only oatmeal, beer, bread, tuna fish, and the .22 stored next to a can of coffee.

"Fuck it, McKay," I called. "There's never anything in this house. There are never any eggs. And there's no butter. What the hell?" I sat at the kitchen table; I began to cry.

McKay came into the kitchen. I covered my eyes. He lit a cigarette and handed it to me. I didn't look at him. McKay sat down at the kitchen table with me. Finally I looked at him: his eyes were dark and warm upon me.

"There's nothing to cook," I said. Tony sat on the wooden floor in the other room.

"Do you want me to take you out somewhere?" McKay asked. I shook my head. "Do you want to get high?" he said softly.

"No," I said. "No."

214

McKay reached for his wallet and placed a five-dollar bill on the tabletop. "Go to the grocery," he said. "I'll wait for you. I'll be here."

When I went into the other room, McKay's arm was around me. But it was too late in the day or the season, and my eyes were already too wide to close. I decided to leave him.

After all the nights, the waiting, the lies, I knew that the Avenue was still the same – it would remain between City Lines, surrounded by fast Chevys and Fords, coated by ice and leather and fine white dust. And the mood would still be there – still wedged between the unturned pages of movie magazines, still breathing in the back seats of convertibles. The same pattern of snow would fall on the sidewalks, the ivy would grow along brick walls; the waves of liquid in the veins would be constant. McKay's eyes would still be as dark, and the tracks of the needle would always find the same vein.

McKay helped me into my winter coat. As I left the apartment, McKay and Tony were already testing cocaine. I walked down the Avenue, past the gas stations, to a small grocery store. I picked up eggs and milk; my eyes felt tired. I followed the length of the dairy case; I began to cry. When I reached inside my coat pocket I discovered I had left the five dollars on the kitchen table – it didn't seem to matter anymore; I was not sure I would have ever been able to decide between small curd and large. I was sure only that if I moved one foot outside the circle I could walk away: what held me was only air, what held me was dust.

The Avenue was stuck in the mood; I was not. And what I left would not be McKay, would not be heroin or the Avenue. It was only the mood. I slowly moved a foot that had been paralyzed by air; I decided to leave the circle.

II

When I woke, the first thing I saw was his arm on the pillow. Abscesses had already begun to form on his skin, pale white marks ran in tracks.

I left the bed, and though the air was cold, and though I stood naked, I threw open the window. Outside on the Avenue was January and ice. I turned from the window. McKay slept with his mouth open. I smiled and lit a cigarette; with the first intake of smoke, I felt my morning blood live. Now I would leave him.

I sat down again on the bed close to McKay; I watched him breathe. I moved my hand along the skin of his shoulder, and in his sleep he moved closer. He was a beautiful sleeper. I reached over to the floor and killed my cigarette in an ashtray that overflowed with matches and ash onto the wooden floor. Beneath our apartment the auto mechanic was already at work; finely tuned engines hummed and shook our floor with a gentle vibration. Winter sun and air fell through the open window; I was not cold because I lay close to McKay.

I slowed my breathing so that our bodies moved and breathed together. I moved my hand along his face as if recording the planes and angles with my fingers; I avoided touching the scar on his cheek. I moved my hand along his body; I touched him as though I were blind, as though I read his body as Braille. I wanted to wake him right away and tell him, and at the same time I wanted to continue watching him sleep.

While I waited for McKay to wake, I began silently listing the items I would pack in my suitcase. The list was not long. There was more sun as time passed, but the room grew colder. I could not wait any longer. Finally I whispered his name. McKay would not open his eyes. He held me close and whispered, "Shut up," but I would not let him sleep.

"McKay," I said.

He held one finger to his lips. "Don't talk," he said.

I moved so that I lay on top of him. "Just let me tell you one thing," I said.

"Quiet," he said.

I touched my tongue to his lips; his arms were around me. "I'm leaving you," I said.

McKay laughed.

Up through the open window filtered the sounds of the

Avenue – engines and skidding tires. Outside pigeons circled, and snow froze hard as ice.

"I'm leaving you," I said again.

"Did you leave the window open?" he asked.

I stood up, went to the window, closed it, and then returned to bed.

"McKay," I said.

"I heard you. I heard you," he said. "You're not going anywhere." I did not answer. "It's heroin," he said finally.

I shook my head. No, it wasn't heroin. I had been with McKay on heroin, off heroin, strung out, hooked again. He had a habit now. He had money enough to support it, and he would get busted again and would kick again. And again.

"What is it? What is it?" he asked. "Nothing's different. Nothing's changed."

"I know," I said.

"So?" he said. "Don't tell me this makes a difference?" He touched the scar on his face.

"Do you mean are you still beautiful?" I asked. "You are still beautiful."

"Uh huh," McKay said. "You ain't leaving."

We made love for a long time. And for once I did not have to fake love; this time I made it. I forgot old movements and sighs; I forgot the Avenue, its spells and faces. I was myself; I felt and moved as myself. It was because I was going that I was able to come. When McKay moved away from me, I did not feel the need immediately to leave the bed; there was no reason to hurry.

"No," McKay said. "No, you're not leaving. Tell me that wasn't good," he said, "and I'll tell you you're a liar."

I smiled.

"I knew it," he said, lighting a cigarette. "I knew it."

I left the bed and reached underneath the mattress where my suitcase was stored. I rested the suitcase on the bed and clicked it open. There would not be much to pack. Dust that had collected around the edges of the suitcase fell in strings onto the sheet.

As I began to go to the closet McKay stood up and grabbed my shoulder. "Stop this shit," he said. I looked into his eyes and then, when he released his hold, began, again, to move away.

He reached out for me again, but grabbed the chain of my silver locket as he touched my skin. The chain broke; the locket fell onto the floor. The metal sounded softly on wooden planks. "Do you hear me?" he said.

"I hear you," I said. "Did you hear me?"

We stood in the middle of the room and kissed. And then McKay laughed. "I don't think I did hear you," he said.

He walked away from me and opened the dresser drawer where the envelopes of heroin were stored. Then he went toward the toilet. I sat on the bed and watched him move away. At the door McKay hesitated and turned. "You wait there for me," he said. When he closed the door of the bathroom, I stood up. I dressed in jeans and a sweater, and then folded some clothes into the suitcase. I looked at the bathroom door and I was slow – there seemed no need to hurry.

As I walked down the stairs and out past the auto repair shop, I knew McKay had begun to roll up his sleeve. When I passed the Chevy McKay planned to race again in the spring, he was already measuring the heroin into a silver spoon. I walked to the subway station, and, as the doors of the train closed behind me, I imagined he had pulled the belt tightly around his arm. The heroin would melt like snow into the blue liquid that ran through his veins. I knew that, as he sat on the rim of the bathtub, his dark eyes were closed.

I slid open the door leading to the next subway car and stood on the platform, my suitcase beside me, the wind around me. Already I imagined his eyes were closed. I lit a cigarette. I rode through the tunnel between cars, unable to see into either because of the underground grime that covered the windows. And as the subway followed tracks, and as it hit hard against the tunnel walls, I traced the letters of my name in the dust of the window. I erased the print with my palm. Then I wrote my name again with the very edge of my fingertip, and I could not help but smile.